A New Renaissance

A Celebration of African American Fiction

Edited by Dr. Rhonda M. Lawson

A New Renaissance

A Celebration of African American Fiction

Edited by Dr. Rhonda M. Lawson

A New Renaissance:
A Celebration of African American Fiction

Edited by
Dr. Rhonda M. Lawson
Published by Meet the World Image Solutions

PO Box 8803
New Orleans, LA 70182
www.mtwimagesolutions.com

Cover design by Dr. Rhonda M. Lawson

ISBN: 979-8-43-368191-0
Meet the World Image Solutions

Table of Contents

Celebrate Our Children

Original Children's Stories

This anthology was a labor of love, and it's surreal to see it finally come to fruition.

The idea was born in 2020, but the inspiration came when I was a sophomore at Loyola University in New Orleans. I took a class called the Harlem Renaissance, led by the unforgettable Professor Brenda Osbey. Her class opened my eyes to such trailblazing writers as Nella Larsen, Claude McKay, Zora Neale Hurston, Alain Locke and so many others. Although I had been writing since I was twelve, the Harlem Renaissance reignited my love and respect for the written word.

This love grew even deeper when I became a published author in 2004. A part of me wanted to make these trailblazers proud. They had set the path for the authors of today, just as we are now setting the path for the authors of the future. Someone somewhere is learning to write by reading our work, just as many of us learned to write because of the Harlem Renaissance. This is a responsibility I take seriously.

The authors in this collection of work share this love for the written word, so it is only fitting that we come together for A New Renaissance. No two stories in this book are the same. Some will make you laugh, some will make you cry, some will make you think. These authors truly brought it with their creativity and originality. I loved reading each story, and I am confident that you will, as well.

What makes this anthology special is its diversity. Some are established authors, and some are being published for the first time. Four of the authors are members of Zeta Phi Beta Sorority, Incorporated. One is a pastor. The youngest writer, my daughter, is twenty-two years old. The oldest just celebrated her seventieth birthday. One is a social worker, while two work in the movie industry. Some are military retirees. Our roster includes speakers, ministers, singers, and foundation owners. And the most amazing of all, two of the authors are visually impaired. Don't you just love it?

I would like to thank all of the Beta readers who gave their honest and helpful feedback: Wanda Herbert-Romain, Phyllis Jones, Renee Livious and Butler's Bookbag. Thanks also go to everyone who lent their support to make this dream a reality, including Gwen Richardson, Lisa Dumas Harris, and Author Anna Bella. Thanks also to my rock, Dedrick Brockington, Sr., for your love and support. It was a lot of long nights putting this project together. Thank you for your patience and feedback. I love you! Most of all, thank you to the authors who signed on to take this journey with me. The process was challenging and selective, but you held on for the ride. This wouldn't be possible without you!

Big things will be birthed from this book, and I thank you for your support. Each sale will support the Meet the World Foundation's Graduating Senior Scholarship Fund. For more information on this annual award, visit my website at www.mtwimagesolutions.com.

Now, without any further delay, let's jump into these stories. May they inspire and entertain you. I think you're in for a real literary ride!

A New Renaissance – A Celebration of African American Fiction picks up the baton and continues the journey into boldly claiming space in the literary world. Twelve well accomplished Black Jalimusos created a familial bond, penned an anthology ensuring space in creating and contributing to a cultural legacy. Black life and the Black diaspora collectively are not a monolith. This rich collection of fictional short stories incorporates vibrant work across genres – adult, young adult and children.

A New Renaissance showcases prolific Black writers who share stories all exemplary of Black lived reality. Although this literary gem is fictional, the themes in each story are interwoven, contextualizing lived experiences with prose filled with love, friendship, family, deception, trauma, resilience, healing and spirituality. Each one an essential part of our collective experience as Black people. Embedded in our DNA, traditionally passed down is the craft of the griot. And so we embrace, hold a sacred space and immortalize our love for the culture.

Consider this an invitation to immerse yourself if you will into each story, and reflect on the lives of the characters and the message they convey. There is a healing power in writing and having your story read. It allows for grace, creates awareness and allows for opportunities to form different perspectives. The conduit is the love for literacy, maintaining tradition and the art of storytelling that will give birth to the New Renaissance, a love letter to the literary world and all of you.

— Author Anna Bella

Ride:
A Quarantine Story

By Tracey Jackson

Chapter 1

It's official. The world has run amuck.

It's a tepid Monday in South Florida, and I just came in from the grocery store dressed in a black hoodie and colorful tights. My purple latex gloves and mask make me look like a weird mashup between a thief and a surgeon about to perform an operation in broad daylight.

I open my front door, go inside, close it, and then lean against it, letting out a deep minty sigh that bounces against my thick n95 mask right back up into my nostrils. It's hot outside, and the sweat drips down my temples.

I drop the plastic grocery bags on the floor and step out of my slip-on sneakers. I peel off my mask, gloves, hoodie and Gucci sunglasses, and then collapse on the couch. The cool air from the A/C cradles me like a newborn in a bassinet. I don't even care that the CDC said you're not supposed to wear your outside clothes inside because your home could come into contact with that damn virus.

Whatever!

I try to exhale the stress of the grocery store lines from my body. Can you imagine Americans lined up outside of "big box" groceries stores for rations of basic items? When I see the local news, I am reminded of documentaries I've seen of third world countries with people lined up outside of stores for bread and milk. The look of their aggravation pierced my TV screen while their leaders had a pissing contest with their opposition as their people were left to suffer in the madness.

In my case, the president is having a pissing contest with the federal director of infectious diseases, and we are left to fight over one-ply toilet paper from off-brand companies that popped up when the big brands popped out. The shelves are empty like Armageddon hit and made a U-turn just to hit again. The gas stations have lines like a Category 5 hurricane is on its way, and don't even talk about going to the hardware store. Or any store for that matter.

And then my mom had the nerve to have a grocery list with items requiring me to go to several specialty grocery stores. She got the basics from the local grocery store double-bagged and left on her doorstep, but I'm not going to six shops for two items here and two items there. I'll do anything for my mom, but I will not go to six stores and stand in six lines. She's just going to have to get her herbal teas from the grocery store instead of her favorite Caribbean spot.

My cell phone rings. I know it's Regina. I'll call her back later. I'm still trying to decompress, and I don't want to hear about another probate case or how her paralegal is letting her kids use the law firm laptops to do schoolwork because the school-issued ones aren't working.

My sorority sisters have been talking about DJ D-nice having a big quarantine party on Instagram over the weekend. As weird as it sounds, I can't wait to dance to old school music in the comfort of my living room while wearing booty shorts and a camisole top. A digital party where everyone stays home: a closet introvert's dream.

I turn on the TV to see the news regurgitate the same updates over and over again. It seems to be the only constant.

My phone vibrates. It's Karyn. She left a text message. It's probably a Bible scripture with a beautiful picture. I don't read it.

I pick up the phone to surf my Facebook feed. I want to see something different. I want to *feel* something different. I see pictures of families encamped in their houses playing the board games that were popular in the 80's. I see my associates in selfies wearing pajamas and headsets, trying to get work done from home. I see people posting healthy recipes that they finally have time to make.

I glance at my colorful workout tights that snuggly cover my legs. The quarantine pounds are starting to wave at me. I stick my tongue at 'em in protest and resume my phone screen swiping. I get an email notification that my flight to Jamaica was canceled. Figures. I'll just add that to the ten-day Caribbean cruise that was canceled the week prior. Life was turning into one big cancel notification with a heaping side of face masks, plastic gloves, hand sanitizers and long lines.

I go to the shopping bag and pull out a bottle of Shiraz and a ready-made cheese 'n' prosciutto board for one. I want to take a nap before my nightly Zoom Happy Hour with the girls.

We might have to think of something else to do during our digital happy hour before we turn into full-fledged alcoholics. Well, except Karyn, who only drinks sparkling grape juice. I killed a bottle of wine in two happy hour sittings. Regina is killing one every other night. This isn't good. This isn't good at all. I'll tell the girls we need a virtual game night with no alcohol. We are down to killing bottles of cheap store wine while staring down the black hole of our laptop screens. We are even having sappy movie watch parties on Saturday nights.

None of us have quarantine men to distract the fact that we're living in unprecedented times. Well, except Sharon, who's reconciling her marriage. She barely comes to virtual girls' nights anymore. She's getting reconciliation lovin', and shouldn't come listen to a bunch of single women crying about the dating scene. Instead, we're getting two for twenty-dollar bottles of Shiraz and Chardonnay, and running our mouths in front of a laptop screen. The world has run amuck, and so have we.

Chapter 2

"I have an idea," Regina says over the phone while crunching away at a bag of popcorn and smacking in my ear.

"What's that?" I ask flatly while looking over yet another work email and eating strawberries.

"Let's join a bike club!"

I laugh so hard, I snort. Is this girl crazy? She must be chasing a man who rides a bike, and for the life of me, I don't understand why she has to chase anyone. Well then again, it *is* South Florida, where independent and successful Black women are at the bottom of the dating totem pole. Regina is five-eight and slim-thick with long sisterlocs and smooth cocoa-brown skin. She is smart as a whip and very infectious. Too damn infectious. She was able to reel me in at a conference some years back when I started my natural hair journey. She made a comment about my dry hair and that a product she uses could help take the ashiness from my hair. Since when is hair ashy? Either way, she knew what to do about it, and we've been talking shop ever since.

"What's his name?"

"Girl, why does—"

"Name?"

"David. We met in this singles Facebook group for locals and he said I should come out next Friday night to ride bikes with him. They call it the Happy Hour Ride."

"We already have happy hour, chick!"

"Didn't you say we need to do something different? And besides, we need to get outside and away from our laptops."

I let out a deep breath. She ain't lying, but riding a bike? I put on ten pounds since being on lockdown. I don't know if I can haul my thighs down the road on a bike. I don't even know if I'm comfortable even doing so. I eat another strawberry. "Yes, but I don't know about this one. There's a walking group right by my condo."

"Old white Jewish women, Yvonne?"

"Listen, they make these chocolate baklavas, and the group leader is my realtor that got me this awesome condo, annnnd—"

"I know, I know. She got me my awesome condo downtown, too. But why old Jewish white women with money, pocketbook dogs and boring husbands?"

"It's good business," I push. "They know all the money gossip in the real Miami. Not the fake stuff on TV. Even if we don't know all the people, it's juicy to hear whose ex-husband brought who to temple on Saturdays."

Regina lets out a deep breath. She is not amused. "You need to be around your people."

"You know my sorority chapter serves historic Overtown."

"You need to be around your people," she repeats. "C'mon, let's just do it."

"All I have is a beach cruiser."

"That's all you need! Bye, chick!"

Click

What kind of hair-brained, third-wheel scheme did I just get myself into? Happy Hour Bike Ride? In Black Miami? And I'm the third wheel. What in the blue hell? I lean back in my office chair and look at the calendar. I have a meeting coming up at one. It's twelve-thirty. I thought working from home was supposed to be some sort of relaxing alternative to fighting Miami traffic. Unfortunately, not. I've been in meetings since seven this morning. Nearly twelve-hour days with presentations and managing clients. Business is good, but more than I and the other managers can handle. We even have a director helping out with all the contract madness.

I get up from my desk in the bedroom that I converted into an office and grab my water bottle from the desk. I look into the walk-in closet for Bessy, my red beach cruiser that I used to ride on South Beach after church on lazy Sunday afternoons. I shake my head at the thought, remembering my bike rides with William, a guy I was in an on-again, off-again relationship with for two years. He was tall and had a smile that was bright like the South Florida sun. We shared our time, our dreams, our beds and everything else, and then he unceremoniously called our thing off out of the blue.

Then he got engaged.

This man decided to get on one knee months after he dumped me after he told me for two consistent years that he wasn't ready for the next step, but I had nothing to worry about and that he was comfortable with where things were with us. The woman who he asked to marry was this mysteriously beautiful Black woman with wild curly hair who just happened to be jogging by while we drank water after one of our bike rides. The woman who he asked to marry just happened to run into us at an ice cream shop on a ride pitstop. The woman who he asked to marry would run into us sporadically with her girlfriends on the way to brunch or alone walking her dog while wearing a sarong and flip flops.

How did I find out about the engagement? I did the cardinal sin: I went snooping on his Facebook with an ice-cold glass of Shiraz at one in the morning. There he was on one knee with the same chick who appeared out of thin air on our Sunday jaunts. I went back and saw that she popped up on his Facebook and liked his pictures right before we broke up. I never slept that night or many nights after that. I went into a three-month depression.

I need to donate Bessy to Goodwill and buy another damn bike.

***

It's Friday night, and I have no place to go but my laptop. Regina's quarantine boo is at her place for drinks and things, and Karyn is running her Friday night hallelujah service. That girl knows she loves herself some church. Too bad those single deacons keep bringing in women they met at out-of-town church conferences.

I really think these church men don't want a church woman. They want a woman they can mold, and Karyn ain't it. She and her cousin co-own a hair salon that was handed down from her mother and aunt. Their fathers weren't alpha males, nor were they beta, gamma or delta. They were just there. Her mother groomed her to be an alpha woman. An exact replica of herself. Too bad no alpha man wants an alpha woman who's had her own money since her mid-twenties and a large house in Miramar with a pool and two-car garage. She deserves to be loved by an equal partner. God needs to answer her prayers.

The phone rings. Speak of the angel. It's Karyn. "Ma'am, you can log into the service, you know. You ain't doing nothing but watching the news and drinking wine anyway."

"That means I'm busy, right?"

"Yvonne, what am I going to do with you?"

"Pray for me. I'm a dues-paying member, you know."

"Tithes. Tithes are not dues."

"Same difference."

"How's work?"

"Draining, but I'm glad to have a job."

"You better praise Him," Karyn says. "I had to file for the relief loan. I have savings and everything, but business is hurting. I've had to do hair out of my garage."

"Geesh, are you being careful with COVID running the streets?"

"Well, you know Mr. Lester, our lawn man who works at the hospital? He's been blessing us with PPE stuff."

Blessing? Sounds shady to me. "God don't like ugly, Karyn."

"I made a donation to their pancreatic cancer support drive in my daddy's name last year. It all works out."

I laugh. Karyn has a sense of humor similar to mine when we're amongst ourselves. We've been friends for a long time. She prayed and even sat with me several nights after I found out about William. I called Karyn crying and she literally prayed me through that dark place when Regina was too engulfed in a "friends with benefits" scenario with a visiting lawyer at her firm.

"So, any other new developments?" Karyn asks.

"I have no idea," I reply. "I blocked him and deleted his social accounts and phone number."

"Again, I'm going to ask. Any new developments?"

"I'm single as a dollar bill."

"It's been a year, sis," she states. "That man is gone, girl."

"Actually, I found out she broke off the engagement!" I exclaim, but immediately regret it. Damn. She got me. She knows I occasionally snoop, and the fact we have mutual acquaintances keeps juicy news flowing to me.

"Umm hmm," she grunts. "Don't you take your butt back over to him, either. Remember the pain. Remember him being unsure about you, sis. Remember me staying at your place for two weeks so you could get yourself together enough to go to work. Remember that?"

"You don't have to worry about that," I assure her. "Whatever you prayed took every romantic feeling away from me. That chapter is closed for good this time."

"I'm glad. I don't ever want to see you that broken again unless it's death. You get a pass with death, but over a man who was unsure about you from the beginning? Nope. You can call our prayer line for that one."

We laugh. Underneath it all, Regina is like my fun younger sister, but Karyn is the older, wiser and more level-headed one, even though she's only one year older than me.

"Well, girl, I gotta go and set up this Zoom for worship service. I texted you the link and password already."

"I know you did."

"May the Lord keep you, girl."

"I'm kept."

"Well, amen then!"

We laugh and then hang up.

Chapter 3

It's a bright Thursday morning and I need to get out of the house and go somewhere other than the grocery store. I decide to go to the bike store since it's one of the only shops in town that's open and has bikes for sale. It also seems to be the only store that doesn't have a line outside. Well then again, they opened a week ago after being closed for a month.

I walk in and see bikes everywhere. Bikes on wheels, bikes on racks and bikes with SOLD signs on them. An older, tall guy with shoulder-length blonde hair and the body of a teenager walks up to me. He's wearing shorts and a short-sleeved button-down shirt with the store logo stitched on it. I look directly into his ocean blue eyes and then notice his white teeth. I'd date him if I were into white men.

"Welcome to Townside Bikes, how may I help you today?" he says with a wide smile. He probably saw dollar signs when I walked into the door. I should have left the Gucci crossbody bag at home and wore my Coach one.

"I need a new bike," I say.

"What kind of bike riding will you be doing?"

"Happy hour rides? I don't know. Maybe on trails or something. Nothing too fancy, but nothing too basic, either." I look around at the different bikes like I know what to look for.

"Well, we have a few hybrid bikes left," he informs me. "Actually, that's what I was going to recommend. They've been selling out quite fast. You need a fifty-six centimeter."

"A fifty who?"

He lets out a laugh. "Bikes are sized according to your height."

"Oh, okay." I say it like I know what he's talking about.

"We have a few Cannondales and a Trek brand bike. Follow me."

I walk behind him, looking at his calves. Clearly, he's a bike guy. He probably wears the spandex, funny shoes and helmet all the time, and rides the skinny bikes I see going north on A1A out of South Beach. I follow him to a row of bikes near the back of the store.

"We just pulled these out of the warehouse," he says. "I put them together myself."

"Oh, so bikes are your thing?"

"Yup, my father owns the shop. I come from a family of cyclists. See?" he says, pointing to the pictures on the wall behind the register. I see old jerseys in frames, older bikes on the top shelf, and trophies. "I'm on the Everglades Bandits racing team. We place first in the Tour of Florida every year. My father is an Olympic cyclist. He won bronze in the Los Angeles Olympics in '84. My mom is a retired triathlete. And my younger brother is in Europe on a developmental team representing the United States for the Tour De France."

"Impressive."

"Yeah, this shop is our little corner of the bike world," he says proudly. "Anyway, I have one purple Cannondale hybrid here and it's a fifty-six centimeter. You're about five-nine, five-ten in height?"

"Five-ten flat."

"Yup! I knew it," he says as his blue eyes twinkle. He turns toward the bike and takes it off the stand. "You want to take it for a whirl in the front parking lot?"

"Ummm, I'll just pay for it," I say. I don't need nobody seeing me fall and bust my behind in broad daylight. I take the bike when something hits me. "Wait. How much does it cost?"

"Well, I can give it to you for fifteen hundred. Its price is at two thousand, but I need to move bikes because we have so much in inventory and more coming now that things are opening again."

"Okay," I say. "I'll take her."

I look at the brand new glistening bike and think of the helmet in my storage room, but it sort of feels like a new beginning. Maybe happy hour rides on this purple beauty won't be so bad after all. It's actually kind of nice to be outside.

Blue Eyes takes my bike to the register and starts typing things into the computer. I look around at the merchandise, visually inspecting the socks, bags and other colorful stuff in the display cases. I hear a ding dong, followed by loud conversation. I turn my head to see a pack of uncouth brothers wearing "City Ridaz" t-shirts. Some of them have those dreadful looking locs in their hair that look fat and unkempt. One is clean cut, another has a beard with a bald head, and the other is a tall chocolate brother who looks like a sore thumb with his low haircut. I wonder if he is the ringleader and these guys are his minions.

"How you doing, Ms. Lady?" the one with the fat locs says to me with a mouthful of white teeth.

"I'm fine, king," I reply with a half-smile. I know when to turn on my Miami Black and when to turn it off.

"Here's a flyer for you. It's for our happy hour ride," he offers, extending a flyer to me. I look at it and realize this is the ride I'm supposed to be doing with Regina and her new friend guy any day now. Oh, lord. What did she get me into? "Bring ya peoples. Everybody comes. We got lawyers, doctors, police, councilmen. Everybody. Get in where you fit in!"

"Okay, then, king. I'll come through."

"Alright, Ma'am!" he said with a friendly smile.

Ma'am? Do I look like a ma'am? Maybe I need to get rid of this natural hair and wear eye lashes and long weave like these young girls.

The taller, more mature one looks at me and smiles while he walks behind the group.

"Aye, my man Ash," the loc'ed guy calls out. My blue-eyed cutie looks up and smiles.

"Hey, Jonny T! What's good?" Ash greets. "Got some flyers for me for the happy hour ride?"

Jonny T slams the flyer stack on the counter with a smile. "Where the old man at? Is he driving the SAG mobile again?"

"He sure is!"

I stand there wondering how in the world Cutie Blue Eyes linked up with this interesting band of brothers.

Jonny T leans over the counter and looks at my bike, and then looks at me. "You buying this?"

"Yes, that's my bike."

"Bet!" he exclaims. "Then I know you coming to the ride. I'll be looking for you. I'ma call you Purple Rain."

The guys laugh. I even laugh. He's quite infectious.

"Miss Purple Rain, this is Jonathan Thompson," Cutie Blue Eyes introduces. "He's the leader of the City Ridaz. We partner with them and the local hospital for the Happy Hour Ride. Bikes are the only thing keeping people sane during these tough times."

"And that's why she's coming to the ride tomorrow," Jonny T says while pointing at me.

Tomorrow! The ride is tomorrow? The quarantine is making me lose track of the days. This is getting ridiculous.

After a few more minutes of banter and me laughing and smiling at the band of bikers, I collect my bike and roll her out to my white BMW SUV that I gifted myself for working harder than hard last year. It was also a pick-me-up after my meltdown when William got engaged.

I wonder why she left him. Maybe because of the same red flags I saw that I kept ignoring. Red flags like his selfishness and borderline deceptive communication issues that made it convenient for him to slide out of tough conversations. If I see him again, I might risk it all and turn my all-white BMW red with his blood after running him over. Repeatedly. Like he did my heart.

Maybe it's time to call my therapist again.

***

"Yvonne, this is David. David, this is Yvonne," Regina introduces with a smile.

We're in a supermarket parking lot in the middle of Overtown. Cars are everywhere. I even see police squad cars with plain clothes officers taking their bikes out of the trunk and back seats.

Regina is wearing simple black leggings and a Michael Jackson t-shirt. David, a nice-looking golden-brown bloke, is wearing basketball shorts with a Miami Dolphins t-shirt. They are about the same height, but he's a bit on the chubby side. He looks like he used to play football in college and struggled to keep his physique after graduation, but his brown eyes, low haircut, low-shaved beard, and earrings make up for it. He's a departure from her normal tall, dark, handsome and slender men. She must be serious about this one.

"Nice to meet you, David," I say. We do a fist bump.

"You, as well," he replies. "Regina told me a lot about you. You're like a big sister to her."

We laugh. He's well spoken, but I hear a little southern twang. Makes him down to earth.

"She likes to get me out of the house on adventures," I say as she smiles at me from ear to ear. Ohhhh, shat! She really likes this one. I've never seen her smile like this before.

I turn toward my trunk and press the button on the remote. The trunk lifts slowly and reveals my new purple toy laying on the pulled down back seats. My purple helmet and water backpack lay next to it. I hear loud music in the distance as I pull my bike out of the trunk. I tug on my too-tight black exercise pants and tank top. My walking sneakers look tired, but hey, I'm here and a participant in Regina's new adventure.

I feel a hand on my exposed shoulder. I look around to see the tall, handsome guy from the bike shop.

"I see you made it. I'm Stephen," he says, extending his hand for a handshake.

"Yup, I'm here with my people," I reply, taking his hand.

"Jonathan is my cousin," he explains. "We started this ride a few months back with a few people from our jobs and old neighborhood. Now, here we are."

Damn. I don't know why I'm drawn into this guy. Must be the cologne. Yeah. That's it.

"I'm the director for Parks and Rec for the Susie B. Holley Park down the street from here," he continues. "I also co-chair the boys group for my fraternity."

"Oh nice!" I never saw him at any of the citywide Black Greek galas. Oh wait, that's my fraternity brother. I see the signature blue and white rubber bracelet. *Holy shhh.*

"Yvonne, come close to take a picture," Regina says while fondling her phone.

"Nice to meet you, Stephen," I say, reluctantly ending the conversation. "I'm going to take a pic with my friends."

"Nice to meet you. Oh wait, I didn't get your name?"

"Oh, Yvonne."

"Pleasure. Enjoy the ride tonight."

I just *know* he isn't available. Someone that put together and committed to things outside of himself isn't rolling around here single. I walk over to Regina and David, who are already looking like two birds on a branch and I'm the random leaf. She holds up her phone and takes a pic of the three of us.

Click!

Picture taken and I start to look around at the huge crowd. All ages, all walks of life, even different races are here. A souped-up Ford Expedition starts to cruise through the parking lot blasting music. It has all black everything with lights and huge speakers in the back. It's a sight to see. So many people wearing neck gaiters and face masks, trying to escape the quarantine life on a bicycle.

Soon, I close my truck, lock my door, and give myself one final look in the window.

"A'ight y'all," Jonny T announces through a microphone next to the truck with all the music. He's wearing the club t-shirt, basketball shorts and brand new black and red Air Jordans. His voice escapes the speaker into the evening dusk. "Stay in one lane behind the truck. No helmet, no ride. If you don't have a helmet, you can be a part of the welcoming committee when we get back. So, ladies, I don't care if you just got your lace front installed. You better put a helmet on it 'cause if you crack ya head on the sidewalk, I ain't cleaning you and your brain crumbs up off the street. And, all the paramedics and EMTs here tonight are off duty and they ain't cleaning up no brains and weave either."

The crowd laughs.

"Ride marshals have on neon shirts and helmet lights, and we have a few cars in the back in case some of y'all too cute to finish the ride or your bike broke from not doing the safety check before the ride. Y'all got that?"

"Yeahhh!" the crowd replies.

"A'ight, let's ride!" Jonny T says before giving the mic to a uniform-clad police offer.

"Okay, listen up," the police officer says. I hear his voice, but I don't hear words. I assume he is talking about more ride stuff, but I'm not listening.

I tune him out and find my handsome frat brother standing with the other bike leaders. A young-looking girl wearing a colorful sports bra, iridescent silver biker shorts and a mile-long weave walks up to him. They exchange smiles and she whispers in his ear, and then walks away smiling. That must be his girlfriend or friend with benefits. Maybe she's his baby mama or love interest. Oh, well. He's nice to look at, though.

A whistle blows, and the sea of people on their bikes moves like molasses from the parking lot, onto the street, and into the Miami summer sunset. I'm not going to lie. It's a sight to see. Some ride skinny road bikes. Some have hybrids like mine. Some ride beach cruisers. I see a few gnarly looking white kids on skateboards keeping up with the mass group of riders.

I ride behind Regina and David, looking like the quintessential third wheel. Wait a minute. Their bikes are matching. They bought matching bikes? We need to talk about this one. I look away from the new love birds and see people with colorful lights on their bike wheels.

Everyone looks free from the cares of the world. At the stoplight, I overhear random people talking about the effects of the quarantine, like working from home, having reduced hours, and sick family members. I even hear one person say the Friday night rides are keeping him alive and sane. To hear a community of people talking about things they have in common since the quarantine brought down the barriers of separation of class, education and race is refreshing. It makes me think of my own life. Am I truly happy? Is everything really peachy with me?

The traffic light turns green, and the sound truck moves forward, followed by the mass of people. As the wheels spin, I think about my upcoming fortieth birthday and my recent promotion. I think about my beautiful condo on the water in Brickell. I think about all that I've amassed and realize I am dreadfully unhappy. The man who I thought would come to his senses one day and choose me didn't, despite all my best efforts. I fought tooth and nail for a promotion, being one of only a handful of Blacks at my firm, and I just know I'll hit the glass ceiling in a few years. I'm nearing forty and still single in a city that cares about looks more than anything. Not that I'm ugly or anything, but being ambiguously multi-racial and slim with long hair wins out against thick with natural hair. Exotic vacations aren't as fulfilling as it once was. Neither is spending money.

I'm here in Overtown on a bike at sunset, wearing workout tights and a tank top while riding through the areas marked for gentrification with people I don't even know, heading toward Wynwood on a purple bike I just bought yesterday. And to be honest, this is the best I've felt in years. Something has to give.

I need change, and I need change now. I'm calling the therapist on Monday.

Chapter 4

"Ms. Clarke, it's good to hear from you," my therapist Anne says. She looks refreshed on my laptop screen. Or at least what being refreshed should look like when getting to work from home. Then again, I'm sure her caseload is through the roof dealing with people having a hard time with quarantining with spouses, quarantining single, quarantining with kids, or quarantining with depression and anxiety that was diagnosed before the world shut down. I don't know how she does it. Therapists are blessed beyond measure to deal with the potholes on the road of our lives. "How are you?"

"Same," I reply. "How are you holding up?"

"Big adjustment. Little by little and at a reasonable pace. It's not about the outcome. It's how we get to the outcome."

Yup, she's a therapist, alright. Such a therapy answer.

"Anne, I'm unhappy," I admit. "I thought I was happy the last time we spoke, but I'm just…unhappy."

"I remember. You recently got a promotion, you got over an ex, you bought a new car, and your outlook seemed to be on the up and up. But I knew that was a cover up."

"Anne?"

"I was waiting for you to really talk to me. Those items were placeholders. You are trying to fill the void and the pain of that lost relationship and the rejection from the fallout."

I feel the hot tears falling down my cheek. I don't even lift my hand to wipe them away.

"We have more work to do," Anne continues. "Success is what it does. It's an external thing. Are you searching for meaning?"

Dammit, Anne! Why are you pulling my cards and we ain't even ten minutes into the session?

"The one thing we all can grasp out of this quarantine is possibly letting go of what we think we want and grab hold to what we need," she says.

My phone rings. It's Regina. I transfer her to voicemail. I sit back in my chair and realize the one thing I want that I do not have: love. I don't tell Anne, though. She's already trying to snatch all my edges in this therapy session.

"Well," I say, "maybe a different profession will help?"

"Perhaps, but how will that serve you?"

"Umm, well something more meaningful. More than marketing contracts and such. I mean the money is good, but—"

"It's not satisfying?"

"Well…"

"Or are you just lonely and in need of pouring into something greater than yourself? I really think you haven't quite healed from the relationship."

That's it, I'm going to close this laptop because she is pissing me off. Why is she reading me for filth right now? Ugh!

"First, I'm going to suggest that you volunteer your time at a homeless shelter," Anne says, ignoring my facial expressions. "But before you go making a major life change in the middle of a quarantine, let's start small and work with reframing your thoughts while you practice servitude. And speaking of thought logs, I need a fresh set of thought logs before we proceed. I need to get an idea of where your head is."

The last time I did thought logs was right before I healed from William's engagement. She revealed my victim-playing in the relationship. But I *was* the victim. Two months after we broke up for good, he finds a damn fiancé. Well, he's single and broken now, and walking through a worse tunnel than I had. What goes around comes around. I will celebrate his pain with a glass of Rose' after this call.

The rest of the session was a bit lighter. I must admit she came out of the gate on fire, but it's what I needed. After this quarantine, I can't go back to the same. I just can't. Maybe these Friday night sweaty bike rides will bring clarity.

***

"Yvonne, I wasn't sure about telling you this, but I think things with David are deeper than I expected them to be. I'm not going to fight it. I want this to work."

It's Laptop Happy Hour Night with the girls. Regina and I decide to log in before everyone else to talk. Her face and voice are different. She's wistfully happy. I have never seen her look like this, not even when she wins cases and buys a new Gucci bag as a celebration. She looks full of life. I sip my cold Chardonnay.

"Wow, this is definitely a shock, but then again, I kinda knew this already," I reply before taking another sip. I laugh and take another sip. "I mean, you guys have matching bikes."

"From candy rings to matching bikes," Regina muses. "Ha! Yeah, we've kinda been talking about our futures and how we fit. It's been surreal."

She picks up her red wine and takes a sip. "Enough about me. What are you up to?"

"I'm unhappy!"

"Well, damn, I thought you had a good time at the ride! You were doing the electric slide with a red cup of rum punch in your right hand and a glow stick in your left at the after party."

"Not the ride, silly. Just life."

"Sis, you just bought that car, you finally got over William, you're a manager now on the path to director. I just—"

"I'm not happy. My therapist says I need to practice servitude to others to gain more clarity before I go making a rash decision like leaving my job to bag groceries."

"Yvonne, it's the quarantine. It has everybody self-loathing. Maybe this is just a phase. What did that therapist say to you? I don't get it. I can't imagine you pulling up in a BMW SUV to bag groceries with a Gucci cross body purse."

"That ride, I got to see people. Real people. It did something to me."

"Sis, pour soup into a bowl at a homeless shelter and be done with this," Regina dismissed. "Miami ain't cheap to be making leaps of faith. Did you go snooping on William's Facebook again? Anytime you bring him up, see his page, or anything that reminds you of him, you get all soupy."

My phone vibrates. I pick it up and see an email from my therapist titled "servers needed." There goes that damn Anne again.

The laptop makes a ding sound, and Karyn signs into the Zoom Happy Hour, with Sharon right behind her. Everyone has on her video except Sharon. Something's up.

You okay? I text her.

No.

Jesus. Reconciliation might not be going as well as we all thought it would.

I text back, *It's going to take time. Reconciliation ain't linear.* I learned this from watching my parents navigate through my father's infidelity.

We had a huge fight earlier. He left to sleep at a hotel.

"Ladies, ladies, how's everyone?" Karyn asks before she sips her sparkling grape juice from a Miami Dolphins cup. Oh, please send this woman her husband. She watches football and has the cups.

"Good over here," says Regina with a huge smile.

"I'm unhappy," I announce.

"My husband is staying at a hotel," Sharon adds.

I watch Karyn take a huge gulp of her drink. She puts down the cup and looks back into the camera. "I keep telling you heffas to come to virtual church. Heck, you guys barely wanted to come to church when the world was open. You know Jesus—"

"Jesus paaaaiiiddd it allllllllll," I sang. The girls laugh, including Sharon, who has now turned on her camera to reveal a face with watery eyes.

"Sharon, baby come to my place tonight," Karyn suggests.

"I'm okay. I'm going to stay home tonight," Sharon says, pulling her braids into a ponytail.

"Well, your hair looks nice, baby," Karyn says. She had installed Sharon's braids a few weeks prior.

"Yeah, it better look good because I'm putting myself back on the market."

"No, no, no," Regina interjects, echoed by Karyn. I just sit back and sip my wine.

I hurt for Sharon. Her marriage has been rocky since the beginning of the year. She'd suspected that her husband Ron was cheating, but she had difficulty confronting him and reconciling. It's as if he was pushing her to make a decision that will benefit him. A decision that will leave her broken and confused. Ron is Jamaican-American. I warned her about island men. She didn't listen, and here we are.

The girls chatter about the goings on of the marriage. I look at all of our faces on the screen. This quarantine is about to be our undoing. Except for Regina, if she doesn't get in her own way and sabotage a love interest like she always does. She has undiagnosed anxiety. I know it. She will not give up too much control. She can't control love, and when it gets too close, she runs. I'm going to give her Anne's number.

"I just want Ron to act right. We've been married for ten years, and he's acting crazy," Sharon says as she drinks a Heineken beer from the bottle. "First, he wants to open up his own lawn care business, so I gave him the money for it. Then he wanted to do property management. I quit my job and we ran both businesses. The money started coming in and now the weird phone calls and him coming home late. Last Christmas was a total farce."

She takes another sip. "I hosted his damn family at our home for three weeks and he had the nerve to come home late every night. His mother still criticizes my cooking. I don't know. Maybe I should call it quits. Oh, and when I say we're done, he starts yelling and saying that this is his house and "him nah go nowhere."

We were quiet at this point. Bad enough he had no green card and she married him. He's a hard worker, though. I'll give him that. He has two successful businesses. They have a nice house in Rolling Oaks, three cars, one beautiful daughter together, and three of his own kids in Jamaica. But everything isn't always what it seems on the outside.

Our happy hour turns into a therapy session for Sharon, and rightfully so. She needs it. She needs us. And we are here for her.

***

I wake up with a mild headache. Happy hour went until midnight, with Sharon eventually going to Karyn's house to spend the weekend. I'm glad she did. She shouldn't be alone right now, especially not in a quarantine.

Sharon's heartbreak last night has me in a sore spot this morning. She doesn't deserve to be left on a limb by that husband of hers. Jesus! I think I'll get a cat instead of a husband.

I look into my mini forest on the balcony and see the sunlight pierce my room through the branches and leaves of my plants. It's seven-thirty. I need to get to the homeless shelter in thirty minutes for orientation. I was just getting used to languishing in my bed until ten. I said I was unhappy, but I'd rather be unhappy and stay in bed until ten.

I hop in the shower, soap up, rinse off, dry off and get dressed. Workout tights, t-shirt and a pair of leopard print Adidas sneakers will be the outfit for today. I gather my unruly hair in a ponytail under a cap and head out.

I literally fly down I-95. This BMW really has a lot of speed on her. I turn up some old school Chaka Khan and get myself into the lyrics. A few quick maneuvers, and I'm at the homeless shelter. There are cars everywhere. Clearly, this must be volunteer day. I find an empty space around the corner near a small enclave of homeless people, shopping carts and cardboard boxes. I immediately sink into the reality that me being unhappy could be unwarranted, especially when I see persistent homelessness right in front of me.

I get out of the car and head to the back entrance. The door is open, and I walk in to see about forty people all somewhat socially distanced. I'm here because my therapist wants to avert a potential mid-life crisis situation. *They* are here to make their companies look good.

I look to my left and I see Mr. Tall 'n' Handsome from the bike ride last week. He is wearing his fraternity shirt. I'm stopped in my tracks. Why do unavailable men captivate me and overly eager men annoy me? Maybe I can unpack that in therapy.

"Good morning, everyone. My name is Carlos, and I am the weekend meal production lead at the shelter," the director announces. "I'm going to break this group up into socially distanced pods, where some of you will be serving meals, putting meal kits together, and assembling PPE kits for our homeless citizens. Saturday is our busy day, so plan to be here for four hours."

Four hours. Really?

"Ok, I need everyone to count one, two, three, four from the front row," Carlos commands.

I hear varying audible numbers until they reach me. I call off four just before my phone vibrates. It's Regina. I'll send her a text later. I need to focus.

Everyone is herded into groups by their numbers.

"Hey, I remember you from the ride last week," a very confident, yet familiar, voice says. It's him!

"Yes, it was quite the experience," I reply.

"I can tell. I saw you doing the Electric Slide."

Jesus. Did everyone see me doing the Electric Slide? So much for being incognito. "I'm quite the dancer."

"That, you are. Hey, what's your name again?"

"Yvonne."

"Stephen. Nice to meet you again."

"Same here, Frat."

"Wait, you're a soror?"

"That, I am. I saw the bracelet last week, but I didn't want to do the whole name, chapter, year thing. It's annoying sometimes.

"Incognito again, huh?" He looks right through my eyes into my mind, as if trying to crack a code or something. Damn! He has the most beautiful big brown eyes.

"Okay, ladies and gentlemen. Group four, follow me," the director shouts.

I walk toward the group behind the director. Stephen follows.

"I see we're in the same group," he says.

Oh hell, yeah. I just need to focus on whatever I'm pouring into a bowl, 'cause I'm not in the mood for another failed almost relationship. "Yes, I see. We will have some fun this morning, eh?"

I'm trying to be cool, but this additional scenery is encouraging and annoying altogether. I just wanted to spoon soup into a bowl and meditate on why the hell I'm unhappy, and now I'm distracted.

I follow the large group into a food service area that looks like an assembly line. Everything is separated into the food groups for a lunch: veggies, carbs, protein, dessert and the utensils and trays. Everyone self-segments themselves to a station. Stephen and I find ourselves in the protein section. Baked chicken and meatballs. We're supposed to put one of each on the plates. We assume our positions next to each other in the assembly line.

"So, I never saw you at the citywide Greek events," I said as I spooned meatballs onto a meal tray.

"I either got off too late to attend, or I was just tired. I only moved down here about two years ago. I haven't really had time to meet the Greeks outside of chapter meetings."

"I get it."

"So, what do you do?"

"Marketing and contracts for large corporations," I replied as if it were no big deal.

"Boss lady."

"Eh, I'm losing my passion for it."

"I used to work in corporate America for a consultant firm in Texas," he stated.

"Oh? Got tired of travel or the perks. Which one?"

"Well, I was losing time with my son, and my marriage started to suffer."

"I'm so sorry to hear that."

"I'm to blame a bit. The money was good, our lifestyle was good, but I was too tired on weekends to do much of anything, including my wife."

"Poor lady."

"Yeah, she started finding other things, or shall I say, another person to do. We divorced and I got custody of my son and moved back home."

"I'm really sorry to hear that." Dang. A divorcee because the wife cheated. This is a first for me. It's usually the other way around. There was an awkward silence between us.

"What about you? Pretty lady such as yourself has got to be spoken for."

"I wish. On again, off again boyfriend who didn't want to get married got engaged three months after we broke up."

"I'm sorry. People can be really shitty when it comes to relationships."

"Well, karma got him get back because that young girl decided to call off the engagement and broke up with him."

"Sister Karma don't play, huh?" he remarked with a laugh.

"Nope! So now I'm trying to find my way. I figure I'd give some time to the people who need it."

We silently continued serving for a few more minutes.

"I hope this doesn't sound too forward, but would you like to get brunch tomorrow or coffee?" he asks suddenly. "You have a cool vibe. I think we have some good stories to share."

Whoa. He just asked me out! I wasn't expecting this. I'd better say something quick. "Sure. Why not? We can all use a good storytelling session over socially distanced food."

Shit! I wasn't supposed to say that.

"Let's connect afterwards, Ms. Yvonne, my sorority sister and fellow cyclist."

***

"I ended things with David. Everything was moving too fast."

"Regina, what the hell are you doing?"

"Just trust me on this one."

"No, I will not." I'd just come home from the shelter and was kicking off my shoes. It's cool in my condo. Welcoming. Just like Stephen's presence. I still smell remnants of his cologne from when we hugged after serving meals. Regina, however, is blowing my high with her foolishness.

"Yvonne, look—"

"Regina, you need to talk to my therapist. I'll text you the number."

"Yvonne, I feel comfortable with my decision. He wanted to get exclusive, and I don't think I'm quite ready for that right now."

"Ma'am, we are in the middle of a frickin' quarantine, and this man says he wants to lock things down while the world is moving out of control. What more do you want? Oh, I know: control!"

"Seriously, Yvonne?"

"You control everything in your life, but the minute you can't control something, out it goes with the bath water," I preached. "Call Anne. She'll get you worked out, 'cause this is the third good man you're about to let go of."

Regina lets out a deep breath, and then goes eerily silent. "You're right."

"Of course, I'm right. Look, life is showing us right now, this minute, we have no control over anything like we thought we did. It's like we're chasing the pavement looking for stability when the stability is within ourselves."

"Well damn, how many therapy books you been reading while knocking back glasses of wine?"

"Don't ask, but sis, let go. Everything will settle to where it's supposed to be."

I put her on speaker while I send her Anne's number via text.

"Really? You just sent me Anne's number?"

"Yes! Now, do you want to hear about me serving food to the homeless while standing next to a handsome man who was at the ride last week?"

Regina laughs and then we have our gabfest. I tell her about the brunch meetup tomorrow. For some reason, I'm excited, which is scary. I haven't been excited over much lately, except for finding out karma made her ice-cold special delivery to William's doorstep, but that's beside the point. I was doing something outside of myself.

Chapter 5

Karyn invited me to a small group church service. Only thirty people are allowed in the sanctuary.

I sit here in casual clothes with a mask on and my brand new Bible in my hand, which makes me feel bad. I have one my mother gave me that is more worn out than this one, but leaves my home under no circumstances unless a hurricane is coming. I look around at the other masked faces whose eyes look tired from all the pandemic drama. They look like they need a word. I need a word, too. We all need a word.

The praise team is spread out in the choir stand. I see the pastor and a new face. The pastor welcomes everyone. Karyn sits a few spaces down from me. I can see her smiling through her face mask. I smile back. She is just happy that I got my butt here.

Karyn texts, *The guy sitting next to the pastor is a guest co-pastor from Palm Beach. He's single!*

I listen to the pastor's message. A few attendees shout their amens and the organist plays a riff every now and then. This quarantine is indeed tough. Everyone is coming either to the end or the beginning of themselves. I'm somewhere in the middle.

I feel my phone vibrate in my purse. I reach for it while still watching the pastor. It's Stephen. I send him a text that I'll see him soon. I then text Karyn, who is furiously taking notes. *I need you to be making eyes at the guest pastor and not at your notebook.*

She reads the message and then looks at me with a "girl hush" look.

"He asked me out for lunch," Karyn says as she gathers her notes and Bible after service.

"Well, good."

"If I never marry or anything, Yvonne, you know I'll be okay, right?"

"Karyn, you're talking like you're eighty years old. You're forty-two. That's young."

"I'm serious, Yvonne. I have my business, my church family and my friends. I'm really okay," she says before putting her purse over her shoulder. "I knew the guest pastor years back. He just moved back down here."

"Just be open, Karyn. I really think you intimidate these men on purpose."

"I'll think of this lunch date as practice for when I'm sitting across from Boaz or Abraham. He is nice looking through."

I laugh. One thing about Karyn is, she never complains about spending the holidays dateless, like we do. She just threw herself into her work, built a successful business and went to church. She seemed content while we weren't. I think I may start going to church more often. Maybe some of her contentness will rub off on me.

***

It's Monday, and after a rather eventful weekend, I am right back at work. The emails start coming in and the meetings commence. From seven until eleven, I am between emails, work and impromptu meetings.

My phone vibrates. It's a text message from Stephen. *I really enjoyed our afternoon. I hope I'm not being forward by asking you out for another Sunday lunch n stroll. If not, I'll be more than content with you still coming to our Friday night Happy Hour Ride.*

I haven't really been on dates after William. Well, if you count the hit and run with a young manager from our D.C. office, and the boring ring-around-the rosey with a pompous community college professor and department chairperson. And why am I still working at this job? Luckily for me, it's almost noon and my session with Anne is about to start.

I run and grab a bottle of water and a bowl of fruit, and then sit on my couch in the living room. I open my personal laptop and log into the telechat. Anne is already front and center.

"Good afternoon, Yvonne."

"Afternoon, Anne."

"How was the event at the homeless shelter?"

"It was great, actually. I'm thinking of going back. I ran into an acquaintance. Very handsome guy. We ended up going to lunch."

"Stay there. Did anything come up in your mind? Sometimes when our focus is off of ourselves, it allows our minds to see things a bit clearer."

"Well, I realized the fact that I'm an only child of older parents may have had an impact on my life choices. I never got a chance to just live or try things. I find myself drawn to men who are emotionally unavailable with no plans because maybe I don't want to have plans for myself."

"This is big, Yvonne. Did you ever have any hobbies or any passions?"

"Well, I'm in a sorority. I traveled a lot."

"But those aren't passion things that speak to your heart."

Dammit, Anne. Can you not snatch my edges so quickly in the session?

"I also realized why I allowed myself to stay with William for so long without a hard commitment. And why men who are stable with a plan don't excite me."

"This is really, really big, Yvonne. I feel once you find your passion and get engaged in something that speaks to you, there will be a groove that will feel comfortable to you. Are you still in contact with William?"

Oh, God, I hope she's not suggesting some sort of closure conversation, 'cause it ain't happening.

"You mentally have unfinished business with William, and until you come to terms with the breakup, you are going to be in limbo about really moving on."

"Dammit, Anne, I don't want to talk to him. Nothing he's going to say will make sense. *Nothing* men say after a breakup makes sense."

"It's not about him making sense; it's about you moving on. Let's table talking about the new handsome gentleman until you finally close this door."

Talking to Anne wears me the hell out. Now I remember why I stopped my sessions with her. I need a glass of wine.

"And, I'd like you to remain dry for the next few weeks. It can be staying away from a go-to snack, drink or whatever crutch you've been using."

"Wine?"

"Whatever it is. We have to get you unstuck."

What the hell, Anne? I just wanted to see if I needed to find a new job. Why are we going back to William? Jesus H. Christ. I think I'm gonna take my bike for a spin tomorrow. I really need to clear my head of this William conversation.

***

By Thursday, I'm laughing on the phone with Stephen. This is the third late night in a row we've talked. I even asked him about the thick brown-skinned girl who walked up to him last week. Surprisingly she is the older sister of one of the boys in his after-school program. She knows she has no chance with him, and he makes it clear every time.

We're going to meet up for a bike ride Saturday morning. This is the most comfortable I've felt in a long time.

The conversation with William still looms in my head. Maybe I *should* reach out to him. Maybe Anne is right. Maybe I finally need to close this door on my own. Just because he closed the door on me, doesn't mean I closed the door on him. I don't want to see him, though. It will have to be over the phone.

After I get off the phone with Stephen, I send William an email. *Hey William, I know it's been a long time and I hope all is well with you. I wanted to reach out to see how you're doing. Give me a call.*

I hit send. I can't even reach for a glass of wine. Instead, I reach for yet another ice cold can of flavored seltzer from the mini fridge in my room. No sooner than I open the can, my cell phone rings. I recognize the number. "Hello?"

"Yvonne?"

"William. How are you?" I sit down on my couch. My heart is racing. Ugh!

"I've been okay, and yourself?"

"I'm okay. Um, thank you for calling me."

"I'm glad you reached out. I've been meaning to catch up with you."

"You have?" I ask. Why?

"Yeah. I, uhh, wanted to apologize for everything."

Snap! It looks like I don't have to say much after all. Whew! Looks like this might just be the easiest door-closing conversation ever. I sip some of my seltzer.

"It was never *you* really. I just wasn't in a place to make that step, and not even with the next woman. I just know I needed to do something with my life. When I realized how messed up I treated you, it was best I just moved on."

"William, you moved on from me before I even found out what was going on."

"That was real crass of me. I just didn't want to let you go. You're too damn good of a woman, Yvonne, and I just couldn't measure up to what you needed."

"So, you go for low-hanging fruit?"

"Be nice. Sonya is a really nice girl."

"I'm sure she is. You asked her to marry you," I state, deciding not to mention that I know the relationship is over.

"I deserve your anger, Yvonne. Trust me when I say, I paid for what I did to you."

"You got engaged after we broke up to the girl we kept running into on our Sunday dates. Like, what were you thinking?"

"I didn't handle things well. But for what it's worth, Yvonne, I always loved and respected you. I just couldn't be what you needed and I just didn't want to try and fail with you knowing what you truly deserve."

"So, cheating on me was your exit?"

"I'm sorry. And yes, karma came and kicked me down. In fact, I'm glad because I started getting cold feet."

Jesus, he was gonna marry this girl with cold feet? Oh, he was gonna wiggle out of that marriage quick. I dodged a bullet! Good for her to kick his trifling ass to the curb. Damnit, I need a glass of wine. Sorry Anne, I'm getting my recompense. I rush to the kitchen to pour a glass of Pinot. "So, you cheat on me, break up with me, ask the girl you cheated on me with to marry you, and then get cold feet in the midst of all that. I don't understand, William."

Now I'm getting pissed. Somebody told me when you try to seek closure from a man, what he says will never make sense. Right now, the math ain't mathin'.

"I just wasn't ready for anything. Your love and her love unfortunately couldn't change that. I'm sorry, Yvonne. I didn't mean to handle you like that, and I hope you can accept my apology."

"I have no other choice but to, William."

"Look, can we meet up for coffee or something? I'd really like to see you."

Snap! He wants to see me? I have pandemic weight. Wait a minute. Karyn told me don't take my butt back to him. This is a trap. "I'll have to get back to you on that one."

"That's fair. I have to get up early for work in the morning, but I'm really sorry again."

"Thank you for the apology, William. Good night," I say, feeling the final chain around my heart falling to the ground of my subconscious.

He sounded so subdued. That carefree light-heartedness I remember in his voice was gone. He seemed more grounded. He sounded serious. I sounded lively. I sounded free. I lean back into the couch and close my eyes as the tears well up in my eyes and slowly fall down my cheek.

I wasn't sad. Just relieved. This man in his brokenness broke me. The other girl had the strength to see it and kick his butt to the curb. Smart girl. I still don't like her, though. She can kick rocks in those cute little Tory Burch sandals she wore every time we saw her. I grab a throw blanket and curl myself under it. A weight fell off me and I need to finally rest.

Chapter 6

"Ready for the ride tonight? David is gonna come!" Regina announces.

"You guys talking again? I'm glad he's coming," I say before taking my bike out of the closet and reaching for my helmet. I'm actually looking forward to the ride. I need to feel the hot South Florida air on my skin, and I'm looking forward to seeing Stephen.

"Well, after two intense sessions with Anne, I realized that I need to stop throwing away men and just let go," Regina says. "I can't control another person. My law practice? Yes. A man? No."

I listen to Regina give me the rundown of her therapy sessions with Anne while I set up my water bottles. I won't tell the girls about my conversation with William. Well, not until our online brunch chat on Saturday. My phone beeps. It's Stephen. I don't click over. Regina is more important right now.

"So yes, I decided to call David. We're going to take things really slow."

"So no more matching bikes and stuff?" I say with a smirk.

"Ha! No more matching stuff."

We hang up and I finish getting dressed. Work didn't even feel like work today. I've just been floating. I even started looking at corporate community outreach positions. I'm ready to stop living my life according to a template of success, I think.

I look at my condo before I walk out of the front door, seeing all the trappings of success, and now I'm looking for myself amongst it all. I close the door behind me and walk to my vehicle. I load up my bike and drive into the sunset.

* * *

After the ride, Regina, Karyn and I jump on video chat to console Sharon. During our ride, she texted us to announce that she's filing for divorce. She isn't crying; she just looks blank. We are quiet while she sits in her bedroom drinking wine.

"Sharon, I'm so sorry," Regina says.

"I'm sorry I didn't listen to you guys," Sharon says. "I saw the signs, but I ignored all of them. He doesn't know I'm divorcing him. I'm sure he's going to put up a fight, but I'm ready. I've changed the locks and arranged to have the papers served to him at the office while I'm not there."

"I'm proud of you, Sharon. You are doing a brave thing," I say. No woman deserves to stay in a marriage that hurts her beyond what she can even fathom. I put down my glass. I'm not even in the mood to drink my normal Pinot. I hate seeing any of my friends broken.

"I'll be fine," Sharon says. "I feel a bit relieved at this point. I knew I couldn't do another year, month or week like this. I'm hoping he doesn't make this ugly. Just split half and leave me alone."

"No, Ma'am! You need more than that. He got his citizenship off your back!" Regina proclaims.

She's right. Immigration papers ain't cheap.

"I don't even care," Sharon says before taking another sip from her glass.

My phone vibrates. It's William asking if I thought about meeting face to face. I don't answer. My mind is floating right now. Another text message comes in. It's Stephen. *I want to see you tomorrow after your volunteer hours. Is it okay?* I tell him yes.

"Who you over there texting, Ma'am?" Karyn asks, desperate to break the weight of the group chat.

"Stephen." The girls perk up. Even Sharon. "He's a good guy."

"I bet he is," Regina says. "I didn't even see you guys after we left the parking lot for the ride tonight."

I smile a bit, mindful that Sharon is the focus. But I couldn't hold the fact that I had spoken with William. "I spoke to William a few days ago."

The girls get quiet. You could hear a Florida roach pee on a palm branch.

"You what?" Karyn says. "I told you not to—"

"Aht aht, the therapist told me to do it," I interjected. "It's part of my closure so I can really handle the other issues I have going on."

Karyn isn't happy. I gotta mitigate her displeasure. After all, she loved and prayed me through that dark time.

"Don't worry, Karyn. I promise you nothing is going on or will go on."

"So, what did he say?" Regina asks, looking just as serious as Karyn. Sharon is checked out at this point with her own pain.

"Well, he told me he had issues going on and he knew he couldn't live up to what I needed and that he did a poor job of handling things."

"He got engaged to the chick he cheated on you with," Karyn says, not giving an inch to my soon-to-be breakthrough explanation. "What other crap did he say?"

"He apologized."

"Of course, that's what he's going to do. That's a man's go-to when he doesn't have anything logical to say after he wrecks your life," Karyn says, her face wrinkled.

"Karyn, it's okay. I got my closure. In fact, I felt light as a feather when it was all said and done. I'm finally free."

I dare not tell her he asked to meet up. That will send her through the roof.

"Okay, Yvonne," Karyn relents. "I love you like my own blood and I never want to see you that broken again. Ever!"

I am silenced. You don't realize how broken you are until someone witnesses your undoing. I completely unraveled after William and damn near went dark when he popped up engaged three months later. I grab my wine glass and take a sip.

"Who wants to have a sleepover?" I suggest. "We need it. Take a damn take-home COVID test before you all come to my place."

"I'm on my way!" Sharon says after she puts down her glass. "The kids are with my mom this weekend. I'll see you in a few."

She closes the laptop.

"I'm coming, too," Regina says.

"I'm on my way," Karyn says before closing out the call.

I smile and then take a deep breath before opening William's text. As much as Karyn's words annoyed me, she was right. The door is open, but do I really want to keep it open? I know what needs to be done.

William, I want to thank you for your call the other night. Thank you for the apology. Thank you for the clarity. I have what I need to finally move on from what happened. There is no need to see each other. Let's keep our chapter closed. I wish you all the best in the future and your healing.

I put down the phone and gather blankets and pillows for the girls. I remember William would pull that same "can I see you" after our on-again-off-again talks. Sorry, William, but I can't look past a whole engagement.

Who knew a bike would bring me such clarity? I don't know where this quarantine ride is going to take me and the girls. Maybe we haven't run amuck like I thought. I think this newfound clarity will usher me into the next phase of my life, just as long as the store doesn't run out of Shiraz and the pandemic finally comes to an end.

Or not.

Mattering

By Angie Wyatt-Braden

Part 1

I heaved my exhausted body from the Uber Black and thanked the frumpy driver, whose coffee-brown head was crowned with a curly, bleached blond mohawk. He smiled at me and flashed all twenty-eight of his snow-white veneers in my direction as he shamelessly surveyed my curvy profile. His perfectly shaded teeth were in stark contrast to the dingy white button-down shirt he wore over his bulgy midsection. I pretended not to notice his intrusive stare as I balanced my weight on the balls of my aching feet and felt the flames shoot through all ten of my perfectly manicured toes.

"Nice building," he remarked as he greedily stared at my bosom.

Looking in the opposite direction of the driver, I scanned the perimeter of the entrance to my building to ensure there was no one outside awaiting my arrival. I grabbed my Coach computer bag and my Louis Vuitton purse from the creamy, leather upholstered seat.

"Have a good evening," I feebly mumbled as I motioned to close the door to the shiny, silver BMW.

"Excuse me, pretty lady. You have plans tonight?" he asked before I could close the door.

Me and this weirdo were trapped in the vehicle for thirty-four minutes as we needled our way through the four-mile commute from my office to my condo. And even though I was glad he chose complete silence as the soundtrack of our ride, I didn't understand why he would wait until I was out of the vehicle to suddenly inquire about spending time with me. Before I used my hip to whip the door closed, I replied with a resounding, "Yep."

I didn't even look back to wave at him as he yanked his car back into the barely moving traffic that surrounded my condo tower like a boiling moat.

I stepped into the lobby of my building and flashed a perfectly lipstick-applied smile at Tony, the faithful, always friendly doorman. He was parked in his usual spot behind a lofty granite security desk.

As a daily ritual, I winked at my mirrored image that was displayed on the 4K security monitor. My ruby lips sparkled like a satin ribbon, complimenting my smudge free, dewy, amber complexion. The whites of my eyes were tinted with evidence of how exhausted I was, and in the crease of my leave out was a slither of silver hair. But yet and still, I was an exceptionally good-looking forty-year-old woman. I made it a point to look my best, even if I didn't feel my best.

I turned my attention back to the doorman, intending to engage him instead of inconspicuously flirting with myself. But before I could part my lips to greet the doorman, two deeply tanned, blonde, exceptionally tall women, who may have well been faceless and nameless, whooshed past me as they exited the place each of us called home. They giggled and pranced on their spiked heels out to their now approaching limo. Neither woman acknowledged me or the doorman, who offered them wishes of a safe evening as they disappeared into the back of their luxurious ride.

Since I moved here two years ago, one of the aspects that I found to be most odd about this condo building is how so many people can share a place, call it home, but refuse to be neighborly. Well, at least, they refused to be neighborly toward me. They planned their ski trips, dashed to happy hour at the most exquisite bars in Downtown Dallas, and discussed stock options around me, but not with me. The color of my dollars had no influence on how they perceived my value as a woman, neighbor, potential business partner, or friend.

My only friend in this building was now a former friend. Turns out he was as unneighborly as the rest.

"Good evening, Tony."

"Hey there, Ms. Grayson. Good day at work?"

"Wonderful," I lied, glancing at the now opening elevator.

I dashed to the elevator and pressed the number fourteen and watched the button flash with promise as I kept my eyes on the lobby's entrance until the doors of the elevator restricted my view. I exhaled and relaxed my nerves as the metal doors clamped and the floor took flight. Tuning out the quintessential elevator music, I silently counted each layer, praying that I would not experience any interruptions before I arrived at my hiding spot.

***

When the doors of the elevator parted, I leaned forward, scanned the carpeted corridor, and rushed to my door with my key fob ready and aimed.

Home free, I thought.

Unleashing my victimized feet from the four-inch, Tom Ford stilettoes had to be the first order of business when I stepped over the threshold of my overly priced abode. I dropped my bags on the hardwood floor, slumped down on my smokey gray recliner, and lifted each one of my feet to my lap so I could unfasten the straps of my shoes. I massaged my feet with care until each foot relaxed into its natural arch.

Next, I stood and grabbed the hem of my gold Dior contour dress and pulled it over my head, not caring if I disturbed any of the curls that snaked from my $2,000 sew-in. I unfastened the front snap of my bra and let gravity have its way. Next, I unpeeled the one-size-too-small Spanx from my waist and breathed deeply for the first time in six hours. I leaned back into the recliner with nothing binding me but a single pair of purple lace panties and some anonymous, Brazilian chick's bundled hair.

"Alexa, shuffle my *I Don't Give a Damn* playlist."

The first of my fifty, carefully selected chill songs poured from the surround sound speakers in my two-bedroom condo.

I closed my eyes and let Lucky Daye steal me away to Paris with his soulful serenade.

If I were a weed smoker, this would be the music I would listen to as I got high. But because I adamantly refused to do any illegal drugs, I would sit in my recliner naked and eat butter pecan ice cream out of the carton as I vibed to the music. Since my normal weight, which was already too much, was now becoming more of too much, I had decided to lay off the ice cream for the next few weeks. The music would just have to help me unload all the burdens of my day.

Before I could deeply slip off into my evening nap, my phone vibrated, startling me out of my blissful sleep. Always regretting that I don't have the nerve to put my phone on do not disturb when I'm not at work, I peered at the screen to see who was calling. Sighing at the unwelcomed disturbance, I bookmarked my chill time to take the call. Being a champion code switcher, I put on my best good daughter voice.

"Hi, Mama."

"Syl, me and Jackie been calling you all day. Where you been?"

Where am I every day between the hours of eight and five? I thought, but said, "I've been at work. How are you, Mama?"

My mother was the not-so-proud mother of two daughters and three grandchildren. Her grandchildren also called her Mama because she was actually raising them as her kids. My younger sister, Jackie, was on her second stint in state jail. This time, she was arrested for shoplifting out of CVS.

Most people would immediately rush to sympathetic judgment, offering Jackie some leniency, thinking she was grabbing items she needed but could not afford. Instead, she was grabbing items she could take back to the hood and sell for crack.

"Everything alright?" I asked.

"Jackie need you to talk to that lawyer for her. She say they tryin' to pin some other shoplifting cases on her."

"Well, he's not talking unless I'm paying."

"But ain't he a friend or something of yours? He can't do you no favors?"

"No, Ma'am. He's not a friend. He's a colleague."

"Well, you can't pay him? Jackie's your only sister," she asserted. "God blessed you with that good job, so you could be a blessing to others. Don't give Him a reason to take it away."

Mama never took into account that I sent her a thousand dollars each month to take care of Jackie's three children, as if I was any one of Jackie's baby daddies. All Mama knew was that my giving was never enough. I guess it's because the needs were never fully met, so she felt like I wasn't doing enough.

Mama excused Jackie's not doing enough because she believed all of Jackie's issues to be a result of her failure to prevent her brother, our uncle, from secretly fondling Jackie from age six to eleven. Mama found out about the hideous transgression when Jackie had a full-blown meltdown after abortion number two and baby number one. Jackie unleashed the truth about her abuse and revealed her abuser's identity to Mama while being treated for depression in the county psychiatric hospital. Her newborn was only three weeks old when she tried to shuck off the weight of the painful secret.

What Jackie didn't realize was that discharging the secret would not alleviate her from the pain of what happened. In fact, the pain was more pronounced when Uncle Howard denied Jackie's claim. After that, Jackie abandoned her first born and replaced it with marijuana, X pills, cocaine, and crack.

Mama never forgave herself for not seeing or either acknowledging the red flags. She wore the burden of Jackie's painful childhood like a scarf that strangled and immobilized her day after day, month after month, year after year, grandchild after grandchild, arrest after arrest, unanswered prayer after unanswered prayer, and heartbreak after heartbreak.

Mama stayed frustrated with me because I had the audacity to take my heavy garment of pain off long enough to try to have a life outside of her, Jackie, and her grandbabies. So, even though I proved to be responsible, gainfully employed, and a successful contract attorney, Mama was no happier with me than she was Jackie.

"Sylvia Ann Grayson, what good is making all that money if you can't help your sister?"

I always knew when I'd struck a nerve with Mama when she'd call me by my full government name. She only calls me Syl when the waters of our relationship are flowing peacefully.

"Mama, please do not say I don't help Jackie," I protested. "I help Jackie by putting money on her books and paying for her jailhouse calling card. I help Jackie when I buy school clothes for her kids. I help Jackie when I buy Christmas gifts for the kids and put her name on the gifts."

"We know what you do, Sylvia. What I tell you about bragging on yourself?"

"Mama, I'm not bragging. I'm just asking for a little credit for what I do."

"Well, since you think you're so helpful, please talk to the lawyer for your sister," she shot back. "Talking to that lawyer gets Jackie the representation she needs to make sure they don't try to pin no more cases on her. She need to be home with these kids. I'm getting too old to look after these kids all by myself."

Even though Mama and I both knew there was no chance in the world that Jackie would get out and help her with the kids, I remained silent. "I'll call him in the morning, Mama."

"Thank you, baby. Mama sho' appreciate it."

We talked for the next fifteen minutes about how the kids were doing in school and what she planned to cook for dinner. Then, I came up with an excuse to get off the phone. "Mama, I better get off of here if I'm going to call that lawyer for Jackie."

I knew if I said I had to get off the phone to do anything for Jackie, she would relent and bless me for the rest of the evening. I was right.

***

Rather than calling my colleague to discuss Jackie's new issues, I decided to turn my music back on and take a hot bath. I slipped off my panties and sat my bottom on the cold surface of my garden tub as I turned the chrome handle to unleash the multiple jets of water surrounding me. I always liked to run my bathwater while I was in the tub. That way, I could elevate the temperature of the water as high as my body could handle. I leaned back in the tub and let my timely playlist caress my frontal lobe while the heat of the water melted away all the frustration and stress that existed in my body.

After rinsing off the last of the soap from my freshly exfoliated skin, I heard a light knock at the door. *Who is that?*

I used my toes on my right foot to lift the stopper and grabbed my towel from the counter as I stepped out of my tub. The knocking persisted, but I was naked, wet, and puzzled as to why anyone was at my door.

Please go away, I thought as I quickly dried off and grabbed my silk robe from the top drawer in my adjoining closet. I scurried to the door as I was putting on the robe and tapped the screen on my security camera. I nearly fainted when I saw my unexpected visitor. "What the—?"

The knocking increased its pace and volume, matching my heart rate. I stepped back from the door, hoping I was still sleeping in the recliner and this was only a dream. But reality gripped me when I felt a tiny stream of warm water slither down my leg to my ankle.

I stepped to the door and unlocked the deadbolt. I inhaled and slightly cracked the door, offering my uninvited visitor a very nasty frown.

"Sylvia, we need to talk."

"I'm not dressed."

"And?"

Our eyes met and the meaning was understood. Jarret had seen me naked dozens of times. Naked in my bed, naked on my recliner, naked in my tub, naked on the kitchen counter, naked on the balcony, naked on my desk at work, naked in the back seat of his Lincoln Navigator, and naked in the bed he shares with his wife.

"Sylvia, how long are we going to do this?"

"Do what?"

He tapped the door and said, "This."

my neighbor, who is usually quite unneighborly, stepped out of her unit. She wrinkled her already wrinkled nose and looked in the direction of my door, piercing me with her familiar suspicious blue-eyed stare.

"See" I hissed in a sharp, whispery tone. "Look at what you've done. The last thing I need is for these white folks to be in my business."

"Well, let me in."

"I'm telling you for the last time. Stop stalking me."

"Stalking you? I live in this building just like you do."

"But you live on the twenty-first floor with what's-her-name. You have no reason to be on this floor."

"I'm looking at the reason."

***

Nine months ago, I went to the lobby to wait for an Uber to the airport, when a beautiful, perfectly postured, tall brother walked from the pop-up cantina into the sunlight-drenched lobby. He was dressed in navy slacks, chocolate brown loafers, a sky-blue button down, and a white lab coat. His gray eyes were a beautiful contrast to his hazelnut skin. The Rolex on his left wrist was a postcard of where this brother was coming from and where he was going.

Our eyes locked before he splashed me with his beautiful smile. I looked away. Not because I wanted to, but because I couldn't look him in the face. His smile disarmed me, sending me into a freefall of unexpected emotion. I wanted to know this man, but didn't exactly know why. It wasn't like he was the first black doctor I had ever seen. He certainly wasn't the most handsome man I had ever encountered. So, what was it that I saw when I looked into his eyes?

I stared down at my phone, pretending to study my Uber app. As soon as the Uber arrived, I dashed out into the safety of the outdoors and hopped into the car. I didn't even look back as we pulled out into the slow-moving traffic.

***

Three weeks later, when I had forgotten about the dreamy brown apparition, I saw him again coming out of the same cantina, holding a cellophane-wrapped blueberry muffin. He smiled at me again, but this time there was no quick escape. I froze in place, like I was an ice queen.

"Good morning. How are you?"

I noticed I was holding my breath when I was forced to reply to his unexpected inquiry.

"Good morning. I'm well and you?"

Extending his hand, he introduced himself. "Dr. Jarret Franklin. It's nice to meet you."

"A charge went through my hand when our fingers touched. I was almost breathless again. I looked down at my Tiffany blue toenails and then back up at his face. His smile was still locked on me.

I reciprocated the smile and said, "Um, I'm Sylvia. It's nice to meet you, Jarret."

He took in all of my sixty-eight inches and hundred-eighty-seven pounds with a sweep of his sexy eyes when he asked, "Do you live here?"

"I do."

He offered me a boyish chuckle when he replied, "Me too."

And that was the beginning of what I thought would be everything. But instead of it being the beginning of everything, it was the beginning of nothing at all.

Jarret and I stood at the door, daring each other to relent in our personal resolve. Him on the outside, and me on the inside, painfully illustrating the difference in our intentions. I looked down at his left hand and noticed his wedding band, which caused me to clinch my resolve even tighter.

"Jarret, I'm not letting you in. I'm kindly asking you to leave."

"Sylvia, I've tried calling you, but you've been declining all my calls. I've sent you dozens of texts, but you never respond."

"There's a reason why I don't respond."

The wrinkly nosed neighbor stepped out in the corridor with her black labradoodle harnessed and ready for their evening stroll. She quickly glanced in my direction and offered a tarnished grin when she passed the entrance to my condo. She looked Jarret up and down before allowing a greeting to seep from her perched lips.

"Good evening."

"Hello, Mrs. Rutherford. Going out for your evening walk?" I asked.

"Yes, Onyx and I are headed out to dinner and a little evening exercise."

Jarret smiled at the stylish pooch and said, "Onyx? That's a nice name."

"Yes, I named him that because he's so black," she explained.

Maintaining his sunny disposition despite Mrs. Rutherford's crude confession, Jarret replied, "Oh, did you? Clever."

"I certainly thought so," she remarked.

He offered the dog an affirming smile as he said, "Beautiful dog, Ma'am."

Eyeing him suspiciously, she replied, "Thank you. He's a very shy little fellow, so don't try to pet him."

He smiled and nodded as she and her pet walked past him and disappeared into the elevator. As soon as they disappeared, his smile and "friendly Black guy routine" also disappeared as he turned his attention back to me. "Sylvia, can we please talk this out inside?

For some very unclear, ridiculous, silly reason, I decided to allow him in. I backed away from the entrance to my door, providing him passage to my safe space. He reached for my hand, but I stepped away. I saw hurt in his gray eyes when I retreated. He walked past me and sat down on the curved, leather navy sectional that sat adjacent to my gray recliner.

"Sylvia, please sit down with me and give me a chance to explain."

I sat in my recliner instead of next to him on the sectional, hoping he would notice the invisible partition that I intended to remain in place. I placed my fuzzy throw over my lap, making sure to hide any view of my thighs that peeked under my flimsy robe. I offered him the icy stare that I should have given him nine months ago.

"Explain what? That you were engaged to a white girl and didn't tell me?"

"First of all, she's not white, and you know that already."

"Yeah, I forgot. Your Latina, Latinx, Chicana, Hispanic girl that you married last month. What's up with them and the different terms? They worse than us. They don't know what they want to be called. And I guess I forgot she was of Latin descent because of that bleach blonde hair she got on her head. Let me ask you this, Jarret: Does she know she's not white?"

"Sylvia, you're way too intelligent for this line of conversation. And do I think you want to be white because of that white girl hair you got sewn on your damn head?"

"Now, you're going to insult my intelligence and take a shot at my blackness, too? How dare you? And for your information, I don't have white girl hair sewn in my hair. It's Brazilian girl hair."

"Really?"

"I knew letting you in here was a bad idea."

I stood up and walked toward the door, my ears registering the sounds around me. The icemaker dropped newly formed ice, the air condition hummed as it kicked on, Lalah Hathaway was loving on what was once Anita Baker's angel, and Jarret was deeply sighing as he stared in my direction.

"Dr. Franklin, did you hear me? It's time for you to go."

He hesitantly stood as he kept his eyes locked on my grim disposition. I reached for the brass handle, prepared to put him out, when he slumped back down on the couch.

"No, Sylvia. I came here to talk. Even if *I* don't deserve this conversation, you do."

***

Soon after we met, Jarret and I entered a fast and furious relationship that was filled with highs and more highs. We went to art shows, went bike riding, experimented on foreign cuisines, discussed the splendors of African resilience, devised several strategies on how the American government could implement reparations for descendants of slavery, unapologetically watched hours of old school cartoons, and made love several times a week.

Our runaway love affair began in the simplest and most complex manner. The second night we went out, we returned to my condo and comfortably lounged on the very couch he currently invaded. Half watching CNN, we debated the merits of AI cleaning equipment.

"People are lazy enough," I remarked. "If they don't have to vacuum and mop, they will for sure become more unhealthy and lazier."

"Well, I don't see you washing your clothes by hand and hanging them out on the line to dry. It's called modern technology."

"That's different," I refuted.

"Not different at all. Just accept it. Technology makes life better and easier."

"Do you have a robotic vacuum, Jarret?" I asked.

"I sure do," he replied with a laugh.

Our chatter was suddenly interrupted. The so-called regular news, which I classified as CNN's obsession with all things Trump and all things COVID, was halted by a breaking story out of Minnesota. A Black man had been killed by a police officer while being arrested.

"Here we go again. Another unarmed Black man gunned down by the cops," Jarret sardonically remarked.

But we quickly learned that this was not the typical run-of-the-mill police shooting of a Black man. This was a Black man being strangled by a white police officer, who was kneeling on his neck for nearly ten minutes. This was a Black man screaming for his mama as an unfeeling, unconcerned, unsympathetic, white police officer used his knee to squeeze the life out of him. This was a Black man dying as several other police officers stood by and watched him being murdered by their blue brother. This was a Black man murdered as a crowd of people stood by and called for the officers to save this dying man. This was a Black man dying while an unsuspecting teenage girl captured the murder on her cell phone.

With every viewing of the now viral video, the talking heads were talking, the rioters were taking to the street, and black rage was magnifying itself throughout the country.

I looked over at Jarret, who trembled as the amateur video ran for the third time. I placed my arms around him as he silently wept for the dead man, himself, and countless other Black men and boys.

That night, we flipped the television from one cable news channel to the next, watching the haunting video over and over. Finally, Jarret removed the remote from my hand and clicked the television off. His beautiful gray eyes were surrounded by a pink sea of sorrow. Tears brewed in the corners of his eyelids. He mumbled one word before sitting the remote down on the coffee table. "Enough."

We sat in silence for nearly ten minutes. Neither of us moved an inch, as if we were paralyzed with five hundred years of sorrow, fear, oppression, disappointment, and betrayal.

Jarret inhaled deeply and exhaled the waves of pain that permeated this dreadful moment. I reached over and placed my hand on his hand. He leaned toward me and rested his head on my chest. That night, we made love for the first time, achieving solace in the loving arms of one another. I understood his pain; he understood mine.

After we shared ourselves with one another, I told him about Mama and Jackie. He kissed my lips and offered me gratitude when I told him I send a thousand dollars to my mother every month for the kids. I told him how my father was killed thirty-five years ago in a fishing accident with his brothers, and how his body was never recovered from the lake. I told him how tiring it was working three times as hard as every white man and woman at my job, but steadily being ignored when I asked for partner status. I told him how hard it was trying to look the part, be the part, and pretend to be the part, all the while acknowledging your failed authenticity. I told him how insecure I was about my weight as he caressed my breast and kissed my soft, round belly.

He told me how he was the only child of a blind woman who taught him how to see the world better than anyone could have taught him. He told me how he travels with her, giving her a chance to touch and feel the attractions. He told me how his father abandoned him and his Mama when she lost her sight to diabetes. He was only seven. He had only seen his father a dozen or so times since then. His father moved across the country and committed himself to raising Jarret's two half-brothers, all the while ignoring his oldest son. He told me how even though he was happy to be a doctor, he was lonely in the occupation.

We held each other tight as our struggles melded us together. Our healing infused us and made us one. This was why I didn't understand why in the hell he didn't tell me he was engaged to be married in seven months!

***

"Sylvia, I honestly didn't know how to tell you about her," Jarret pleaded. "When I met you, I thought I had met a really wonderful woman who would end up being a great neighbor and friend. I didn't know I was going to fall in love with you. And once I did, I was too in deep. Too in deep with you, too in deep with her, too in deep with commitments, too in deep with wedding deposits, too in deep with familial responsibilities, and too in deep with twisted emotions."

Staring down at his downcast face, I replied, "Too deep in BS then and now."

"I deserve that. I know I was wrong. I know I'm wrong now. But here I am, asking you to give me a chance to make this right. "

"Make this right?" I waved my French manicured hand between us. "How are you going to make this right? Jarret, you're married."

"You're right. I should've told you about her. And I should've never gone to the altar with her, knowing what you and I have. So, until I can fix all my wrongs, can we be friends? Not friends with benefits. Just friends, who have their love for each other on reserve."

"On reserve? Jarret, my heart ain't no damn library book."

"You're right. Your heart is way more than that. Your heart is everything."

He looked up at me, pleading for my concession, but instead of offering him deference, I further withdrew into the sanctity of my personal will to choose what was right for me. I looked him directly in the face and watched my next few words land on him like hot lava rocks on virgin sand.

"Jarret, you need to leave."

We intently stared at each other and offered each other pain-streaked silence as Robert Glasper anointed our silence with ringing expressions that swirled around us like falling tears from a sorrowful sky. I wished I could hide in the caverns of each note instead of standing plainly and painfully in front

63

of Jarret. I considered conceding, but before I could fully consider wobbling on my resolve, Jarret stood, demonstrating his acceptance of my decision to fully withdraw from this twisted game.

"I'm sorry. I really am," he uttered.

He reached for me, and I hesitantly allowed him to circle me in a full embrace. This man who hurt me so badly was the very one I now wished could heal me. Hot tears streaked my cheeks as I rested in his safe—but unsafe—embrace. He softly kissed my tears, sending my emotions into a freefall.

"Jarret, you should've told me about her," I whimpered.

"I know."

"You took away my ability to choose what kind of relationship I wanted to have with you."

"I know. And I'm sorry. I can't tell you that more."

The tears kept flowing, and Jarret kept kissing them away. And with every fallen tear and every accepted kiss, I melted within myself. I crashed. I imploded. I ignored my usually faithful mind and let my usually deceitful heart guide me to a place that felt good, but wasn't good for me. His kisses went from my eyes, to my nose, and then to my mouth. Next, my robe slipped down and I gave Jarret all of my nudity, even though I knew he or I didn't deserve my shattered vulnerability. Even though I knew what I was allowing was wrong, in that moment, I chose to neglect what I wanted and needed so I could feel the gratification of what Jarret wanted and needed from me.

I allowed him to steer me to my bed, where we collapsed in the depth of our unbridled passion. But only a moment after the deed was done, the fullness I felt evacuated, and emptiness barged its way back in and cuddled in the bed between us.

What have I done? I thought as I pulled my body away and unlocked myself from his embrace. He pulled me in tighter and held me there.

"Sylvia, I swear this is not what I aimed to happen here tonight. Please don't think I came here to trick you into doing something you would regret."

"Do *you* regret what happened?" I asked.

"I only regret the situation we're in. I could never regret being with you."

Even though confusion shrouded my heart, I replied, "Well, let's not talk about it then,"

I snuggled myself deeper in the ark of his embrace, determined to further sink into the moment rather than reflecting on the past or peering into the future. We rested together for nearly an hour when the stressful reality of both of our situations blasted its way through. Our phones buzzed almost simultaneously, catapulting us from our newly constructed arrangement. We reluctantly released each other and reached for our respective phones. I answered my call, while Jarret sent his to voicemail.

"This is a prepaid call from a correctional facility," uttered the feminine automated voice.

"Hello."

"Syl, I been calling you all day. You been ignoring my calls?"

"No, Jackie. I've just been working."

"You always trying to shoot slugs."

"I don't have time for this. Let's cut to the chase. Jackie, Mama already told me what you need. I'll talk to the lawyer."

"Good. These white folks tryin' to give me more time. I need to get out of here so I can be there for Mama. She told me you don't hardly go see her and the kids. The least you could do is go see them. A visit to your only mama don't cost you nothin'."

My body tensed and Jarret rubbed my arm to help calm me down. "Well, that's because I'm busy working."

"There you go again with those slugs. I'll talk to you later. I don't have time for this."

"Okay. Take care of yourself, Jackie."

"Hey…"

"Yes?"

"Please don't forget to call the lawyer," she squeezed in as the friendly automated voice disconnected our call.

"That was your sister?" Jarret asked.

"Yep. Was that your wife?"

"Yep."

And that was how my evenings transpired each night. Jarret would sneak to my condo. We would forget ourselves in one another. I would take my "back to reality" phone calls from Mama or Jackie, and Jarret would get his "back to reality" phone call from his wife, whom he always ignored in my presence, but quickly returned to shortly after the declined phone call was tossed to voicemail. And despite all of my hard work to not be in a situation that looked anything like this one, I was pronounced, crowned, and anointed the side chick.

Of course, being a side chick was not what I wanted for myself, but with everything I had going on in my life, it wasn't about what I wanted. It was about what *they* wanted. In my life, everyone mattered. Mama mattered, Jackie mattered, Jackie's kids mattered, Jarret mattered, my colleagues mattered, and even a deceased George Floyd mattered. The only one in my life who seemed to not matter at all was me.

Part 2

Singing the Stevie Wonder version of *Happy Birthday*—
the one Mama prefers—I wiggled around my mama like a
voluptuous brown hula girl and tossed a lei made of brand new
twenty-dollar bills over her head.

Next, I handed her a bouquet of carefully folded bills
masquerading as a dozen green roses. Finally, I placed a tierra
made of impressive fake diamonds on her head.

"Syl, what's all of this for?"

That's odd, I thought, but said, "Mama, it's your
birthday!"

She scrunched up her round face and said, "Oh?"

"Yes, Mama."

"You right. It *is* my birthday."

The kids poured into the living room and locked their eyes
on all Mama's gifts. Next, they spotted the three-layer birthday
cake I specially order for Mama every year and circled the
dining table with greedy amazement.

I looked at each of their lovely faces and noticed that the
three children didn't resemble each other at all. Moxie, the
oldest, looked just like Jackie, with undertones that looked like
she was molded with red clay by God, Himself. Although only
sixteen years old, her eyes resembled the knowing you see in
the eyes of old women who have seen so much. Her curly hair
spiraled on her head, just like Jackie's did when she was a girl.
Only her wiry frame differed from Jackie, who was short and
thick.

LaTyeshia, the nine-year-old, was tiny with perfectly
carved features. Her complexion was as deep as the midnight
sky, just like my daddy's. She was timid, but when she smiled,
the room glowed with warm content. She was always the first
of the three to rush to me for a hug.

Daniel, the baby, was only four years old and the lightest of the three. Mama said the father is white, while Jackie said he was Hispanic. All I know is that Daniel don't look Black at all. People always looked at us strangely when we went out, almost as if they thought we'd stolen him from some pitiful non-Black mama.

"Mama, I know these kids want some of this birthday cake now, but we need to hurry up and get to the restaurant. We have reservations."

The children squealed with excitement over the prospect of going to a fancy restaurant that required actual reservations. However, Mama's face crumpled at the idea.

"What's wrong, Mama?"

"What's wrong is that we don't have no money to be spendin' on no expensive restaurant. Plus, this COVID stuff is out of control. I done cooked anyway."

Moxie looked at her grandmother with worry brimming her expression and said, "Mama, you didn't cook anything today."

"Yes, I did too cook. I've been frying chicken all afternoon."

"Mama, that was yesterday," Moxie replied.

"Yesterday? Nah, baby. That was today."

"No, Ma'am. That was yesterday."

What's today?" Mama asked.

"It's your birthday, Mama."

Mama's confusion straightened up once she realized everyone but Daniel was staring at her. He was still staring at the birthday cake, looking like he was at high risk of dipping his tiny fingers in the surface of the buttercream icing. But all the rest of us had our eyes locked on Mama.

"Mama, are you okay? "You sleepy or something?" I asked.

"Yes, I'm fine. And no, I'm not sleepy. This here fast ass girl always trying to make me look like a fool." Looking directly at Moxie, she scolded, "God ain't gon' bless you for trying to always embarrass your granny."

Moxie lowered her head in embarrassment and replied, "I'm sorry, Mama."

"Mama, look at me," I requested.

Her frown shone in my direction like a fog light splitting the darkest night. Her coffee brown skin radiated heat as she eyed me with blaring perplexity.

With a hint of a wobbly tone, she replied, "Look at you for what?"

"Mama, your speech is slurred."

Stumbling over every other word, "Don't come over here, judging me, Sylvia Anne Grayson."

"Um, Mama Can you smile for me?"

Her frown dipped even further, but I noticed something a little off in her facial expressions. I think Moxie noticed it too, because she also stared at Mama's face.

"Please smile," I begged.

"Alright! Even though I ain't got nothing to smile about right now, I'll smile."

Moxie said, "Mama, you do have something to smile about. It's your birthday."

"It's who birthday?" she asked with a puzzled expression.

"Mama, please smile for me," I implored.

She begrudgingly flipped her frown into a smile, but the right side of her lips didn't quite rise to the occasion. I reached both of my hands out to her and commanded more actions.

"Mama, squeeze my hands."

She squeezed my hands, but the right hand was limp in its efforts to clinch. My concern heightened with each request, matching Mama's frustrated suspicion of my requests.

"Sylvia Ann Grayson, what is this about?"

"Was her speech this slurred a few minutes ago?" I thought.

The following minutes nudged and squeezed in together, seemingly freezing the moment. Without warning, Mama rocked on her feet and suddenly slumped to the floor. The children scrambled and tears escaped their frightened eyes as

I rushed to Mama's side and checked her head to ensure she didn't injure herself too badly.

"Mama, you okay?" I screamed.

No words, no movement, no response escaped her. Panic gripped me, but I knew I had to remain calm and focused to keep the children at ease while I tried to get Mama some help. I quickly dialed 911 for the first time in my life, and then barked out instructions to Moxie to please watch the younger kids in another room while we waited for the EMS to arrive.

***

Four hours later, I was sitting in a waiting room that would have been crowded before the COVID pandemic, but now looked sparse. Speckled throughout the waiting room were worried brown, white, black, yellow, and red men and women who looked frightened and anxious. I wasn't sure if they were afraid of what was happening with their family members without them, or if they were afraid of catching COVID while at the hospital. Thankfully, everyone was masked, which was a mandate here in the state of Texas. I prayed to God their vaccination status was on point.

The buzzing of my cell phone also kept me busy. Every half hour, I received a text message from Moxie, asking about her grandmother/mother. Jarret texted me a few times, trying to figure out if I needed him to come to the hospital to use his doctor privileges to check on Mama. I thanked him and passed, knowing I would likely need to take him up on that offer later. Even Jackie called. Not sure how she knew Mama was sick.

"Syl, what's wrong with Mama?" She erupted as soon as the call connected.

"I'm not sure. Looks like it might be a stroke," I replied.

"Stroke? Why would she be having a stroke?"

"Mama got a lot on her plate, Jackie."

"Syl, you got to start helping Mama more. Stop thinking everything is about you."

I took a deep breath as I stared at the black and white C's that posed on my purse. With every judgmental word Jackie spoke, the C's budged together and morphed into ugly loops that seemingly noosed around my neck.

"Jackie, I'm going to hang up the phone before I hurt your feelings."

"Hurt my feelings? My feelings already hurt. How do you think I feel being up in here while Mama is out there?"

"I guess you may feel fine since you return so often."

"Oh, here we go. You know, Sylvia, it's not enough for you to be doing better than me? You got to always find a way to make me feel like crap."

"Jackie, I don't have time for this. I'm trying to see about Mama."

"Well, you're too late, lil sister."

The next voice I heard was the prerecorded automated woman telling me the call to the correction facility had been disconnected.

"Fine, Jackie." I huffed.

***

Hot tears poured from my tired eyes as I scrolled through the browser on my phone. I tried to find articles about strokes, attempting to forget about my frustrating conversation with Jackie. I hoped my suspicions about Mama's symptoms were off base.

An hour into my phone research, I looked up from my phone and peered across the room, noticing something I hadn't seen in the five hours I had been there. The most beautiful aquarium with breathtaking exotic fish stared back at me. I stared through the translucent glass of the massive aquarium and wondered if these beautiful sea creatures could empathize with me. Like the fish, I was trapped in a see-through cage that looked great, but was void of any depth and freedom. I wondered if they were as miserable as I was. I wondered if they were as afraid of what is in their cage as what is on the outside of their encampment. I know I certainly was very afraid. This thing with Mama only magnified my fears.

What if Mama really had a stroke? I thought. *No, no, no, no. Don't be negative.*

Two additional hours transpired and then finally a short, plump nurse called my name. I quickly grabbed my things as I yanked my body from the pleather seat. She beckoned me to follow her to the back, where a tall, lean doctor waited to speak to me. His young face looked curious, but deeply concerned. I could tell what he needed to convey was not good. I would soon learn I was wrong. What he had to tell me was actually horrific.

"I'm Dr. Hurwitz. You're Mrs. Grayson's daughter?" he asked.

I nodded and offered him an encouraging smile, beckoning him to continue.

"Thank you for getting your mother here so quickly. We've run a series of diagnostics that have luminated what's going on with your mother."

"Go on."

"It seems that your mother has an aneurysm on her brain. We need to take her into surgery to try to mitigate any further damage."

"Surgery?" Flaring with concern, I asked, "On her brain? Isn't that dangerous?"

"We have to try to drain the aneurysm before it ruptures. If it does, we can expect sudden death. Surgery is our best option."

My heart climbed out of its tucked away home, balled up its fist, and started banging on the wall of my chest. I squinted my eyes so I could focus.

"Okay. When do you need to do the surgery?"

"We have a neurosurgeon prepping everything for a surgery first thing in the morning. We just need your consent."

Tears escaped my eyes and the loud boom of my heart picked up its rhythm. The doctor and nurse looked to me for a response, but I was paralyzed with fear. I wanted to take the advice of the doctor, but I didn't want to make the wrong choice. I had heard stories of people going into surgery and never coming out.

"We'll give you a chance to think about it," the doctor said. "Please let us know within the hour. I know that's little time to think about it, but we don't have much time if we're going to help your mother."

He turned and walked away and left me with the nurse, who displayed empathy in her expression.

"Ma'am, I know you're concerned about your mother. What the doctors are recommending is the best course of action. Yes, it's risky, but there is only one way this can end if you don't consent to the surgery."

I silently cried and nodded my head.

"I'll take you back to the waiting room so you can call anyone who can help you make this decision."

But that was the thing. There was no one to call. Jackie was locked up. Mama's brother, Uncle Howard, had nothing to do with any of us since Jackie accused him of molesting her when she was a child. And Mama never remarried after Daddy died. All of those facts were a painful reminder that Mama was really the only family I had left. Yes, there were Jackie's kids, but they were kids. I certainly couldn't depend on Jackie for anything. And Jarret, my unofficial boyfriend, belonged to another woman. So, I decided to throw the dice and do whatever I could to keep Mama with me.

"No, I've made a decision. We can do the surgery."

"You've made the best choice for your mother. I would do the same."

She ushered me back to the waiting room as she explained that they would need me to sign the consent before they got started with the surgery. I signed the consents, and Mama indeed had the surgery.

***

Three weeks later, Mama was sitting up in her bed, demanding to go home. She had a mound of gauze taped on the left side of her scalp. Her salt and pepper, gray hair had been shaved on that side to allow the doctors to conduct the surgery. Being partially vain, she screeched at me when she found out I allowed them to cut her hair, but her fussing didn't bother me. I was just glad that she was alive.

"Syl, you need to convince these doctors to let me out of here."

"Mama, you need to get more physical therapy before you go home."

"I can do outpatient therapy. They just want to run up this Medicare bill. These doctors ain't no good. I probably didn't even need no brain surgery. They probably charged my insurance a million dollars for that bogus surgery."

Medical mistrust in the black community is a real thing. Black folks in America have never trusted their doctors nor the police. It seemed the only individuals they trusted were their pastors, and pastors were slowly working themselves up the list of entities the black community didn't trust.

"No, Mama. You needed the surgery. You think I would let them operate on you for no reason?"

"Sylvia, you may be smart, but you ain't no doctor. These doctors can tell us anything. You included—"

"Mama, the kids are doing well," I interrupted, disguising my silence as deference and switching the topic. "I've been making sure they have everything they need."

"Where they been staying?"

"At the house."

"By themselves?"

"No, Ma'am. I've been staying with them."

For those three weeks, I took care of Jackie's kids, ran into the office to take care of business items that just couldn't be ignored, met Jarret for an hour at my condo for a bit of my own brand of physical therapy, sat with Mama at the hospital for a few hours, and cried myself to sleep every night. And each morning I would get up and do it all over again.

"Mama, I think the doctors said you can probably go home in a couple weeks."

"Well, I ain't going home on no walker. That's for sure. So, they need to get me back better since they making so much money off of me."

"You'll get better. I promise."

"You can't promise me nothing. You ain't God. But Mama sho' appreciate the encouragement."

***

Six weeks later, Mama was doing much better. Despite her very loud protests, she had to use the walker to maintain her balance. Nevertheless, she continued to get stronger each day, week after week, and with the change of every month.

For the next few months, I took care of Mama by staying at her house a few days a week to help in whatever way I could find myself useful. It wasn't easy, but I managed to ignore her incessant fussing:

"Syl, you don't ever cook no home-cooked meals."

"Syl, stop babying them kids."

"Syl, your dress too tight."

"Syl, why you don't have a husband?"

"Syl, you gettin' bigger and bigger."

"Syl, wash those kids' clothes on warm instead of cold."

"Syl, you always got it too cold in this house when you're here."

"Syl, you need to start going back to church."

"Syl, you work too much."

But all I heard was, "Syl, you're never gon' be good enough for Mama to be proud of you."

Nevertheless, I persisted in taking care of Mama, Jackie's three kids, my open cases at work, Jackie's criminal case, and keeping Jarret pleased. The only person I managed to ignore was myself. The toll was adding up, and the bill was past due. If my body was a bill collector, my phone would be ringing incessantly.

But I kept ignoring the calls from the bill collector. I kept acting like everyone else mattered and I didn't matter at all.

In those three months, the menagerie of priorities proved to be a balancing act that left me discombobulated and dizzy. Still, I pranced around everyone, not giving anyone the satisfaction of knowing that I was truly a mess. I kept my weave and spanx tight, never hinting how fragile I felt on the inside.

I, and I alone, was the only one who knew that I was the daughter of a woman who persisted in reminding me that I was never enough. I was the only one who knew my oldest sister, who was in jail, blamed me for Mama being tired from raising her children. I was the only one who knew that I was the aunt of two beautiful nieces and a striking nephew whom I would prefer to send a check to raise than to offer myself as a surrogate parent. I was the only one who knew that I ate butter pecan ice cream four times a week, even though the doctors told me that I was pre-diabetic. I was the only one who knew I had almost two hundred thousand dollars' worth of student loan debt that financed training for a career that I abhorred.

I was the only one that knew that all my credit cards were maxed to the limits because of my incessant need to purchase expensive clothes and shoes to costume my pain. I was the only one who knew that even though I lived in a fancy high-rise, my credit score was in the basement. I was the only one who knew that I was the willing, self-serving side chick to a man, who insisted he loved his side of cabbage more than he loved his lamb chop. I was the only one who knew I had a full bottle of Zoloft sitting in the bottom drawer of my nightstand that hadn't been opened since the doctor prescribed it a year ago. And I was the only one who knew how unhappy I was, as I did everything in my power to make everyone else happy. So, I persisted in my efforts, despite the lingering toll it took on me.

***

Keeping with my normal dysfunctional, yet highly functional routine, I scurried to my condo one evening after work to meet Jarret before what's-her-name was scheduled to be home.

"When are you going to start staying at the condo every night again?" Jarret asked as he unraveled himself from my embrace. "I miss you. Don't you think it's time to shift your priorities back here?"

Even though I had answered this question more than a dozen times before, I sat up in the bed and begrudgingly offered him a response.

"Jarret, I'm not sure. Mama and the kids need me. You know that. And you also know that we've already talked about this a few times before. The situation has not changed."

"And the situation probably won't change. And in the interim, what about *you*?"

"What *about* me?" I asked.

"You're going to continue to split your time between here and there?" You still need a life. Sylvia, you've been living between your mother's house and here for the last three to four months. You got to add yourself back on the priority list. And you also need to think about how much time you and I are being restricted from having together.

Realizing that Jarret's proposed concern was likely a strategy to manipulate me into being more present to serve his wants, anger seethed beneath the surface of my then stiffened disposition. I felt that Jarret's advocacy for me to have a life was more about him advocating for himself and for what he wanted more than what was best for me.

Snatching the bedding away from Jarret, "*You* split your time between two places," I exclaimed. "Do I complain? Do I accuse you of making a choice to be somewhere else, with someone else, other than me?"

"That's different. And you know it is."

"The difference is that what I'm doing is honorable. What you're doing isn't."

He responded to that unexpected jab by further pulling away from me. He sat on the side of the bed and began putting on his clothes.

"Sylvia, that's not fair. I'm just trying to point out that I see you changing. And it's not good changes, either. All I'm trying to do is tell you that maybe it's time for you to start spending more of your nights here."

"What do you mean, I'm changing?"

"Sylvia, don't worry about it. I overstepped." Sliding on his Ralph Lauren, teal and white polo and his relaxed-fit jeans. "Let me take my dishonorable self home. I have work to do."

"No, you started this. Tell me what you mean about I've changed."

"My bad. I shouldn't have gone there."

But you did. So, fess up. How have I changed for the worse?"

He waved his hand in front of me and pointed in my direction. "That right there, Sylvia. The attitude. You used to laugh. You used to make me laugh. Now, you hardly talk. And when you do, you're acting all mad."

"Oh, so now you want to call me an angry black woman? I'm sorry I can't be all sweet and giddy as what's-her-name. I happen to have real issues I'm dealing with. I have a sick mama, a sister in prison, and a serious job. And unlike her, you don't help me with these bills here. So, I got a lot of BS to think about."

"See, this is exactly why I didn't want to bring this up. Black women always trying to deflect when you try to point out they are being impatient or outright mean."

I snatched myself from the sheets and stood, not caring if my flawed nudity was being seen outside of a sexual haze. "Jarret, I'm not being mean. I'm just tired. Have you thought about that? Have you ever considered that I'm just stressed?"

"I don't have time for this. You're yelling at me as if I've done something to you," he remarked as he placed his Rolex back on his wrist. "I'm out of here."

"Don't bother coming back."

"Really, Sylvia?"

"Yes, really. You're right. I do need to put myself on the priority list."

He turned his back to me and retreated to the living room.

Trailing him, I asked, "You're leaving?"

"Yes, I'm leaving. You've made your choice."

Without uttering another word, he stepped into the corridor and didn't turn to look back to see how his dismissal had impacted me. I closed the door on him, us, and any future we never had. I leaned against the oak door and sobbed for the life I never truly had. Here was the truth: Jarret was on loan to me. He didn't belong to me. And I didn't belong to him. It really made no sense why I expected him to be there for me during the difficult moments of my life.

***

I went back to my bedroom and slid on a pair of baby blue joggers and an Aliyah t-shirt, and then grabbed my journal and began writing through my tears.

My Priorities

Forget everyone. Forget Jarret, Mama, Jackie, the kids, work, and everything. I'm only the Black life that matters.

I scanned the words on the paper as tears reformed in my eyes. I yanked the page from the journal and tossed it to the floor.

"I'm not going to let Jarret dictate what's right or wrong for me," I proclaimed. "My life is mine and mine alone. And I got to do what's right for me."

I took my pen and wrote a new declaration.

My Priorities

I promise to take care of Mama and the rest of the family, but only after taking care of myself. I promise to do well on my job, but not at the expense of my health. I promise to allow room for an emotionally and physically accessible man to care for me. Taking care of others is fine. I just have to be at the top of the list. I matter!

As if I were in elementary school and tasked by my teacher to write fifty times what I wouldn't do anymore, I wrote *I matter* over and over.

From page to page, I wrote. *I matter. I matter. I matter. I matter. I matter.* Over and over, I wrote until the ink from my pen and the tears from my eyes began to dry. Next, I put down my pen, picked up my cell phone, scrolled through my contact list, and hit the call button.

"Yes," I said once the answering service picked up. "My name is Sylvia Grayson. I need to schedule an appointment to begin therapy."

This action was not intended to be the healing balm of all my problems. However, this call that I should've actually made years ago was the beginning of me taking the steps to set the record straight.

I, Sylvia Ann Grayson, matter so much that self-care has to be at the top of my priority list. So, every night, like a ritual, I reminded myself of why I must put myself first. I would pick up my journal from my nightstand drawer and meditate on the words that washed over me like a redemptive flood.

I matter. I matter. I matter. I matter.

What I didn't know then was that particular declaration that seemed to be so liberating at the time was merely the beginning of me trudging up the steepest mountain in my life. Mattering to myself was truly the hard work that would break and remake me. And so the journey to matter, first to myself, began.

THE BEAT GOES ON

By B. Danielle Watkins

Welcome! I'm so excited to see you here, and to personally escort you through Beat System Studios. Before we get started, I just want to give you some background about the studio, the owner, and hopefully we see a few artists while we're here.

Beat System Studios was founded in 1998 by Steven "Randy" Richardson. He's Buffalo's version of Puff Daddy if you ask me, but I could be biased. Randy knows music better than anything else and it shows. Look at these records on the wall. These artists were nothing until Randy touched them. He goes hard for his artists, and he delivers on everything he promises.

Like any other studio, Beat has its share of drama, scandal, and skeletons, but that is part of what makes us great. It makes us real, and it makes you feel like you belong to something bigger than yourself. That last part is important to know because of people like that lady right there, Ms. Lora Styles. I happen to be curious as to why she's here right now, but let me tell you about her first.

The first time Lora Styles walked into Beat System Studios, I didn't see anything special about her. She was the usual mixed breed—half Puerto Rican, half Black, light skin, long hair chick—who is always sashaying her ass up and through the studio trying to be the next J. Lo. She walks with her head high like she's better than all the other *video hoes* the Beat's artists attract, but she could never fool me.

Lora had been fuckin' and suckin' for as long as she had been able to fuck and suck. Walking around like her pussy was the cleanest in the business. Bitch, please. Her problem was she was hungry for a life she was hardly even ready for. BET and MTV got the game twisted and had these foolish little girls thinking all that glitters is gold. It ain't, and to take it a step further, Andre 3000 said it best: "Roses really smell like boo boo." Boo boo, stupid ass girls.

Anyways, like I was saying, Lora has been through any and everything that could be done here at Beat System Studios. When she was sixteen, she thought she was going to walk in and be the next Melissa Ford or some shit. I don't know who told her Buffalo was known for video vixens, but she figured she would be the one to break out.

She did a few videos, got a few rappers' attention, but it never went anywhere. All those niggas wanted from her was ass. They didn't think she was a talented model. They thought she was a good fuck. Any referrals they were doing to other artists were based on pussy game, not model game.

After about two years of being handed off from artist to artist, Lora changed her name to DJ Pyre, like fire, but spelled P-Y-R-E. I will give her credit: it was clever. The name, not the disk jockey idea. Randy pumped her head up one day after hearing a mix on her iPod. Let me just say I heard the same mix and I didn't think it was such a masterpiece. That fool believed Randy and went around advertising that she could DJ small events around town.

She ended up landing a nightly DJ gig at a hole-in-the-wall strip joint down behind the old auditorium downtown. I can't even remember the name of it. That's how significant it was. She was surrounded by liquor and hoes five nights a week. That child didn't know if she was coming or going. Pimps trying to put her on the streets, getting caught up with money-throwing playboys out to have a good night, even fucking with some of the strippers, thinking that someday she would be in the right place at the right time.

Randy realized that maybe the whole DJ thing wasn't the best idea after going down to the club one day and seeing that the strippers were taking off their clothes to Fleetwood Mac and Madonna. Embarrassed, Randy called Lora back to the studio, this time as a producer for some of his new artists. He truly saw something in her that no one else could see.

As I said earlier, she was talentless, but she had a look. All she needed to do was find the right fit. Talent or not, she would make it. Maybe you've heard some of the songs she produced: *Not Shit Niggas*, *Alone in the Club*, and let's not forget her biggest flop, *He Never Called Back*. I know you know those cuts. Needless to say, she wasn't cut out for that, either.

Lora's Pyre

"Lex," Lora whispered into the phone as she stood in the lobby of the studio. "I have to get on Phases's album before they close the session."

Alexis sat silently on the other end of the line.

"Lex!"

"What, Lora?" Alexis snapped. "What do you want me to say? I have been telling you for weeks to talk to Crank J, and you haven't done it, so what the fuck do you want me to say?"

Crank J is the one and only successful producer here at Beat System, and since Phases is the main focus right now, his was the only album being produced. Lora knew getting on Phases's album would surely lock her into underground queen status.

"You're my assistant. Isn't that *your* job?" Lora hissed.

"Your mouth isn't broken. You'll figure it out," Alexis snapped before hanging up in Lora's face.

As Lora hung up the phone, Crank J walked from the back of the building.

"What up, Pyre?" Crank J said.

"Hey, Crank!" Lora greeted with her devastatingly beautiful smile. "How's the recording session going?"

"Man, it's cool," Crank J started. "The kid is doing his thing back there. I'm proud of him. We only have a few more tracks to lay, and the shit is finished."

"That's what's up! What's the name of the album?"

"What you want to know for?"

"Just tell me."

"No."

"Come on, Crank," Lora whined.

"Alright man, damn. It's going to be *Addicted to the Game*."

"That shit is fire!" she exclaimed, lighting up with excitement. "All you need is Pyre on a track."

"Get the fuck out of here," he dismissed, walking away.

"I'm serious, Crank," Lora pushed, following him in desperation. "I'm trying to get down. What you got to lose? I can do this shit. You just have to give me the opportunity."

Crank J kept walking toward the studio door, but Lora ran to block the entrance. "What is it? You want me to spit right here?"

"No. I want you to move," he snapped.

"I will do anything."

He laughed. "Tell me something I *don't* know."

"I will do anything," she pressed.

"Get out of here with that bull shit, Pyre. I'm not about to go through this with you."

Lora began rubbing the front of Crank J's pants. Her look went from desperate to seductive as she watched his demeanor change. She slowly, yet seductively, began kissing his neck while whispering in his ear, "Just one track."

A few more kisses, and her hand found its way into his pants and her lips at his mouth. "Just one track."

Crank J withered before finally responding, "I can't do it."

"Can't should never be in a man's vocabulary," she mumbled as she went in for the kill.

***

"Damn, Crank, where you been?" Phases exclaimed, jumping from the soundboard. Before the producer could answer, Phases noticed that he had company. "Hey, Pyre. What you doing here?"

Lora smiled and looked over at Crank J.

"Phases, bruh," Crank J stuttered. "I was thinking. You don't have any features on the album. Why not let Pyre get on?"

"Fuck out of here. Are you for real?"

"Just hear me out, Phase," Crank J pushed. "You were filming the video for *Perfect Imperfections* tonight anyways.

You needed a leading broad. Why not let Pyre drop a few bars and play the lady? Kill two birds with one big ass stone."

"It doesn't need a feature. This bitch can't even fuckin' rap!"

Lora finally got offended. "Aye fuck you, Phase, okay? I could spit just as hard as any other bitch out there. You need me on your track, so chill out and let me do what I do."

Lora set down her purse and rolled her eyes as she walked into the booth.

"This must be a joke," Phases grumbled as he sat down on the speaker in the corner of the room.

"Go ahead and test the mic, baby," Crank J said into the microphone, not making eye contact with Phases.

"1, 2, 1, 2."

"She even sounds whack she's checking the mic," Phases screamed and stormed out.

The engineers in the room laughed at Phases's mini temper tantrum, but Crank J got instantly irritated.

"Run the playback and let her get a feel for the lyrics," he instructed, causing the laughter to halt. As the prerecorded track of *Perfect Imperfections* played through the speakers, he explained, "Pyre, Phase is talking about the ins and outs of holding down a relationship while being married to the game of Hip Hop. In the first verse, he spits heavy about his love for his girl. The chorus is simple: 'I'm addicted to the game, ain't a damn thing changed. I see my future, deep introspection. I love you, girl, that's no exchange, but still I come with perfect imperfections.'

"What I need you to do is be the woman he's speaking about and spit how you're down for him and shit. Can you do that?"

Lora nodded nervously as she tried to feel the beat in her head. Soon, words started coming to her mind and smoothly flowed from her mouth. A hit was born.

And The Beat Goes On...

***

Let me use this time to put out my disclaimer. I am not hating on Lora at all. I think she's a beautiful girl. She just lacks talent and the know-how to make up for it. That's where you would think her personal assistant/ best friend would come in.

If there was a picture of jealous bitches in the dictionary, it would be a picture of Alexis Cunningham. Lora and Alexis had been friends since they were thirteen and fifteen, so roughly about ten years. I don't know how Lora dealt with her. She was rude and downright surly, if you ask me. She followed Lora around Beat System with daggers in her eyes, and Lora just turned the other cheek.

I remember one time Alexis outright told Lora, "You talentless slut. I should be producing and being in the videos, not you!"

And do you know that foolish girl laughed it off and kept it moving? She had to be a fool because Stevie Wonder could see that girl's ways. Lora got irritated and frustrated with Alexis, but never enough to let her go. She trusted Alexis with everything. Even her life if she had it to give.

Since I'm talking about Alexis, I might as well go ahead and tell you about the "Wicked Witch of the East Side." I can't stand that little bitch, either. I have no shame in my game; I'm too old to fake the funk. She's a trip, and I'm not interested in her ignorance.

Alexis favors Lil' Kim before the plastic surgery. She's short, chocolate brown, and thick as hell, something like Kandi from Xscape. I will say she's cute for the most part, but her soul is rotten, so it makes her ugly. I think she was jealous of Lora because she was light-skinned. I don't know what it is with these young Black girls thinking that the lighter the better, and the finer the hair the better. Be happy with yourself. My hair has been nappy all my life, I'm *still* beautiful. My skin has always been a shade from cocoa, and I have yet to complain!

As I told you before, she'd been friends with Lora for the last ten years, and she has been *jealous* of Lora for the past 15.

And with her envy came rage. Alexis and Lora became friends because Alexis tried to fight Lora. Lora was in seventh grade, and Alexis was in ninth. So many people talked about Alexis for targeting a kid that she eventually let go of the idea.

Anyhow, she still needed something to bring her closer to Lora. You know the saying, keep your friends close and your enemies closer? She hooked her up with Lora's little brother. His name is not of significance because their relationship didn't last twenty-four hours. Alexis's ass told Lora a series of lies to make her think that she was being a friend, and they have been inseparable since. Inseparable in the unhealthiest way possible.

Lora never knew that Alexis lied to her, so she couldn't recognize the behavior getting worse and worse as they got older. When Lora started here at Beat System, she was just an intern, but she brought Alexis along for the ride. I'm pretty sure that just like the rest of us, Alexis wished that Lora would have left her right where she was. No matter where they went, Lora always got all the attention, and Alexis was left in the shadows, so she rode Lora's coattail, for lack of better terms. Lora had the looks, and Alexis had the diabolical mind to accompany it.

Alexis's Rise

Randy realized Alexis's smarts way before Lora even paid her any attention. He was the one who suggested that she get on as Lora's assistant. He saw the potential in her business sense and figured that she could help steer the mentally blind Lora in the right direction, not realizing she would use it for her own evil and dethrone Lora. What that did was open the door for Alexis to act a damn fool and embarrass Lora every time she got a chance. It also opened the door for her to slide in and find other people hanging around Beat Studios to join her "shit on Lora" crusade.

The first person she scouted out like a moth to a flame was eighteen-year-old Teyana Astire, the girlfriend of Beat

System's leading artist Phases, also known as David Pace. Teyana is Randy's goddaughter, whom he raised since she was seven. Her parents were killed in a bad car accident on Highway 33, and he took her in immediately. He sent her to the finest private schools and molded her into a very respectable young woman. She is just as cute as she can be. She reminds me of Monica when she first came out. Tall, slim, caramel complexion, with a short, cute cut. But the girl was so shy; she made me nervous.

Alexis spotted Teyana one day after Phases got the studio session. As the two girls left together, Alexis instantly turned on her charm and became one of Teyana's closest confidantes. I told you the girl was shy. And naïve, too. Teyana had no business getting involved with the likes of Alexis, especially since Phases's career was taking off the way it was. And that damn Alexis knew better.

"You got it?" Alexis asked Tenaya with a slick smile.

"What will happen if she finds out, Lex?"

"Why are you worried about that? Just stick to the plan and I'll handle the rest."

Bless Tenaya's little heart. She knew nothing of the streets. Randy protected her from that shit! When Alexis approached her to join the "Let's fuck up Lora's life" crusade, she really had no fucking clue what she was getting into. All she knew was Alexis was cool, and she believed every word out of her nasty ass mouth. I watched the shit happen, shook my head, and kept it pushing.

"Hey, Teyana!" Lora greeted as she bounced into the studio one morning.

"Lora, can I talk to you?" Teyana said so low, it was almost a whisper.

Lora stopped in her tracks. "Oh god, what's wrong?"

Teyana looked around with the most innocent of faces and motioned for Lora to get closer. Lora cautiously approached Teyana and then noticed that Phases and Crank J were in the studio. "Why do you keep calling me Lora?"

"Because I need you to know how serious this is."

"What, Teyana?"

"I overheard something from David the other night and I think you need to know," Teyana whispered, pausing for a hell of a dramatic effect and drawing Lora in further. "I know this isn't any of my business, but I think they are going to cut your verse from *Perfect Imperfections*."

Lora's eyes widened with tears. I can't even lie. I felt bad for her. As talentless as she was, she worked hard to secure that feature. Not the normal work, but work is work. You know what I mean. And in that moment, you could tell that everything she ever thought could go wrong did.

"Teyana," Lora managed to get out while trying to keep herself together. "What did you hear him say?"

Tenaya thought for a second. "David was talking to Crank J—or Randy, I really don't know who—but he said that he felt a girl on the track would have been cool if it was someone else, but you don't have the right fit."

"So, he lied to me?"

"What did he say to you?"

At this point, the tears were freefalling down this child's face, and it was pitiful to see. The craziest thing of it all was Alexis standing behind the door the entire time smiling like the goddamn Cheshire Cat! Had I been in the mind to do it, I would have yelled and spoken to her right across the room. Snake!

"When we finished the video shoot the other day, he came to me and apologized," Lora said. Teyana's face changed. "He said he was wrong for calling me whack, and that I was a perfect fit for the song. He said that the video was what he needed, and he thanked me."

"Wow."

"He lied to me."

Teyana began to panic slightly. "No, no, wait. David isn't a liar."

Lora's eyes focused on the session happening on the other side of the glass. The daggers coming out of her eyes were something fierce! If there was a moment when she needed to get some smarts, that wasn't it. But in her reality, it was.

Teyana looked in Alexis' direction for a second, but Alexis silently directed her to run interference on Lora.

"Pyre, listen—"

"Don't defend him, Teyana! I know that's your man, but fuck all of that!"

I blinked and next thing you know, Lora's psychotic ass had burst into the session, interrupting everything. Everything, you hear me? What Lora didn't know was Randy was sitting in on this particular session, so her real boss watched her show her natural black ass.

Alexis came from her space in the shadows and watched through the window as the silent argument unfolded in the sound booth. Arms were flying, fingers were being pointed, and I'm sure if we could hear, names were being called. Watching it from the outside truly looked like some B level Hip Hop movie, starring one of those *Love and Hip Hop* girls. Come to think of it, I should call Mona Scott-Young and tell her it's time for *Love and Hip Hop Buffalo*!

Sorry, I got off track. Anyways, I knew the argument was over when Randy stood up.

"This is the part I was waiting for," Alexis whispered.

"Alexis, this ain't right," Teyana whispered to Alexis. "I didn't know she would do all of this."

"Grow up, Tenaya!" Alexis snapped, careful not to let Randy hear. "I knew she would do this. I did what I needed to do to get her out of the way."

Teyana's eyes widened with horror as the door swung open.

"Get all your shit and get out!" Randy yelled as he held the door. "Forget about the album, and damn sure forget about the feature! You're dead around here."

Phases looked sick when he looked past Lora and saw Teyana, who immediately hung her head in shame. Alexis smiled and waved at Phases.

Randy had rage in his eyes until he realized his baby girl was standing almost ten feet in front of his face. "My love, I'm sorry you had to see this."

"See, she didn't even tell them you're the one who told everything. Plan was amazing, admit it," Alexis whispered to Teyana as she smiled proudly.

Teyana instantly began crying. Phases ran from behind Randy and attempted to console her. Randy shifted his focus to Alexis after realizing Phases could handle his woman. "What are you smiling at?"

"You," she replied with a smirk.

"Why?"

"Sounds like you need a new leading lady around here," Alexis said confidently and rhythmically.

"And?" Randy asked, clearly annoyed.

"And you need me."

"Fuck out of here!" Crank J yelled from the soundboard.

Randy sized Alexis up for a moment, and then smiled. Alexis took the smile as an invitation and began walking into the studio. Randy stopped her while continuing to smile.

"Nah, I think we're good with what we got. Thanks, though."

Boom! He pushed her out and slammed the studio door in her face. *Jokes on you, bitch*, I thought with a cackle.

But as we know, *the beat goes on.*

Teyana's Phase

One of the less dramatic relationships here at Beats would be Teyana and David, or as we all have come to know him, Phases. Phases was created by the man who raised Teyana, so he was taught how to treat her, and she knew nothing less. Flowers every Friday, notes in the lunch box, and date nights for the gawds! She had everything any girl could ever want. Beautiful love story, but in the end, a man will be a man.

David and Teyana had been together for six years, all through their middle and high school years. They were both in the same school and had similar backgrounds, so it was only natural that they would get together. They were each other's first loves, and first lovers. Love like that is rare in today's society.

When they got to high school, David began showing an interest in Buffalo's underground Hip Hop culture and started hanging around the Beat System Studios without realizing that his girlfriend's guardian was the owner. Randy started taking David under his wing after Teyana hipped Randy to game. He gave David small assignments to do around the studio just to see if David was made for all that he wanted to pursue. David passed with flying colors and was finally granted studio time. He first challenged David to express his love for Teyana.

"You got ten seconds," Randy told David.

"My love, my heart, my soul, my life, past a phase, the kid, he fell into her like his heart was an FBI informant and she was the Niagara River, dazed."

Randy was so impressed he immediately signed David and gave him the name Phases.

***

Randy finally agreed to let David propose to Tenaya, and it was beautiful. As most of the world doesn't know, the city of Buffalo, led by our handsome black mayor, has spent millions of dollars building up the downtown waterfront area, and it is breathtaking. When the sun sets and the breeze is just as it only can be on a Buffalo summer night, it's one of the most romantic backdrops I've ever seen.

David paid for a twenty-seven-piece orchestra to sit canalside. He contacted all the closest people to Teyana (ain't many, so imagine the intimacy of the setting) and set up a photoshoot for the two of them.

After the photoshoot, David took her heels from her feet (I get misty eyed just thinking about it) and walked her down to where everyone was waiting. Once they were in sight, the orchestra began playing *The Roof* from Mariah Carey's

Butterfly album (Thank me later. As you would say, it's slappin').

Mariah is Teyana's favorite artist, so when Mariah appeared as the intro played, that was it. He became the G.O.A.T. Teyana didn't have to say yes. Anybody who can pull Mariah's diva ass for a proposal shouldn't have to ask for anything else. Debate your mama because I'm not in the mood.

***

Wedding planning was in full swing, and Randy was pulling all stops. Musical guests, doves, top shelf liquor, the finest china and silverware, and money as wedding favors. The issue came when Teyana turned into a bridezilla out of nowhere.

"I hate pink!" Teyana screamed at the wedding coordinator.

David and the coordinator looked at each other in clear confusion as Teyana stomped around the room.

"Lavender?" the coordinator slowly suggested.

"I hate purple!"

"Babe, what is going on with you right now?" David asked.

"Do you really want to know what's going on with me right now, David?"

"Yes!" David and the wedding coordinator spoke simultaneously.

"You! You are my freaking problem!"

On that note, the wedding coordinator quickly gathered her things, put up that good church finger, and let herself out of the conference room. David stood in shock as Teyana stared him down with what looked like steam coming out of her ears. David approached this with the utmost delicacy because I would have just cursed her ass out!

"Babe, what did I do?" he asked.

"This!"

"What?"

Teyana screamed in frustration, "You did this, David. You put me in this position, you threw me into the forefront, and you're taking my life from me."

David was just as shocked as I was at this point, but his pain was unimaginable, and I wouldn't wish it on my worst enemy. Not even Alexis.

"Teyana, what are you saying?" David asked, fighting tears.

"I don't want this, David."

"What is *this*?"

Teyana stood tall, with confidence and poise, and then broke this man down to nothing. "I am too young to get married and have the weight of being a wife put on me. I love you, but I don't want this."

And like that, Teyana was gone.

Landry

Landry Cunningham, Alexis's younger sister and the biggest bone in her closet, is another regular here at Beat System Studios. Though she's low key, she has the key to a lot of the things that happen here in the studios.

Landry looks just like Alexis, except for one tiny flaw: she has a nasty, skin-crawling scar straight down the center of her face from her prostituting days, when a trick took a brick to her face. She was fifteen at the time, and has been treated like the Hunchback of Notre Dame ever since.

Randy found her down on Chippewa one night about five years ago and took her home for a night full of fun. It wasn't until he got her in the house and turned on the light that he saw the scar on her face. Appalled, he immediately ordered her out of his house. Disheveled, Landry began pleading with Randy to finish the job so her pimp wouldn't whoop her ass for coming back empty-handed. Uninterested, Randy agreed to allow the girl to stay, but he began interrogating her about her life.

Not knowing she was speaking to her sister's boss, she began revealing secrets about their lives as little girls, the trials she had to face as a young girl, and ultimately living on the streets. Randy slept with her out of pity. Had it been me, I would have rather gotten my ass whooped rather than get fucked for pity.

Randy kept her around. He allowed her to live in the studio and work as a janitor and his permanent jump off. Landry's relationship with Randy became very fulfilling on both ends. Landry provided Randy an ear when artists were fucking up and the video hoes were fucking around. Eventually, the sex faded out, but he still confided in her and told her things no one knew, which allowed her into the lives of those who didn't even notice her around the studios.

As Celie said on *The Color Purple*, "I just stand back, and I wait to see what the wall gonna look like. See what kind of colors Shug's gonna put on there now." I watch with silent eyes and see the changes at Beat System Studios.

But I will tell you one thing: *The Beat Goes On...*

***

"Landry, I love your hair like that! I think it looks really pretty on you," Teyana said as she studied in the lobby sipping her tea.

Alexis had been hovering ever since she used Teyana for that little stunt with Lora, and it wasn't making sense to me. I knew if I waited long enough, the truth would come out in one of the most fucked up ways.

"Yeah, sis," Alexis said with a smirk. "You're looking exceptionally creepy today. Real Morticia swag."

Landry gave a soft smile as she naturally ignored Alexis. "Thank you, Teyana. I like it, too."

Alexis cackled something serious. "That's a problem in itself!"

Teyana looked to ache for Landry as she emptied the trash, grabbed her cleaning items, and disappeared down the hall. "That's your sister."

"So?"

"So, why would you treat her like that?"

"Teyana, look," Alexis began. She flopped on the couch next to Teyana, making her noticeably uncomfortable. "You don't know where we came from and what we went through. That's my blood, but she damn sure ain't my sister. Enough about that waste of air. What's going on with Phases? You talked to him?"

Teyana paused for a moment and then closed her textbook.

"That bad, huh?"

"I messed up, Lex. I messed up bad. He won't talk to me, and I don't blame him. Uncle Randy said to just give him some space, but I don't know."

"You pulled some little bitch shit, so you deserve whatever happens to you at this point," Alexis hissed. "By the way, he will be here at three. I saw the studio schedule. You should leave to save yourself some heartache."

Teyana's eyes filled with tears as she looked down at her phone and realized it was 2:55.

"Yup, he's probably outside right now." Alexis smiled.

I had never seen Teyana move so fast. Chile, she grabbed them books, that tea, and all the little things she had scattered and hauled ass out of there, crying silently, but moving quick. I'll be damned if Alexis wasn't right because as soon as she made it out the back door, Phases walked in, and Alexis was right there willing and waiting.

"What's going on, Lex?"

"Can't call it, Phases. How you been?" Alexis replied, turning on the charm.

"I've been better, I've been worse. You feel me?" Phases gave a heartfelt smile and then turned toward the studio.

"I know why she called it off."

Phases stopped in his tracks. "What?"

Alexis brought her voice down to what could have been mistaken for a caring whisper. "I know why Teyana called your wedding off."

"Why?" He was no longer Phases. Every bit of kind and gentle David came out.

"She has someone else. I met him today. Nice kid, but not you, though."

Did I mention I hate this bitch? That poor boy fell apart, and she was there to pick up the pieces. Alexis grabbed Phases and hugged him as he shed a few tears, and then pushed her away.

"I'm good, yo."

Alexis rubbed her hand on his face and looked him in his eyes. "Are you really?"

Then she kissed him! In the mouth! I can't with her ass! You know what? I just realized she is a fucking predator. That's it, that's all, ain't nothing else to it.

Phases hesitated for a moment, and then the male weakness sank in. He was brokenhearted, and she knew exactly what she was doing. They ended up doing *it* right there in the lobby. Unlucky enough for Alexis, Landry hadn't gone far and her speech about her sister put her right in the position she needed.

Days like this I wish it wouldn't, but *the beat goes on.*

Landry's Cypher

"I don't know what you thinking, but I got us Chinese tonight," Randy said.

He had become fond of Landry to an extent. They had weekly meetings in which Landry informed him of what she'd heard during the week, and Randy would bounce promotional ideas off her, get her thoughts on up-and-coming artists, and even play tracks for her. Landry had become a bigger asset to Randy than all of his artists combined.

Thing about it all, she was good at all of that. She had an ear for music like Quincy Jones, or even Berry Gordy. The girl was good. She also had a knack for marketing. Some of Beat Studios' best marketing campaigns came out of these weekly meetings.

"Alexis has to be stopped," she stated.

Randy stuffed his mouth with chow mein and looked up. "What that bitch do now?"

"She slept with Phases."

I think the temperature in the room dropped when she dropped that bomb. Randy stopped chewing and looked Landry in her eyes. Once she nodded in confirmation, he jumped up and reached for his phone. "I'ma kill him!"

Landry kept her cool because she knew that in reality, there is no doubt that Phases loved Teyana. Alexis puppet-mastered that thing, and Phases fell into her trap. "He isn't the one you need to be mad at."

"It's *his* dick, right?"

"That, it is."

"Then, he is who the fuck I need to be mad at."

Landry, my girl, leaned back on Randy's irrational ass and remained cool as a cucumber. "Alexis told him that Teyana was cheating, and that's why she didn't want to marry him."

The temperature got down to about zero Celsius at this point. Randy froze in place like Jack Frost came through and crashed the party.

"She did all of this," Landry said. "She had Teyana lie to Lora a couple weeks ago, too."

Randy's voice got low and raspy and shit. "Saying what?"

"She had Teyana tell Lora she heard Phases telling someone that she was going to be removed from the song, and the video would be reshot."

"You mean to tell me that I lost thousands of dollars because of her stunt? And not only was Alexis's bitch ass the reason, but now she's hurting my baby girl, too."

Landry gave another nod of confirmation.

"I'ma kill this bitch."

"Or," Landry interjected with a crooked smile that revealed more of her scars than I'm sure she would like, "we could beat her at her own game."

Randy sat down. "I'm listening."

***

"The fuck do you want, Landry?" Alexis snapped.

Nobody knows you like your siblings. Whether you want to claim them or not, a person who grew up with you, ran the streets with you, and taught you what they know and don't know, knows exactly how to play your game. The difference is, they have been watching you play it so long, they've mastered it.

Alexis walked into the house just as arrogant as she wanted to be. If you haven't noticed, when the drama pops off, I make myself scarce.

"Tell me what you're doing," Landry demanded.

"No."

"Alexis, I'm serious."

"My no was serious, too."

"You're playing chess with these people, and I'm trying to figure out when you get to checkmate, what the outcome will be."

Alexis leaned into Landry's face and clapped. "That was a clever analogy. Did you come up with that yourself, or did you read it in one of those books you read when you're locked away in Randy's tower?"

"Why do you hate me so much?" Landry asked, fighting tears.

"Look at you!" Alexis spat as she began to circle Landry. "How could I ever be close to someone so hideous?"

"I look like this because of *you*!" Landry shouted back. "You didn't protect me from that pimp! You let him do this to me!"

Alexis turned her back. "Mommy let it happen to me. You needed to know what it felt like."

101

"Do you hear yourself right now?" Landry asked, grabbing her sister and turning her so she could stand close to her face. "I am your baby sister. I should have never even been there!"

"Cry me a river, bitch," Alexis hissed as she snatched away. "Is that why you called me down here? Get over your past and get with your future if you even have one."

"I looked up to you." Landry conceded.

"Make sure you use that good eye so you can see me when I get to the top." Alexis laughed as she took a seat on the stairs.

"The top of what?"

Alexis jumped up and began to ballroom dance with herself around the room. An odd choice if you ask me, but she is a piece of work, and it would only make sense that she thought she was Belle from Beauty and the Beast.

"Beat System Studios, my dear, ugly little sister," she announced. "I have positioned every single person, including you, right where I need them to be. Lora is a figment of somebody's stale imagination, Crank J is letting me do a demo, Phases tasted me, Teyana is out the way, and Randy knows I'm the best thing here. He's just waiting to see it. Then there's you. The snitch. The little run-her-mouth, who likes to tell every single thing she knows. Not the sharpest, or the brightest, but the loudest bitch in my way.

"Do you think I didn't know you saw me and Phases the other day? Of course not. You thought you had me, didn't you? I saw you, and I made sure I moaned loud enough that if you weren't sure what was happening, you got a clear fuckin' picture. I don't give a fuck about Teyana or Phases. I need my spot secured."

"Is that right?"

Alexis stopped dancing as she turned around and saw Randy and Lora staring her in her eyes. Egg on that face! Alexis looked over at Landry so quick, she bout broke her neck! Betrayal didn't feel that good to her. Not when she was the one being betrayed, it didn't. Felt great to me. Damn, great.

Landry smiled. "I did know you saw me then, I actually hoped you knew I was standing there, but what you didn't know was I heard you when you told Teyana that we shared blood, but we weren't sisters. That is something you should probably say when the coast is clear, before you plan to show me your hand."

Alexis backed off and turned her attention to Randy. "Randy, I-I-I…"

"No, you probably should have made sure we were alone before you started running your mouth in here," Landry interrupted. "Not too clever, sister. Did you get your tactics from one of those books you didn't read? Interesting thing, isn't it? Sometimes irony works against you."

Randy was hotter than fish grease. That boy was so mad, his face turned red. He paced the floor. I was scared for the girl. Randy ain't no woman beater, but I thought for sure he was going to beat her ass right then and there.

"You sacrificed my blood because you thought I was going to hand you some shit?" Randy managed to get out, but you could tell he had a lot more to say.

"Randy, I-I-I…"

"Stop stuttering, bitch!" he shouted. "Say what you got to say so I can do what I got to do."

Suddenly, Alexis had the nerve to get bad. "What the fuck you gone do? You trust a disfigured bitch with your most precious secrets. You think I'm scared of you?"

Randy pulled out a gun and put it in her face. That was it for me. I knew everybody was going to jail. This is not Death Row! I'm not for the shit!

"She ain't worth that bullet, or your freedom, and you know that," Landry softly stated. "Lora, care to add anything?"

Randy had hot tears running down his face, and Alexis' eyes widened as Lora moved closer.

Lora reached back and punched Alexis in her nose, causing it to bleed. "Bitch! You tried to end my fucking career! You have been my friend for my whole life! How could you?

Lora kicked Alexis to fall to the ground. Landry pulled Lora back as she broke down crying.

"I was never your friend!" Alexis hissed with blood running down her face.

Landry walked over to Alexis and kneeled until she was nose to nose with her. Alexis turned her face away, but Landry made her face her.

"Look at me," Landry growled. "Face me. You did this to me, and you did *this* to yourself. I don't give a damn where we came from. You never turn on your blood. You left me to die in these streets and turned me into a monster, but you ended up at the bottom just like me."

Alexis began to cry. "If you don't turn on your blood, then what is this?"

"I learned from the best, Sister, and I'm not turning on you. I'm saving you from yourself."

Landry walked away with Lora, leaving Randy and Alexis alone.

"I never want to see you again. I won't give a fuck about freedom next time," Randy said.

I'd been waiting for her to get put out. It did my heart good for this to end on such a positive note. *The beat goes on.*

***

Well, this is the end of our tour of Beat Systems Studios. I wish I had more to tell you, but as I say, the beat goes on, and there are things left to do here.

I realize I never introduced myself, or who I am here. Hello, my name is Ebony Richardson, Randy's wife. Close your mouth. I know what you're thinking. *How could she tell this story with a straight face when Randy is her husband?*

To your question, I would say, because it comes out a lot better from the horse's mouth, than the other end.

Yes, in this story I had to admit that my husband was cheating on me. I had to admit my adopted daughter got manipulated. I had to admit that there were things going on that were threatening to my business. That, my dear, is your first lesson in being a woman. I wouldn't be true to myself if I couldn't articulate my reality. Does it always feel good? No, it doesn't, and I won't pretend that every time I tell this story it gets easier, because it doesn't.

What I do know is, here at Beat System Studios, we are a family, and like most families, we have our issues. Nobody is perfect, and everyone plays their role, but you best believe when the shit goes down, we are still here to pick up the pieces and ensure that we are all good. Bet that.

By the way, Teyana and Phases are getting married next week. Maybe I'll see you there, but if not, I'll see you soon.

Always remember...*the beat goes on.*

Dead Girl Walking

By Dr. AudreyAnn C. Moses

Prologue

Sometimes I wonder about the thoughts going through the minds of parents when they name their children. Do they name kids after their great-grandma and grandpa because they want to honor their ancestors? Or do they name their precious babies to declare their allegiance to or represent some worldwide or political cause? Or maybe by the time they get to the last child, they have run out of ideas and just name them something that popped up on a commercial or in a magazine.

Every day I stand in front of my class preparing to call attendance and pray that God help me pronounce the names of the girls in my class whose names all begin with "Me/Mi" and ended with "sha/shea/shia", with who-knows-what combination of letters in between. My Ph.D. is in Psychology, not Mythology. Only God knows why they put these combinations of letters together and how to pronounce them. Do parents not realize how important names are to the human spirit and that their child's name will make or break their entire life?

Let me tell you a story of a client who had such a name. She was referred to me by her social worker at the New Orleans Department of Social Services.

The year is 1989. The December weather is normally quite mild in New Orleans. There may be one or two cold weeks, but for the most part, winters were pleasant. This particular day was beautiful. Everyone was out running errands, getting ready for the holiday season, eating beignets, drinking hot mochas for breakfast, and basically enjoying life.

Everyone, except one terrified young lady trying to save her life. In the tiny house she lived in on the West Bank in Gretna, Louisiana, she was, once again, attempting to shield herself from another blow from her drunk at nine o'clock in the morning, trifling and very abusive husband. Unbeknownst to her, this was the last straw for her neighbor, who called the police and Department of Social Services.

With her permission, I am telling her story. All names, except hers, are changed to protect the innocent and the guilty. Her name is Mrs. Janedoah Smith Burton, and this is her story.

Session #1: JEEZ-ZAS ... another one...

Mrs. Janedoah Smith Burton sits in my office with a black eye, a broken arm and a two-year-old child clinging to her neck.

"Hello, Mrs. Burton. My name is Dr. Roxanne Matthews. How are you feeling? Can I get you something to drink? Coffee, water?"

"No, Ma'am. I'm fine."

"I am a Christian life coach. My specialty is personal growth and transition. It basically means I help people make positive changes in their lives if that is something they want to do. Is that something you may be interested in?"

"Maybe ... I guess so ... I don't know."

"Don't worry, most of us are not sure which direction is the right one to take, especially after dealing with the type of trauma you have had to overcome. As a Christian life coach, I will help you find the course you feel would be right for you and your child. What we discuss is between you and me unless you decide to tell someone or give me written permission to do so. We have childcare here that can take care of your baby while we talk. They will be right here in the next room and you can look in on her as much as you need to. Is that okay?"

"Yes, Ma'am, that's okay."

"So, we can start by telling me why you were referred to me today?"

"I'm sure the social worker already told you, but I guess you want my words." She said, agitated. "I have this neighbor who walks around passin' out her Jesus papers and being nosey. Anyway, one night I ended up going to her house for help. I asked her if me and my baby could come in. It was cold and rainin', and my husband had locked the door and I didn't have a key because my purse was in the house. She let me in, but I could tell she was turning her nose up at me in her head. I guess she remembered she is always leaving her Jesus papers on everybody's door and how would it look for her claimin' to be a Christian while she was rollin' her eyes and turnin' up her nose at me and my baby. You know what I mean, Dr. Matthews?"

I smiled. "Yes, Ma'am, I know what you mean. So, if I might ask, why did your husband lock the door with you and your baby still outside?"

She smiled, obviously embarrassed. "He was drunk. He's always drunk. He's the same age as me, but he acts like an old geezer drunk, like he's forty or something."

I'm sure I raised an eyebrow at the thought of forty being identified as old and geezer.

"Makes me sick. It's not my fault he got hurt and didn't go to college to play soccer. It's not my fault, it's his fault. He lost his scholarship. Then I got pregnant and he married me. So, neither of us went to college. I didn't tell him to marry me. He said he was gonna marry me and take care of me and the baby proper-like. My momma was glad because she already had a bunch of grandchildren running around because my trifling sisters and brothers don't take care of their own children. That's not my fault, either. Nobody told my momma and daddy to have eight children and fifty-nine grandchildren. Nobody. What were they thinking that they were only gonna have eight grandchildren? NOT! All of them, except one, have three or four kids. I'm not having no eight children. I can tell you that RIGHT NOW!"

Mercy, I was praying my outside face wasn't repeating what my inside voice was saying. Mercy Me!

"Anyway, he locked me out because he wanted chicken for dinner when he got home from work and I made meatloaf 'cause that's all we had. He was screaming and pacing the floor like that naked man in the caves that Jesus had to heal. You know who I'm talking about, right? Mrs. Johnnes—that's my neighbor—gave me a paper about him and about how Jesus can heal crazy people. Well, I wish he was here now to heal my crazy husband! Anyway, I went outside to get away from him and calm down the baby and he locked the door and wouldn't let me back in. That's how I got locked out and ended up at Mrs. Johnnes's house that day. It was just by luck I had my phone in my pocket. He eventually called and said to come in the house, like he had no clue why I was out there in the first place. Crazy, don't you think?

"I don't have a job right now. He's always blaming me about something dealing with money. I told him that just because I don't have a job someplace don't mean I don't take care of things around the house. Also, because I don't work, we don't have to pay daycare. Do you know what he said to me?"

Eyes closed, heavy sigh.

"I'm trying not to cuss in your office, Dr. Matthews, since you're a Christian and all. He said I would be paying for daycare out of my paycheck because *I* was the one got pregnant."

Another heavy sigh.

"Can you believe that mess? Like he wasn't there inside me like a jackhammer having a spasm!"

She was not smiling, so I did not smile.

"Anyway, after he said that, he stormed out the door cussing, like he always does, and drove down the street. I sat there for about an hour fuming and crying because how could he say such a thing and think it's alright? How would he act like I got myself pregnant and this baby is not his responsibility, too?

"As it got on towards dark, I realized that he would be coming in drunk, cussing and hitting on me and then try to make me have sex with him again. Dr. Matthews, have you ever had sex with a drunk? Disgusting! Anyway, I knew what I had to do, and fast! I packed a few things for me and the baby and I called my sister to come get me, but she wouldn't 'cause she has another boyfriend and he was sleeping over there. I knew I couldn't call my momma with all of her grandchildren running around. So, I did the next best thing. I went to Mrs. Johnnes's house again. It was dark by now and I was afraid he was gonna see me before she came to the door. I banged on that door FOREVER. Finally, she came to the door looking like she was sleep. Who goes to sleep at eight in the evening?

Christians, I guess. They don't have much else to do. Anyway, she clearly didn't want to let me in, but she did and she let me stay there for about three days.

"You know what, Dr. Matthews? I was hoping he would not come home because he had been hit by a car or shot by another drunk in a bar someplace. Unfortunately, that did not happen, and the same day I decided it was safe to go home and get a change of clothes, he showed up claiming he had been all over the place frantically looking for me. He is such a liar. He had not been looking for me because if he was, Mrs. Johnnes would have been the first place he looked. Anyway, I knew he was at the bar every night, and I guess at work during the day. I never understood how those shipyard people could allow a stone cold drunk to work on those ships every day. I'm surprised they didn't fall apart as soon as they turned the darn things on.

"Anyway, he started acting like he was so sorry, like he always does. Then one thing led to another, and we ended up in bed. Well, not physically in the bed. We was still in the front room, so on the couch. The first time I just let him, the second time I said no because I had to go back to Mrs. Johnnes's house and get the baby. He got mad and started beating me and throwing me all over the place and pulling my hair and…"

She was clearly distraught, crying and pacing the floor. It was clear these were not love-hurt tears. These were angry, why-didn't-someone-shoot-him-in-the-bar tears.

"I don't know what made Mrs. Johnnes come to the house, but I'm glad she did. I'm not mad that she called the police. He would have killed me if she hadn't called for help. I'm so glad I left my baby with her. Who knows what he would have done to her?"

"Mrs. Burton, do you feel you have someplace safe to stay for the next few days? We can make arrangements for you and your baby, if needed."

"I'm good, thank you. I will stay in my house or by Mrs. Johnnes since he is locked up. Dr. Matthews, I thank you for listening. No one ever listens to me. Never. Other than my baby and Mrs. Johnnes, nobody cares about me, either."

"Call me if you need me. Have a great evening."

"Yes, Ma'am. Thank you."

Her session time was over, but I allowed her to sit for a few minutes to calm down. I would have continued the session a little longer, but I had another client waiting, and Mrs. Johnnes was waiting for her in the lobby. With her husband in jail, she was safe for now. I scheduled her next appointment, gave her my card, and told her I looked forward to seeing her on our next visit.

Session 2: Who is Janedoah Smith Burton?

Mrs. Burton came to my office today for our second session. She looked rested. Her bruises were healing nicely. Of course, she was still in a cast. She did not have her baby with her today.

"Good morning, Mrs. Burton. How are you doing?"

"Good morning, Dr. Matthews, I'm fine, how are you?"

"I'm fine thank you."

"I took your advice and got some rest. I'm grateful to Mrs. Johnnes for helping with Ruth—that's my baby girl's name, Ruth. I named her Ruth because it is such a calming name. He was going to name her Hazel, but I said no because there was a girl in high school named Hazel. She was horrible. She was a bully and she got along a little bit too well with the boys, if you ask me. Even my husband. He was my boyfriend then, knew her well. I should have taken the hint and left him then. I was so stupid for love. If I knew then what I know now, I would have left him a long time ago. Anyway, I did not want my child's name associated with the likes of her.

"Do you know how important it is to name your children the right kinda name, Dr. Matthews? A name sticks with you the rest of your life. 'Bout the only good thing I got out of this marriage was I changed my last name. Thank God for that, since there is very little I can do about my first name."

"Why do you think a name is so important?"

"I know you are not going to say anything because you are so nice, but you know I have a ridiculous name."

She shook her head.

"What were my parents thinking, you ask? They weren't thinking, and they didn't mind telling me they weren't thinking."

"My invisible life began on December 5, 1969 in Biloxi, Mississippi. My parents already had seven other children, four boys and three girls. Two sisters are twins. How could they have ran out of girl names that quick? I'm sure if they weren't just plain lazy they could have come up with a decent name for me. Well, obviously, that didn't happen.

"Like I said, we lived in Biloxi, Mississippi. We were dirt poor and I was the last thing on earth my parents or siblings wanted to see. And…(*a long pause and sigh*) and they treated me as such. You know that story about Cinderella? Well, she was treated like a princess compared to me. But it's my parents' fault. Why would you name a child Janedoah and pronounce it Jane Doe, just like a dead girl no one wants to claim? And then to top it all off, my last name was Smith! So basically, my name was the name of an unidentifiable dead girl!"

I could see tears welling in her eyes, so I asked her if she wanted a break, some water, or coffee. She said no and continued.

"When I was old enough to understand, I asked my momma why did she did that to me. Why did she name me something that would cause me to be teased and bullied all the time, even by my own siblings? She looked me in the eye and said what difference did it make what my name was and that I should be glad she named me anything because she didn't want any more children and she would have aborted me if it wasn't a sin. That was the day I knew I did not matter to anyone on this earth. I was eleven."

It bothered me that she didn't cry as she told me this. When it comes to her mother, it seems that her spirit is numb. This is disheartening and may explain some of her decisions.

"Mrs. Burton, how did you combat the bullying and teasing, especially from your siblings?"

"When I was little it used to hurt my feelings because I didn't know why nobody loved me. But then I figured it all out when one of my brothers told me I was as ugly as my name and that I wasn't his real sister. He treated me the worst. In school I learned about birth order, and that's when I realized he was jealous because he was no longer the youngest. But you know what Mrs.…I mean Dr. Matthews, I don't even know why he acted out all the time because he was still treated like the youngest and I was still treated like a straggler that wandered into the house and forgot to leave."

"What about your father?"

"What *about* him? He went to work, came home, got drunk, went to sleep and did the same thing the next day until he died from ptomaine poison because he fell in the barn drunk and scraped his arm on a rusty nail and never went to the doctor. That is the only time I felt sorry for my momma. I remember her begging him to go to the doctor and he kept saying *with what money*? He would wash it with peroxide and tie an old rag around it. Next thing we knew he was too sick to do anything. My mom had to call an ambulance. He died on the way to the hospital. The good thing—if you can say such a thing—was that I was fifteen. My brother was seventeen. Everybody else was grown already and having babies of their own. This was a good thing because my daddy had no insurance except for a couple thousand dollars. They paid the insurance man every month and all my momma got for my dad was a lousy two thousand dollars. He had another three thousand dollars from his job.

"You know who else jerks my nerves? Funeral people. They are the biggest crooks on the face of the earth. They are worse than used car salesmen. They stand there smiling at you with their palms itching, trying to take every dime you got. Me and my momma did not have a right kinda mother-daughter relationship, but I was glad I watched this show about how to keep the funeral people from stealing you blind. She knew my older sisters and brothers were not gonna help her bury him, so for some reason, she decided to listen to me. I told her she could cremate him, but she didn't want to do that just in case he was going to hell and she didn't want him to be burned twice. And if he was going to heaven, she didn't want him to smell like smoke when he got there. I just said okay and helped her pick out a nice, CHEAP casket and everything. They were not church folk so we had a graveside funeral and called it a day. She was able to keep some of the insurance money. The one smart thing he did that she did not know about was he had a third insurance policy that paid off the house. That was a blessing if you can say such a thing when somebody dies. If I ever buy a house, I will definitely do that.

"Do you want to know what's *not* surprising? Within a month or so of my dad's funeral, my momma was back to treating me like the ugly duckling. Her trifling grown a-- …um…behind children were nickel and diming her trying to get every penny she had left. They were worse than the funeral people. I never asked her for a dime and she never gave me one. Now her precious children drop their precious little gremlins off at her house and don't come back for a week or two to get them while they do whatever it is they do.

"Why do you call them gremlins?"

She smirked.

"Did you see the movie? Don't you remember what happened to those cute little cuddly creatures when they got wet? They turned into demons! That's them. Demons!

"My twin sisters looked alike, but otherwise were as far from identical as twins could get. One of them joined the Navy and never came back. Well, she did come back for daddy's funeral. She brought her family. They flew in that morning and flew out that evening. The other twin had a baby when I was about ten. She went to buy a loaf of bread and some milk, left town, and never came back, not even for daddy's funeral. She sent money or a coloring book or something every now and again for my nephew, but not enough to amount to much. Half the time we didn't know where she was. He's a preteen now, giving momma all kinds of hell. My momma never filed child support papers on her. What's the point now?"

"Mrs. Burton, you said earlier that your name caused you a lot of issues throughout your life. Would you explain what you meant?"

"Dr. Matthews, my name is Janedoah Smith. Even though she tried to spell it fancy, it is still JANE DOE SMITH. Everybody knows that Jane Doe is the name they give dead women with no identification and Smith is the name people use when they don't want anyone to find them; you know, because there are a trillion Smiths in every city in the world.

"My mother made it clear neither she nor my dad wanted me, or, I guess, no other child after my brother. After that, she maintained the necessities—food, shelter, clothing—and the clothing was hand-me-downs from anybody. I always wondered if they continued having sex after I popped up."

This was the first time she actually laughed out loud. Progress.

"I remember one time in high school, I was asked if I wanted to be on the school float for Mardi Gras. I was so excited, until I found out that, since my name was Janedoah, they wanted me to be a zombie – Dead Girl Walking. At first I was more devastated than mad. I wanted so bad to tell them all where to stick that float but my teacher talked me into going through with it. She was always nice to me, even when I wasn't in her class. She said that if I never got another chance to be on a Mardi Gras Float I would regret throwing away this opportunity to prove to myself that I could be an important part of something. I'm glad I participated because I had a lot of fun, even though I was asked because my name was Jane Doe – Dead Girl Walking."

"I could tell you a lot of stories, but what difference does it make now? I learned a long time ago that people treated me the way they did because of my name, and I let them."

"Why did you let them?"

"Why not? What difference would it make? They were gonna talk about me regardless of how much I protested. My own parents and siblings didn't protest on my behalf, so why should I? They did not love me then and they do not love me now. Do you want to know how I know? Because when this happened to me," she said, raising her casted arm, "NOT ONE of them came to my rescue. When he would beat me, I would call them and half the time they wouldn't even answer the phone. Brothers are supposed to protect their sisters, but not mine."

"So the reason you are here today is because you have allowed …"

"I'm tired of talking now. I've used a week's worth of words in the forty-five minutes I've been sitting here. I have to go. I'm sure Mrs. Johnnes is ready to give me back my baby so she can go pass out her Jesus papers."

"Will you return for our next appointment?"

She looked at me as if she was trying to see past my face to discern why I didn't already know the answer to that question.

"I have to come back."

"Why?"

"Because you listen."

I made her next appointment and wished her a good day. When she was gone, I collapsed into my chair and prayed because my spirit was overwhelmed with the pain she carried. I don't see how Jesus carried the pain of the entire world to the cross when I'm struggling with the pain of one little girl.

Jesus, thank you for your strength, because I need you to help me with Mrs. Janedoah Smith Burton.

Session 3: Tears of a Clown

Janedoah rescheduled her last appointment. I was concerned that I had hit a raw nerve. Actually, I know I did. Fortunately, her willingness to continue her sessions spoke loudly of how much she wanted to stop the pain in her spirit.

"Good morning, Mrs. Burton. How have you been since we last met?"

"I'm fine, thank you. I had a lot going on lately that I had to deal with. That's why I rescheduled my appointment."

"Do you care to discuss any of what you have been going through?"

"Some of it had to do with my husband. He's out of jail and I had to get a restraining order so he would leave me alone. I didn't know he was getting out. I was hoping for a couple months before they let him have bond.

"I was sitting on the porch when the police came with him to get his things out of the house. Every time the police weren't looking, he said something ugly to me. He took the car. I told them I needed the car, but it's in his name, so he took it. He used the house bill money for bail and so now the rent is due. The courts don't care where the money comes from. I had to try to find help to pay the rent and light bill. I won't be able to pay it next month, so I will more than likely have to move. I don't work, so I don't have any income. He took all of the money out of the bank. And I don't have anywhere to go. So I guess me and Ruth will be homeless. I don't know where he went and he obviously don't care that his daughter will be homeless. How could a human being be so trifling and so mean towards another human being? Especially one they claimed to love at one time. And especially his own child. But why should he be better than his people or mine?

"Mrs. Johnnes said I could stay with her a little while longer, but her kids are complaining about me being there mooching off of her. I don't mooch off of her. I keep her house clean and she lets me stay there. That's not mooching. Anyway, I can't stay there too much longer without having to cuss out her grown kids. They are big time business people who claim to be Christians. They all think they're better than me. What a joke!

"But the worst one is her preacher son. She is so proud of him. Driving to her house in his Cadillac acting like he's God Himself. He about choked on his iced tea when I walked in the house and he saw me. You want to know why? He recognized me. You want to know why he recognized me? It would break Mrs. Johnnes's heart to know that her preacher son is cheating on his wife in the hood with my girlfriend. So when they are not treating me like the maid, they are trying to get rid of me. Especially him. He is terrified I will 'slip' and tell his mother about his girlfriend. He better worry she and I don't show up to his church in our Pretty Woman Sunday Hoochy-Mama Best, big hair included! I wanna see what kind of praying he'll be doing then! If I didn't despise him so much I would laugh, but there is nothing worse than cheating men."

I wanted to laugh, but she was serious so I prayed my inside thoughts wouldn't show on my face.

"They can treat me anyway they want. Mrs. Johnnes's house is very big, and she is getting up in age and can't keep it up the way she would like. Her kids don't come and help her. Her house needs repairs. Do you think either of them will call a plumber or an electrician? Nope! I guess it doesn't matter if you are rich or poor; your children can still be trifling. I'm thinking about asking her to hire me on as her housekeeper full time and maybe rent one of her rooms for me and Ruth. That will at least keep me on my feet until I can do better."

"Mrs. Burton—"

"Please call me Jane. I want to be known as Jane Burton. Mrs. Johnnes calls me Jane and I like the way it makes me feel when I respond to that name. Jane is a name I can be happy with."

"Jane, I remember during our first session you said you were stuck with your first name forever. I'm glad to know you decided that was not the case. You have told me who Janedoah is and is not. You have told me how you allowed yourself to

become that person. Who is Jane Burton? Where does she want to fit in the world?"

I could see the moisture welling in her eyes and her body tense.

"Why is that important? Why is it important for me to be able to tell you who I am…who I want to be? Why is that so important! I'm no different! I had dreams for my future. You see where that got me. Beat up and homeless."

"Until you can say who you are and what you really want out of life it will be difficult to find your true place in this world. God created all of us for specific reasons in order to touch the lives of specific people. Satan will deceive us by making us believe that others are correct in their misrepresentation of us. His goal is to have us believe the lie to the point that we cannot hear the Holy Spirit telling us who we really are, and more importantly, whose we really are. In your case, Satan enticed people to tell you that you were worthless because of your name. They believed his lie and you believed their lie."

"Dr. Matthews, you sound like Mrs. Johnnes now. She is always talking about how God has a purpose for everyone. I told her the only reason I was born is so the world would have someone to mistreat. That's my purpose on this earth. She said no human born or waiting to be born was put on this earth to be mistreated. Satan decided it was his job to make as many people as possible as miserable as he is. She is always telling me to read something and that I have to affirm and decree that I am better than my name and my circumstances. I never grew up with people going to church and talking about God. I told you my momma said she didn't know if my daddy went to heaven or hell. He probably didn't know either. All I know about me is what I've been told all my life. Dead Girl Walking. Nobody never talked nice to me. I'm not pretty, but at least somebody could have lied."

She smiled.

"Well, one person did. How do you think I ended up in the situation I'm in now? Remember I told you about the

Mardi Gras parade? Well, he was the only one that didn't tease me. He said that even dressed and made up like a Zombie, I was still pretty. I thought it was a trick for people to laugh at, so I told him to leave me alone. But he didn't. Every day at school, he would find me and tell me I was pretty or something. Eventually, I fell for it. We dated junior and senior year. I had planned to go to the community college and he had a scholarship to play soccer at a college.

"I told you he got hurt and lost his scholarship. He went to community college and learned how to be a mechanic. I wanted to go for Early Childhood Education, but I got pregnant. Then we got married. Then I couldn't work because we couldn't afford daycare. When he got a raise, I wanted to work at the elementary school as a teacher's aide, but he said no. He wanted me to stay home with Ruth.

"Things were going well for us until he got passed over for a promotion because he didn't have a bachelor's degree. I remember that day well because it was our second anniversary. I didn't have money for presents, so I cooked his favorite food—fried chicken smothered in gravy with rice. He didn't come home that night nor the next night. When he finally came home, he said it was my fault he had to work double shifts to make ends meet and that he didn't get the promotion because he didn't finish college, which, of course, was my fault also. That's when he started drinking more and more, staying out more and more, and complaining more and more about the bills, about me, about Ruth, about everything. Then he started hitting me, mainly when he was drunk. At first it was a slap or a shove or something, then he would apologize and make love to me. The next day he would bring flowers or something."

"What I didn't know before I married him was that his father drank and beat his mom on a regular basis, until they both died in a car accident. He was driving drunk and ran the car off the side of the road. We were in high school when the accident happened, but I didn't know the details. He lived with his aunt and uncle until we got married. Out of the two and a half years that we have been married, we have only had a few good months if you add all of the good days together. He is broken and I am broken. A marriage made in hell."

"What do you want now…for yourself and Ruth?"

She sat there for a couple minutes in silence. Wiping her eyes a little bit. Staring at her hands. Not saying anything. As I waited, I prayed for peace in her spirit.

"You asked me who I am. I don't know who the real Jane Burton is going to be. I've never met that person. What I do know is who I want the real me to be. I want to be the Jane that can keep Ruth safe. I want to be the Jane that is happy to be alive. I want to be the Jane who is able to take care of herself and raise Ruth the opposite of how her father and I were raised. I want to be the Jane who believes it when people say she was put on the earth to help people, not to be hurt by people.

"Did I tell you why I named my baby Ruth? While I was pregnant I read one of Mrs. Johnnes' Jesus papers that told the story of a girl name Ruth. I'm sure you know the story, being a Christian yourself and all. Anyway, to make a long story short, Ruth learned how to leave the muck of where she grew up and walked into a life of love, kindness and happiness. She no longer had to smile so people wouldn't see her tears. That's what I want for Ruth. That's what I want for me. But you and I both know that *that* Jane does not exist. She only lives behind my tears."

Jane looked at her watch.

"I have to go now. I told Mrs Johnnes I'd come straight back so she could run some errands. I told her I could bring Ruth with me, but she wouldn't have it. She has fallen in love with Ruth. Maybe she is Ruth's Naomi. Maybe she is my Naomi, too."

"Thank you, Dr. Matthews."

"For what, Jane?"

"Listening."

"You are welcome. And Jane…"

"Yes, Ma'am?"

"I will be praying that you find clarity and peace in your spirit."

"Thank you."

When Jane left, I again prayed for her. I prayed she would find peace in her spirit, enough so she could hear the Holy Spirit talking to her. Peace enough so she can hear her voice and the voice of the Jane of her dreams and realize they are the same voice—hers.

Session 4: Timing is everything…

The moment I saw Jane's face, I knew something had happened since our last session. She sat still as a board and would not look in my direction, not even when she spoke.

"Jane, it's a nice day. How about we go for a walk? I've been holed up in here all morning and could use some fresh air. Are you okay with walking while we talk?"

With an agitated look on her face she said, "If that's what you need it's fine with me."

After a few moments of very silent walking, I asked, "Jane, what's happened? Did your husband violate the restraining order? Did he attack you again?"

"No, Ma'am, he didn't. He didn't do anything. I just got a lot on my mind, that's all."

"I see. So, we can walk until you are ready to tell me what's on your mind."

She almost rolled her eyes at me and muttered, "You don't know how to live in silence for too long, do you, Doc? I love the way you listen, but that doesn't mean I want to talk all the time. Sometimes, it's too hard to say the words."

"Like now?"

"Yes. Like now!"

So, we had a very brisk and very quiet walk around the block. Twice. What was I thinking recommending a walk on what had to be the coldest day in the history of New Orleans? Finally, Jane decided to speak.

"Dr. Matthews, something terrible happened and I don't know what to do about it. If I tell the person that needs to know, I know the outcome will be devastating, especially for me. I'm just wondering if I should just worry about myself. I don't know what to do."

"If I'm understanding you correctly, if you tell, it will cause trouble for you, and if you don't tell, it will cause trouble for you. So, my question to you is who will get hurt most?"

We walked a little further in silence.

"I'm pretty sure I'm pregnant. Well, actually, I know I'm pregnant."

She sat on a bench and started to cry.

"I missed my cycle last month. I just thought it was stress. When I missed it this month, I knew it wasn't just stress. I bought a test. I'm pregnant.

"I haven't spoken to my husband at all since he left. He has not returned my calls. To be honest, I don't want to tell him because I don't want him to think he can come back, or worse, that I got pregnant on purpose, even though he raped me. Well, he didn't rape me, but you know what I mean. What if he says it's not his? I swear to God I will catch a charge. Regardless, I am so done with him.

"I haven't told Mrs. Johnnes yet, although she's old and I'm sure she already knows I'm pregnant. You know how those old women are. All they have to do is look at you and they know. It's like there are pheromones for pregnant women that only the grandmothers can smell. You know what I mean?"

Jane smiled even while she shook her head in disbelief.

As we were finally entering my office, I asked, "So Jane, what did you mean when you said you don't know what you're going to do?"

"Did you forget that I already have a baby and that we are homeless? How can I take care of two babies by myself? No education, no job, no house, no money, NO NOTHING!

"I did think for a second or three about an abortion, but that's not my thing. It's not this baby's fault he or she has a jacked-up daddy and a momma with no means to take care of him or her. It's not the baby's fault. The baby deserves a chance to make the world a better place. I will not be trying to explain to God why I decided something he caused to have life didn't deserve to live. So no, I'm no longer considering an abortion. But, it did cross my mind, which is sad and disturbing in itself. Don't you think that shows just how unstable I am right now?"

She started to cry again as she stood and began to pace the floor.

"Oh God, what am I supposed to do now! Mrs. Johnnes says, 'You have all of the answers, so what is your answer to this piece of mess?"

As I handed her a tissue box and a bottle of water, I told her, "Jane, you must tell Mrs. Johnnes. I'm sure she will be able to help you. Also, have you made a prenatal appointment yet? The sooner you do that, the sooner you will be able to get other prenatal services, including WIC, which will help to keep you, Ruth and your baby on a healthy nutritional diet. If you are using WIC now for Ruth, they will increase it for you while you are pregnant and for the baby once he or she is born. I'll have my secretary help you make the necessary appointments."

"Thank you. That would be fine. I already made a doctor's appointment at the free clinic. I go on Thursday. That's another reason I will have to tell Mrs. Johnnes. I'm gonna need her to watch Ruth if she's not busy."

She shook her head again as she sat down on the edge of her chair.

"After I had Ruth and he started beating me, I prayed not to get pregnant again because I knew I could only figure out how to take care of me and Ruth by myself. I took precautions, but I guess God has a very warped sense of humor and other plans for me and Ruth."

"And your husband."

"If you say so. Right now I'd be okay if the police came and told me he fell off of a cliff someplace."

"Jane, God don't like ugly. Also, you do know that you and your babies are going to be just fine. God has never—and will never—leave you or forget about you. Believe that."

Jane started to cry again, slowly rocking in her seat.

"Dr. Matthews, you say He won't ever leave me or forget about me, but God has been mad at me all of my life, and my punishment has been all the trouble I've had to deal with. So why should this baby be any different? My entire life has been a disappointment for someone, including me. Mrs. Johnnes always says God don't make mistakes. I guess you believe the same thing – that God don't make mistakes. This baby, in His eyes, may not be a mistake, but when I can't feed it, someone is gonna say I made a mistake letting myself get pregnant. The only mistake I made was letting my husband inside of me, but if I had not, I'd be dead now for refusing him. The problem with that is Ruth would have lost the only family member that really loves her. One family member that truly loves you is all that anyone ever really needs, don't you think?"

"Yes, I think. I also think when we are hurting we don't allow ourselves to believe that we actually deserve better than what we're used to. Because we have only experienced a life full of deceit, hurt, loss and pain. But God is a God of many chances. Everything about our lives is timed right down to the moment, So—"

"So, are you saying God orchestrated this mess I'm in on purpose? How is that possibly a good thing!"

"It's important that we understand that God does not create mess; we do. The Bible says in 1 Corinthians 14:34, 'For God is not the author of confusion, but of peace.' So, what I'm saying is at some point in our lives it is up to us to choose a life without confusion, or as you put it, mess. We have to understand that there comes a time when we are in control of our destiny and the only way we miss that timing is because we are so busy looking back that we can't see where we should be going. Life is about timing, and God points us in the direction we should be going at the time we should be going there. Again, it is our choices that point our feet in the right or wrong direction."

"Dr. Matthews, I guess you and Mrs. Johnnes have been talkin' to each other about me. I'll ask you what I asked her: how am I supposed to make a choice when I don't even know how to get out of where I am now?" God has not shown me anything except grief."

Before she could stand to leave I sat on the couch next to her.

"Before you leave, let me give you something to think about. The day your husband locked you out of the house, how did you know to go to Mrs. Johnnes? How did you know you could go back to Mrs. Johnnes when you ran away? How did you know you would be able to trust me? And most importantly, why have you continued to come?

"I don't want an answer from you now. When you are ready to answer, call and make an appointment. Okay?"

"Yes, I guess so, if that's what you want."

"Jane?"

"Yes, Ma'am?"

"It's important that it be what you want. I'll see you next time."

"Yes, Ma'am."

Jane hesitated before walking out of the door. Her facial expression said she had no clue what her next step would be. I prayed that she would allow herself to hear God talking to her.

Session 5: Jesus is the Answer...

"Hello, Dr. Matthews. How are you? Since it's been three weeks since I've been here, I know you probably thought I wasn't comin' back."

"Jane, I was happy to see you had made an appointment. I left it in the hands of the One I knew had all the answers."

"You and Mrs. Johnnes say that a lot. I told her about your questions. She added one. She asked me do I want to hear the truth about who I really am. Am I ready to agree that I am forever God's child and that God's children are not all of those ugly things people labeled me with all of those years?"

I smiled. "I see Mrs. Johnnes is trying to take my job. I'll have to start splitting my fee with her."

She laughed. "I thought your fee was free?"

"It is!"

We both had a good laugh. "So, what is your conclusion about the questions we asked you? How do they connect to your current situation?"

"So, Mrs. Johnnes house is about three doors down from where I lived, but in the curve. She could literally look directly at my house from her front door. When he wouldn't unlock the door, my two neighbors between our houses were not at home. The other house is an old man that I don't trust. I never talk to him. So Mrs. Johnnes was the next available house. Then when he left drunk and my family was conveniently not available, there was no one else but Mrs. Johnnes. I just assumed it was fate.

"Now that I have listened to her talk and your talk, I guess God was makin' sure I went to the right house. I came to you because my social worker told me to. I'm accustomed to doin' what I'm told. She said you were safe, but the way you talk and the way you listen is why I let myself trust you, and that's why I continue to come back. I came back because you listen. I know you want me to see 'God's handy work'—that's one of Mrs. Johnnes's favorite sayings—'God's handy work' in this, 'God's handy work' in that. I know you want me to see His handy work in my life, but I'm still strugglin' to understand if He loved me so much, why did he allow all of those bad things to happen to me? If you love someone, you are supposed to protect them, not hurt them. When I asked Mrs. Johnnes this questions, you know what she did: gave me one of her Jesus papers. She love her Jesus papers. This one was about Job. I guess his momma was lookin' at an employment commercial and decided to call him Job to remind him to get a job."

She had to laugh at herself after saying that.

"Jokes aside, I asked her why would God allow Satan to do all of those terrible things to him. Why was Job used to prove a point? How is that love and what point is He tryin' to make with me? She said the story teaches that even though God knows that Satan is gonna tempt us to do wrong and even hurt us into thinkin' God does not love us, it is our choice to choose God over Satan. She said that Satan's job is to kill, steal and destroy, but God's job is to show us unconditional love. She showed me that scripture, John 10:10. The first half is Satan killin' and destroyin', and the second half is Jesus givin' people a better life. I told Mrs. Johnnes I wish I could get a better life. She said I could if I honestly believe that God would give it to me."

"It sounds as if you and she had a very serious Bible study."

"Yes, I suppose we did. Well, I came here to tell you I'm ready to do the work."

"Work?"

"Yes, I'm ready to work on my relationship with me. Are you ready?"

Session 6: The caterpillar has to die first...

Jane and I have been working on some strategies to help her build her sense of self-worth, self-identity, and self-esteem. She has been making progress, slow but sure, especially in building her self-worth. She is realizing that she is worthy, even if no one else agrees. She is identifying immediate and long-term goals she would like to accomplish.

Today, I noticed an immediate difference in Jane. Her hair was styled nicely. Usually, it's pulled back in a quick ponytail. She had on no makeup, except a little bit of lipstick, along with pearl earrings and a necklace. She wore a simple dress that fit her nicely with a pair of low heel pumps. This time I wasn't able to keep my inside voice off of my face. She smiled.

"Hey there, Dr. Matthews. How are you doing?"

"I'm well, Jane. How are you doing?"

"Good. I guess you almost didn't recognize me when I walked in. I read in one of those books you gave me last week that I have to look the part I want to achieve, so that's what I plan to do from now on. Now mind you I did not throw away my jeans and things. I still like that look too, but when I'm conducting business, I want to look like a business woman, not like a neighborhood girl."

She laughed. She's been laughing more lately. This is good.

"Mrs. Johnnes told me that God gives me permission to move any mountains that are in my way. Do you know that scripture? Mark 11:22-25. She said mountains in this scripture could represent my obstacles. It says that if I tackle an obstacle in Jesus's name, it has no choice but to dissolve. Satan can't live in the same house where Jesus lives. You know Mrs. Johnnes is gonna make sure I know that Jesus is the answer to turn every frown I have into a smile. You were right when you said God sent me and Ruth to her house. I learned what has become my favorite praise song."

Jane began to sing: "If you have some questions in the corners of your mind; and traces of discouragement and peace you cannot find. Reflection of the old past, they seem to face you every day. There's one thing I know for sure that Jesus is the way. Jesus is the answer for the world today; above Him there's no other, Jesus is the way..."

"Jane, I see there are a few talents you have been hiding. You have a beautiful voice. I hope you use it more often. And yes, I love Andrae' Crouch's music. He was one of my favorite gospel singers. Yes, that song is an affirmation for how to create a Jesus atmosphere around your life."

"Well I have something to tell you that you are probably not going to like, being a Christian and all."

She laughed again.

I filed for a divorce. It will be final in a couple months. I decided that I could not live my life in fear of never being able to be more than what I was."

"You was?"

"Yes, Ma'am, *I was*. I have learned that I am somebody special and that I am worth more than I've been taught and treated like all of my life. And definitely worth more than a name."

Suddenly, she replaced her smile with a deep sigh.

"I have something else to tell you that might make you a little bit sad. It made Mrs. Johnnes very sad. I'm moving away. I called my sister that is in the Navy. She lives in Beaufort, South Carolina. She will be retiring soon and she bought a house in Beaufort, not far from the water. She and I had a long talk. Do you know she said that she always hated the way everyone treated me, like it was my fault I was born? She said it was not my fault, none of it. She said she was sorry for leaving me to deal with it all, but she had to leave in order to save her own life. She said that if I wanted, Ruth and I could come live with her and her family and that I could have my baby there. She would help me get the proper services I need. They have an apartment over their garage that they planned to rent out and I could rent it if I want. I could help take care of her boys and keep her house until I got a job and finished school."

"Beaufort? Finish school?"

She smiled again.

"Yes, Ma'am! I'm going to finish my degree and become a special education teacher. I know that I can make a difference for children who feel they have been ostracized because they are different. What do you think of that?"

"We leave in a few weeks. I have another doctor's appointment and I have a few other things that still need to be wrapped up. I have to pack out my little bit of stuff. Mrs. Jones had labeled a bunch of stuff in her house to be sent with Ruth and me. She also had started a nursery for the baby. I told her she didn't have to do that, but she insisted. She said she will come to help me when I have the baby. I'm sure her children will have a cow. She is more my mother than my momma would ever be."

"Have you spoken to your mother? Does she know you are leaving? Does she know you are having another child? How does she feel about it?"

"I told her. She don't care. To be honest, I think she does care, but she don't know how to express it. All my mother's favorite children still don't check in on her like she thought they would. The only time she sees them is when they are dropping their kids off or coming to ask for money. They use her and she lets them. Even her favorite little boy. He does at least check on her and make sure she has what she needs, but he don't live there. She lives alone. She is alone. It's sad. I will try to keep up with her. Maybe I'll come back once in a while so that she can see my children. Maybe."

"What about your husband?"

"He's in jail again. He don't care about us, either. When I get to Charleston, I'll file for child support and let the state deal with him. I'm done. Maybe Mrs. Johnnes will send him some of her Jesus papers."

"Jane, do you remember when you first came to me and you described yourself as a 'Dead Girl Walking'? Well, Mrs.

Jane Burton, I am happy that you no longer refer to yourself in such a way." It has truly been a pleasure working with you, and if you ever need to just talk, please call. If you need a personal recommendation, I will be happy to write one for you. Continue to walk with your head high. The view from the balcony is lovely. Don't go back to the basement, and don't leave anyone down there that you can help lift up…even your momma. You be blessed, and I know you will be a blessing to others.

Dr. Matthews sat next to Jane and handed her a laminated index card. Read this card whenever you need to."

> *If you want to become successful in life…*
> *Change your mindset: You don't get in life what you want, you get in life what you are.*
> *Practice OQP: Only Quality People*
> *Develop your communication skills because once you open your mouth, you tell the world who you are.*
>
> *—Les Brown*

Tears filled her eyes as she read the card. "Dr. Matthews?"

"Yes, Jane?"

"Is it okay if I pray for you?"

Is my inside voice again showing on my outside face? Now, I'm in tears. "Yes, of course. Always."

She reached out to hold my hands. "Mrs. Johnnes said it's always good to hold hands when possible."

She cleared her throat and bowed her head. "Our Father, who are in Heaven, hallowed be thy name. Thy kingdom come, thy will be done on earth as it is in Heaven. Give us this day our daily bread, and forgive us our debts as we forgive our debtors. And lead us not into temptation, but deliver us from evil. For thine is the kingdom, the power and the glory forever and ever. Amen."

She sat for a moment before releasing my hands. I could not stop the tears, hers or mine.

“Thank you, Jane. That was a beautiful prayer.”

“You are welcome, Dr. Matthews. Thank you, Dr. Matthews.”

“For what, Jane?”

“Listening.”

THREE WOMEN ON THE ROAD

By Debra A. K. Thompson

"This is going to be so much fun," Janet said to her two besties as she drove down Interstate 10 from Mobile, Alabama headed toward the Florida line. It was a beautiful bright summer morning as they drove down the tree-lined open highway. "I've never been to Jacksonville before, and it has been a long time since I've gone anywhere without my kids."

"I'm with you on that," Carla agreed with a laugh.

"My husband has our two boys," Queenie said playfully as she adjusted her position.

"Yeah, girl," agreed Carla, a full-figured woman with beautiful hazel eyes and full rounded hips. "I left my kids with their dad, too, so I'm definitely going to enjoy myself at this concert. It's so rare I ever get to go anywhere without them, so this is going to be my chance to let my hair down and just be myself."

She waved her hands in the air in time to the oldies but goodies music playing on the radio while Queenie bounced in her seat in time to the music.

"I bought a new outfit just for this occasion," said Queenie, a cute petite woman with a bubbly personality and easy smile.

"I'm ready to put on my party clothes and get down!"

Well, ladies, we've been traveling over three hours," Janet announced with a smile, "and at the rate we're going, we should be in Jacksonville in about two and a half hours. That should give us plenty of time to check into the hotel and get dressed for the concert tonight."

"That's not too bad," Carla said. "It's good we stopped at the McDonald's right outside of Pensacola earlier this morning and had a little breakfast. Otherwise, we'd be starving by now."

"Yeah, I think you're right." Queenie agreed.

Janet, who was a beautiful, tall, dark-complexioned woman had been friends with Queenie and Carla since their college days at Alabama State. They'd experienced life through careers, marriages, and even a couple of divorces, and still remained close. This trip to Jacksonville was one of the threesome's many adventures.

As they continued to laugh and talk, Queenie announced, "I'm gonna need to use the bathroom soon. I guess I had one too many cups of coffee at breakfast this morning and now I need to pay my water bill."

"I know what you mean," Carla agreed with a frown. "That's why I try not to drink too much when I'm traveling because I know I'm gonna have to go. Coffee and stuff like that seem to run right through me, too."

She chuckled as Janet shook her head and said, "Well, that's okay. We've got to stop pretty soon anyway to get some gas, so we may as well use this bathroom break to stretch our legs and get a little lunch. After this stop, our next stop should be Jacksonville."

"How much time do you think we have before we reach the next rest area?" Queenie asked. "I'm not in a big hurry to go yet, but I just want to know how long I've got to wait."

The traffic had picked up significantly, and the cars seemed to fly past her, causing the SUV to swerve a little. Before Janet could answer, she heard a loud noise and felt a sudden hard jolt on the rear left side of the SUV.

"Hold on!" Janet yelled as she gripped the steering wheel. Janet knew she was a good driver, but she wasn't quite used to handling such a heavy vehicle. She didn't want to risk losing control and crashing into someone as the rear of the SUV wobbled and dove-tailed so close to the other vehicles.

"What's happening?" Queenie screamed as she gripped her seat and pressed her feet hard against the floor to keep from jutting forward. "Did someone hit us, or what?"

"Oh, my God, girl. That was a pretty hard bump," Carla said as she grabbed the seat in front of her to keep from falling over.

"Yeah, it sure was, but I don't think anybody hit us," Janet said, as she regained control of the truck. She tried to sound calm, although she, too, was nervous. "I think it might be something going on with the tire. It feels like something exploded or hit my side of the car."

Carla grimaced. "I've never heard a flat tire sound like that before. It sounded like an explosion or something worse."

Queenie gulped hard, trying to catch her breath as Janet continued to slow down the SUV. When she managed to maneuver the vehicle off the road, she coasted out of the left lane and stopped in the median. After catching her breath, she rolled the windows down and lowered the radio's volume before turning the engine off.

"Let me catch my breath and I'll take a look and see if I can figure out what is really going on," Janet said.

Carla took a quick look around at the steep grassy trench to her left and the heavy flow of speeding traffic to her right and then said, "I was always told you should pull off the highway on the right side of the road instead of the left side. We should be on the other side so we're out of the flow of traffic."

"Yeah, you're right," Janet agreed, "but I didn't think I could get across to the right side of the highway with all this fast-moving traffic going by. You know I'm not use to driving a big vehicle like this one. Walter was nice enough to let me use it because my birthday is coming up, and I know he thought he might be able to get some extra brownie points with me. I think we'll be okay if we just stay close to the car and wait for the tow truck to come and help us. I guess I'd better check to see what we're dealing with before I call them."

She looked into the rear-view mirror, brushing her hair back and wiping her face before gingerly opening her door and walking to the back of the SUV. "Oh wow! This tire looks a mess."

She yelled out to her friends, "I'm not sure exactly what happened, but it's a blowout. I'm sure lucky I was able to keep control of this big old thing."

"Yeah, you are so right, because that was pretty scary," Queenie confessed as she unbuckled her seatbelt.

Janet walked back and slid into the car. "I guess I don't have any choice but to call the tow company and get somebody out here to change this tire for us. I don't think it should take too long for them to get here. We're on a major highway so we shouldn't be hard to find."

Hopefully you're right," Carla said. "It's pretty warm out here and Queenie already said she has to use the bathroom."

"Yeah, girl, I do have to go, but I should be able to hold it in without a problem while we wait," Queenie said with a broad smile. She laughed. "I'm just glad I didn't wet my pants with all this excitement going on."

"Me too," Carla agreed, laughing even harder. "That was enough excitement to make anybody have a little accident."

They all laughed out loud.

"I just don't understand how that tire blew out like that," Janet said, sighing. "Good thing I wasn't going any faster or we would have been in some serious trouble. Walter said he had all this stuff checked out for me before he gave me this car to drive."

"Janet, don't you think you should call Walter and let him know what's going on?" Queenie said with a serious look on her face.

"Nope," Janet replied. "Independent women like us ought to be able to handle a little thing like a blown-out tire. There's no need in making him worry when there's nothing he can do from home. I'm just not sure why he wouldn't have said anything about the tires."

"Well, I don't think you can blame him for this blowout unless he already knew the tires were bad," Queenie said. "I feel like he would have said something if he thought there'd be a problem."

"Otherwise, I don't think he would have let you use it," Carla added.

"I know you guys are probably right. I shouldn't jump to any conclusions," Janet replied. "You know how antsy I get when anything goes wrong. I guess I'll have to deal with that later because the first thing we've got to do is find that AAA card. Then we'll be back in business. Walter made sure he told me where to find it in the glove box before we left on this trip."

She turned to Queenie. "Will you reach into the glove box and give me the packet of papers inside?"

Queenie did as she was asked, grabbing a folder lying on top of the pile and handing it to Janet. Janet thumbed through the folder and found the insurance card and tow company number.

"Oh wow," Janet groaned, looking at her phone. My phone doesn't have a signal and on top of that, my battery is low. I guess I forgot to charge it."

"Where's my charger?" she wondered aloud as she rummaged through her purse. "I think I musta forgot it. Do either one of you guys have your phone handy?"

"Yeah, mine should be in my purse somewhere," Carla replied, searching through her own purse. "Hmmm, I know I had that thing in here somewhere, but I don't see it right now. Queenie, will you call my phone so I can see where it is? It's got to be down in here somewhere with all this junk."

"I'm dialing your number right now, Carla," Queenie said. "Can you hear it ringing?"

"No, girl, I don't hear a thing," Carla replied with a nervous laugh. "I must have forgotten to take it off silent the last time I used it. We sure make some pathetic road dogs, don't we? I guess nobody would believe all the trouble we're having trying to have a little bit of fun."

The ladies giggled in spite of themselves.

"Queenie, it seems like you're the only one with a working phone right now," Janet said. "Will you please let me use your phone to make this call?"

"Hey, no problem, girl," Queenie replied. "I just need to turn my voice-over off."

"Voice-over?" Carla asked.

"Yes, it's the accessibility feature Apple has on their phones to help visually impaired people use their phones through voice instructions, or I wouldn't be able to do anything with it," Queenie explained. "I know you can't hear the talking because I have my Bluetooth in my ear so it only talks to me."

"Technology is amazing," Janet said. "I sometimes forget how much you're able to do."

"Yes, I'm truly blessed," Queenie replied as she swiped her fingers across her screen. She then made a few tapping motions to turn off her Bluetooth, and then took her phone from around her neck and handed it to Janet. "My signal seems to be pretty strong, and I have plenty of battery power."

Janet took the phone from Queenie and quickly dialed the number.

"It's ringing," she said with a faint smile.

A woman answered with a soft professional sounding voice. "Hello, may I help you?"

"Hello?" Janet shouted into the phone. "My name is Janet Castleberry, and I'm stuck out here on Interstate 10 with a flat tire. Will you please send someone?"

"Where are you located? What mile marker are you near?" the operator asked.

"Well, I think we are close to Crestview. I'm not sure what mile marker we passed by last, but I am sure we're near Crestview."

She turned to her friends for help. "Queenie, did you or Carla notice the number of the last mile marker we passed?"

Queenie and Carla shrugged, moaning in thought.

"I don't remember seeing a mile marker," Carla said to the woman. "If they come up near Crestview on the interstate, I'm sure they'll see us without a problem."

The operator replied pleasantly, "We should have someone out to you shortly."

"Alright, Ma'am," Janet confirmed. "We'll be waiting."

"Hmmm, I guess while we're waiting," Carla said, "I think I'd better check my tote to see if I left my phone in there when we stopped for breakfast. I know I had to have left it somewhere in this car. I sure hate to think I left it back at the restaurant."

As the cars continued to whiz by, Carla opened her door slowly and waited for the coast to clear.

"Be careful," Janet shouted, trying to yell over the noise of the heavy traffic. "I don't want anything to happen to you, but I definitely don't want anything else to happen to this vehicle while it's in my care. Walter was nice enough to let me use it while he takes care of the children this weekend, but I sure don't want to have to hear his mouth."

"I can understand that," Queenie said with a smirk. "I know how funny men can be about their cars."

"Yeah, you are right about that," Janet agreed. "They can sure make a big stink about nothing when it comes to these cars."

Carla suddenly jumped into the car, exclaiming, "Woo hoo! I found my phone! I guess I must have put it back in my tote so I wouldn't lose it. I am forever misplacing this thing."

"At least you found it," Queenie said.

"I'm glad you found your phone," Janet said.

"I wonder if Dennis or the boys have tried to call me this morning," Carla continued. "I know they're probably wondering why I haven't answered my phone since we left."

"Girlfriend, I am sure Dennis knows how careless you are with that thing," Janet said. "You are forever leaving it somewhere."

The ladies laughed again, and then Queenie shook her phone in the air. "If it wasn't for this body strap on mine, I know I would have lost mine a long time ago."

"Now roadside assistance has all our information, and the only thing we can do is wait. The lady said it shouldn't be too long before they get here," Janet said.

"Um hum," Carla said with a shrug. "I guess we can turn the music back up while we wait."

Janet turned up the volume just in time to hear Michael Jackson's voice blare through the speakers.

"Oh yeah," Queenie exclaimed, snapping her fingers. "This is thriller, thriller night!"

The ladies clapped their hands and sang along, trying their best to perform the moves while strapped into their seats.

"This sure brings back memories of when I used to be able to dance all night and not even get tired," Carla mused as she twisted in her seat to the music. "I guess if anyone saw us, they would probably figure we don't get out much. That would be the truth!"

They all laughed.

"It sure has been a long time since we've been able to do anything besides work and take care of children, and *that's* the truth," Janet said, turning down the music. "Although Walter and I have been divorced about a year, I'm glad we still get along because it sure makes it a lot easier on the kids."

"I know you guys aren't together anymore, but y'all seem to have a good rapport with one another," Queenie said.

"I'm thankful we've always had a good relationship since our divorce, but that doesn't mean he can't get on my last nerve," Janet replied with a smile. "I hate to have to call Walter and ask him anything, because I'm sure I'm going to get a lecture that I just don't want to hear about how independent I am. We were married a long time, and after all these years I know he knows I'm usually a very careful driver, but I don't think he'd be able to resist the temptation to get on my case."

"Yes, you are definitely right about Walter, girl," Carla said. "He can be a trip when he wants to be, but he sure came through for us so we could go on this trip."

"I'm really looking forward to this concert tonight," Janet said after a moment. "I think it's going to be a blast if we ever get there."

"Speaking of blast," Carla said, "I'm getting hot. She patted her hair lightly. "We've been bouncing around in here and I'm starting to sweat. I sure don't want to mess up my new 'do in all this heat. You know these hairdos don't come cheap."

"You're so right about that," Queenie agreed, laughing as she patted her own hair.

The ladies continued singing, laughing, and talking for almost an hour when they realized how much time had gone by.

"I hope we don't have to wait too much longer. I really do need to go to the bathroom," Queenie said, looking out the window for the tow truck. "Do you think you can call the tow people again to find out if someone is on the way? If they don't get here soon, I'm going to need to hide between the two doors so I can pee."

"Girl, we are out here in the open," Carla said with a laugh. "I don't think you will be able to hide too much out here the way we're parked."

"Well, I've got to do something soon," Queenie said, "or I'm going to wet my pants."

"Mmmm," Janet moaned, "I guess it's been a while since we called. The lady said they were sending someone right out. I certainly didn't think it would take them this long to find us."

"Me either," Carla chimed in. "It's not like we're in the backwoods somewhere; we're on a major interstate. I would think they should be able to find us without a problem."

"Well, that's what I would think also, but who knows what you can expect from people in this day and time?" Janet replied with a frown. "We have all this modern technology, but somehow it doesn't seem to be doing us any good right now."

Queenie grabbed her phone from around her neck and handed it back to Janet. "I guess you guys are right about making another call to these people."

"This is ridiculous for us to have to wait this long," Janet muttered as she punched in the numbers. After four rings, she said with a huff, "Hello, Ma'am, this is Janet Castleberry again, and I'm still waiting on someone to come from your company to help us.

"Ms. Castleberry, our technician says he can't find you," the operator explained.

"What you mean he can't find us?" Janet snapped as her voice began to rise. "Ma'am, we're sitting right here on the side of the road. I told you we're parked on the left-hand side of the interstate, but he still should be able to see this big old blue SUV without a problem with three Black women sitting inside of it."

"Please calm down, Ma'am," the operator replied. "Tell me again where you are located."

"Ma'am, I thought I told you the first time we spoke we are not too far from Crestview. It's possible we might be a little further away, but I know we can't be that far away from where I told you."

"The driver says he looped several times around the area and he didn't see anyone with your description on the side of the road."

Janet's expression and voice changed from disgust to frustration. "I'm not trying to say your guy is lying, but we've been sitting here and we haven't seen a tow truck yet. I know we've been waiting over an hour and it's hot out here."

"We'll dispatch another truck immediately."

"Alright then," Janet said, "we'll keep a lookout for your truck. Thanks so much. We'll be waiting."

"What all did she say?" asked Carla.

"Well," Janet explained, "the lady said the tow driver says he's been looking for us since we called. He says he has been circling around Crestview and he hasn't seen us yet. I know we shouldn't be that hard to find because the last sign I remember seeing was a sign that said Crestview/Niceville, so I know we've got to be somewhere close to that area."

"I think he just missed us," Queenie said flatly. "It's around mid-morning and he probably didn't feel like lookin' too hard, anyway."

"Girl, you probably right about that," Carla agreed. "You know people nowadays don't hardly want to work. They just do enough to get by. I think they do only what they have to do to collect a check, and the heck with everything else. I bet if I was in charge of that company, they'd know how to treat people if they want to get paid."

"Maybe he'll come pretty soon," Janet assured them, sighing, "but in the meantime, we'll keep a good lookout for the truck."

"I guess we might need to get out of this SUV and stand outside so he won't have any excuses for why he didn't see us," Janet suggested. "We've got a few bottles of water in the cooler in the back. That should help us keep cool while we wait."

"Oh, no," Queenie interjected. "Don't mention water. I'm doing my best to keep my mind off water."

"Yeah, I guess you're right about that," Carla said with a giggle, "because I know how the mind will make you think you have to go worse than you really do when you start talking about things like water."

They all howled with laughter.

"Even though we do seem to be in a fix, there's nothing that says we can't have fun while we're waiting," Janet said.

"Ladies, since we've got to wait anyway," Queenie urged, "maybe we should look in the back and see if we can find a jack and a spare tire. I think we can change that tire ourselves so we can get back on the road."

Carla shrugged. "How hard could it really be to change a tire?"

"Have either of you ever done it before?" Janet asked.

"No, I haven't," Carla admitted, "but I don't think it should be that difficult. It's not rocket science, you know."

"I suppose you're right, but I just got my nails done yesterday, and I sure don't want to break one," Janet muttered, checking out her fresh manicure.

"Naw, I don't want to break mine, either," Queenie replied, "but we can either sit here or we can see what we can do."

"I suppose you're right, Queenie," Janet conceded. It's better to try and do something constructive, rather than sitting here complaining about our circumstances."

As Queenie started to ease her door open, Janet said, "Hold on and let me come around on your side and help you.

These people are flying by, and I don't want your hubby getting on my case if something happens to his Queenie."

"Listen, girlfriend, I know Nate is a bit overprotective, but I'm always telling him he doesn't have to worry so much about me," Queenie said as she held the door in place. "I have to remind him that I am grown, and I can take care of myself without him."

Janet crept to the passenger side, glancing to her right to check for cars. Once she was clear, she walked to the door and held it open for her friend. "Yeah, 'cause you are the most independent visually impaired person I've ever met. It's truly amazing to me how you're able to do all the things you do."

"Janet is right, Queenie," Carla agreed, stepping out of the car to assist. "You don't let any grass grow under your feet. I can't even imagine what else you would be doing if you had 20/20 vision."

"I know people are always surprised at the things I do when they get to know me, but that's the way I was raised," Queenie said, cautiously exiting the car. "My mama always told me that nobody will feel sorry for me just because I can't see well. She used to say, everybody's got problems and mine is no better or worse than anybody else's. It's just life and we all have to learn how to work with our own limitations."

Janet grabbed her before her foot hit the ground. "Alright fassie-mae, I know you got this, but I got you. Let's get around to the back before more cars start coming and we all end up getting hit."

Janet then smiled and patted her fanny. "I know I've got a lot of junk in this trunk, but it's no match against all these flying cars."

The ladies slid along the truck, trying their best to avoid any speeding cars. Once they all reached the back of the SUV, Janet said wearily, "Okay the first thing we've got to do is find the jack. I'm sure it's back here somewhere, but we've got to take all our luggage out first."

She opened the hatch, greeted by piles of bags.

"Wow!" Carla exclaimed. "It seems like our stuff has multiplied since we first put it back here.

"Alright," Janet groaned, "I've got the first bag."

She grabbed a black oversized duffle bag and dragged it away from the pile, letting it fall to the ground with a thud. "I didn't think it was this heavy when we first put it in, but this sure seems like a lot of junk for just a weekend."

They all agreed as they worked feverishly to move each bag as quickly as they could. Before long, six bags were piled into a wall behind the truck. Queenie shook her head and wiped away the sweat pouring from her forehead.

"I know I definitely over-packed my bag," she said as she tried to catch her breath. "I have five pairs of shoes and three extra purses in my luggage just in case I need them."

"I know what you mean," Carla huffed in agreement.

"This is a lot of junk for just a couple of days," Janet moaned. "I always plan to pack lighter, but somehow I always end up with a lot of just-in-case stuff that I probably won't even use."

She looked around and noticed that they stood on an uneven slope. The falling pebbles and dust confirmed her fears. "We've got to be careful how we sit this stuff down. I don't want anything tumbling down this hill.

Carla looked around, her eyes landing near Janet's feet. "Yeah girl, that would sure be a mess to have all our junk falling out on the side of the road. I can't even imagine having to run around trying to collect bras and panties from everywhere."

Janet laughed, picturing underwear rolling down the hill, and then moved her mind back to the mission at hand.

"Now that we've got all of this stuff out of here, where are the jack and the spare tire?" she wondered aloud. "I know they've got to be back here somewhere. This is crazy. I don't know why we can't seem to find a jack. I'm pretty sure there's one in here somewhere. I can't believe Walter would drive around in this car without a spare or a jack. He is usually so conscientious about things like that."

"Yes, he is," Carla agreed.

"Walter assured me he had this car thoroughly checked out before he let me use it so I'm confused about what is really going on," Janet muttered as she continued to feel around. "It's so crazy that the tire exploded like that. I don't think I ran over anything, unless it was a nail or something in the road and I just didn't see it. And now we can't find the jack."

As she continued to search, she said, "I think we have to fold the back seat down and then we'll see the tire compartment. Give me a little room, ladies, so I can lay this seat down out of our way."

Queenie and Carla stepped back as Janet pulled a latch on the side of the seat. The seat folded down easily, revealing a flap that covered a spare tire and a black bag that held the jack.

"This tire looks pretty big and it's probably going to take all three of us to get it out of here," Janet said.

"I think you're right," Carla agreed. "Queenie, you get around on the other side so we can help Janet lay this thing on the ground and get to work."

"I sure would hate to have this tire land on my foot or roll down this slope," Janet remarked as they struggled to maneuver the tire out of its compartment. They managed to free the tire and slammed it on the ground with a thud. "I know I wouldn't be able to run and catch it."

"Me either," Carla said. "My shoes are definitely not made for running."

"Mine either." Queenie motioned with her hands down toward her sandals. "They are strictly made for comfort."

"I don't think I've ever seen a jack quite like this one," Janet commented, ogling the oddly shaped tool. She pulled the pieces from the bag and squinted. "This looks like a foot pedal and a couple of sticks. Is there anything else in the bag?"

Queenie bent over to get a closer look inside the bag to make sure they hadn't left anything out. "Well, this seems to be all there is, so I guess we'd better get to work figuring this thing out. Now, let's see what we can do."

"Ummm, do you see any instructions for this thing?" asked Carla as she turned the pieces around to get a better look.

"No, I don't," Janet replied, frowning. "One thing I know for sure is that this bar has to go in this thing somewhere, or else how will we get the car to go up?"

"I think it fits right here by this bumper," Queenie suggested, pointing to the edge of the truck.

They tried attaching the jack, but it fell apart before they could even pump the handle.

"No, girl," Janet said, holding up the jack handle. "I think it fits right here, and somehow you have to push this thing up so it will lift the car."

"Well, if we get this side lifted up enough, how will we get the tire loose?" Carla asked as she scratched her head.

"I know we have to use a wrench of some kind to loosen these big bolts," Janet said, picking up the wrench and trying to demonstrate. "These things look like they are screwed on pretty tight, if you ask me."

"It's hard to believe no one has stopped to see if we need any help," Carla stated as she placed her hands on her hips in exasperation.

"Where is a police officer when you need him?" Queenie laughed. "It is kinda unbelievable that we are having so much trouble. Maybe that tow truck will get here soon.

As they continued to struggle to put the jack together, a big rig pulled up behind them. Elated, Janet thought the tow truck driver had finally come to their rescue, but to her surprise, it was a good Samaritan.

The man exited the truck and strolled toward them. "What seems to be the problem, ladies?"

"We have a flat tire," Janet replied.

He looked at them concerned, and then glanced at the traffic whizzing around them. "Do you know you're in a dangerous position on this side of the road?"

"Yes, I know," Janet answered, frustrated, "but that was all I could do at the time. The tire blew out and there was too much traffic for me to pull over on the right side safely. We had no idea it would take this long to get some help."

Carla jumped in to defend her friend. "We've been waiting out here quite a while expecting a tow truck to come, but no one has shown up so far. What's worse is our friend Queenie needs to use the bathroom. That's why we thought we could change the tire ourselves, but we can't get this jack to work correctly, and we don't know how to get the tire off, either."

The man smiled. "Ladies, if you would like some help, I think I can get you back up and running in no time."

"Oh, yes!" Janet cheered.

"You are truly a Godsend because we were getting nowhere fast," Queenie said with a chuckle.

"Glad to help," he replied, taking the jack pieces from Carla and Janet. He put the jack together correctly and changed the tire with lightning speed.

"You made that look so easy," Carla remarked with a laugh. "I guess it's true what they say about knowledge—it's the key."

"I don't know how we can ever thank you for all your help," Janet said with a broad smile. "There's no telling how long we would have had to wait if you hadn't come along. I'm not sure what happened to our tow truck. We've been waiting here over two hours."

"That's strange," the man said, scrunching his eyebrows. "Did he at least call?"

"No," Janet said with a disgusted tone. Nobody has called us back or shown up to help. We told them we were near Crestview, but somehow they can't seem to find us."

"I guess they wouldn't find you," he said with a smile, "because you guys aren't near Crestview at all. You're near Panama City, a little over an hour away from Crestview."

"Say what? Panama City! Oh, my God!" Queenie exclaimed with a laugh. "No wonder they couldn't find us!"

Placing her hands on her hips, Janet chuckled. "I had no idea we had come that far from the last sign we saw. I guess we must have been talking and having too much fun, and we didn't pay attention to where we were."

"Evidently, that's true," the man said with a smile. "However, for future reference, always pay attention to your mile markers because that will tell you where you're located every time. Another thing, always remember no matter what happens, pull off on the right side of the road. It's too dangerous over here and people are reluctant to help you because it's such a bad spot to try and do anything with all the traffic coming so close to the median."

"Yes, Sir," they all said in unison. "Maybe that's why you were the only person who stopped to help us."

"Hopefully, we won't have another blowout before we get to Jacksonville, or we won't be able to make our concert on time," Carla pointed out. She smiled at the man. "You know we wouldn't have been able to do this without you. How much do we owe you?"

"Nothing," he replied. "I'm glad I could help. Just get to your destination safely and make sure you pay closer attention to where you are."

"You don't have to worry, Sir," Janet assured him. "We will."

The ladies moved back to the doors to get back to safety, but Queenie stopped and motioned toward the man. "Ummm, I have one last question, Sir. How far is the next rest area where we can find a bathroom?"

The man smiled and winked at her. "Once you get back on the highway, go down about a mile, and you'll see a sign for the Flying J. You'll find all the restrooms you need along with a place to get food and gas. Do you think you can make it that far?"

"I don't know," she said with a little shuffle of her feet. "It's going to be a challenge, but I think Janet can make this buggy move fast enough for me to take care of business before it's too late."

The man waved goodbye as he jumped back into his truck. Although the ladies had lost more than two hours of time, they were glad to be safe. Once they were all buckled up, Janet eased out onto the highway and made a beeline for the Flying J. They'd had an unexpected adventure, but now it was time to get back to business!

Forbidden

By C. Damon

Opposites attract, and forbidden fruit is definitely the sweetest.

Dylan was as atypical as anyone one could be. In fact, he worked hard to defy stereotypes. He graduated high school as valedictorian. He ignored his family's legacy of attending HBCUs and attended a PWI on a full scholarship. He finished undergrad and grad school in five years and immediately entered the workforce.

Athlete, thug, ghetto, or hood were never used in the same sentence as his name unless someone was describing what he was not. Determined to demonstrate his intellect and decorum, Dylan always wore slacks, a button-down shirt, and a tie unless he was at the gym. His command and execution of standard English, as well as his vast vocabulary and eloquent speech, astounded even the greatest educators.

And then there was Landon, the walking stereotype of Black men. Although a proud HBCU alum, he cared nothing about academic accolades and honors. He worked to pay his way through undergrad because partying in his freshman year had cost him his scholarship. Because he messed up his first two semesters, Landon took longer than four years to earn his bachelor's degree and had no interest in earning anything beyond it.

He was no dummy, but didn't see the point in proving himself to anyone. He spoke however he felt at the moment and had no regard for subjects and verbs agreeing. Every pair of pants he owned hung off his behind, despite wearing a belt. He was often mistaken for an overaged college student rather than an employee professional.

Anyone who knew either of these men would never expect them to have anything in common beyond their complexion. The likelihood of them becoming colleagues or anything else defies logic. The relationship they developed is one no one saw coming, not even Dylan and Landon.

Chapter 1

Dylan had loved rain for as long as he could remember. There was something about the way it fell from the sky that seemed to catch his attention, take him to a faraway place and soothe him. Today was no different. He couldn't wait until five o'clock. He planned to drive straight to the lake and watch the rain fall. This has been a hard week at work, and it was only Wednesday.

He needed something to get his mind off the drama that was his job. As director of a group home that cares for adolescent boys who, for whatever reason, had become wards of the state, Dylan's job was perfect for him. He loved children and always tried to secure some kid's future by exposing him to positive situations and showing him someone cared. That was why he took this job in the first place.

Today had been one of those days that made him consider a career change. One of the boys had been beaten up at school, which meant there would be a Social Services investigation. On top of that, the behavior therapist resigned—effective immediately—and the roof over the dormitory was leaking.

To pour salt into an open wound, Landon, the home's recreation director, seemed to be everywhere. Dylan didn't know whether or not Landon was "family," but Landon did something to him.

Landon Joseph embodied everything Dylan found attractive in men. He was handsome, masculine—a little thuggish even—had a nice body (if that bulge in his pants held what Dylan thought it did, Landon made someone very happy), and he dressed well. This man was fine and sexy, and therefore was to be avoided at all costs.

Five o'clock finally came and Dylan couldn't get out the door fast enough. At about 4:30 p.m., the sky erupted, and rain started falling in sheets. It was still falling as Dylan left the home. Just as he stepped out of the door, Landon stood under the small awning that covered the door, trying not to get drenched by the rain.

Dylan tried to rush past him without acknowledging him. He had enough bugging his brain and he didn't need an image of Landon with wet clothes clinging to his body, further complicating his day. But his attempt was unsuccessful.

"Yo, Dylan, hold up, man," Landon called after him. "Can I get a ride with you? My car is broke and it's raining too hard for me to walk. I only stay about a mile away."

Dylan knew giving him a ride would be a big mistake. He desperately needed some solitude, and Landon would disturb that. "Sorry man, I have something to do in the opposite direction. Use the van. Just make sure you replace the gas."

"The opposite direction?" Landon exclaimed. "Man, we're six blocks from the lake. The only thing down there is restaurants and the lake. I know you not going to the lake in all this rain. Let me ride with you. We can eat together. I'll even pay for it, unless you're going on a date."

Dylan never could lie with a straight face, so he wasn't about to say he had a date. He just wanted to be alone, but he would never be able to put up a convincing argument for not giving Landon a ride. "Okay, I'm going to Landry's. You eat seafood?"

"Yeah."

"Cool. Let's roll. I hope you brought enough cash. I always get the seafood platter with an appetizer and at least two strawberry daiquiris. You agreed to pay, now it's time to pay up."

"Two daiquiris? Dang, dawg. You seem like such a church boy. I wouldn't expect you to drink anything stronger than soda. It seems like butter doesn't even melt in your mouth. It's cool, bruh. I got you."

With that, they ran to Dylan's Kia Sportage.

"Man, I'm surprised you're not rolling like a big baller," Landon said, looking at Dylan's car. "Rolling around in a Kia and you're making the big bucks around here, you secured the bag for sure."

"Let's be clear," Dylan stated. "I do alright, but the bag is not secure and I'm surely not rolling in big bucks. I got a car that would take me from point A to point B comfortably. I'm not trying to impress anyone."

Other than that, the six-block ride was quiet as Tasha Cobb Leonard's *You Know My Name* played on the radio.

Chapter 2

Landry's wasn't crowded. They were seated immediately, which is one of the reasons Dylan wanted to go there. The other reason was the view. Landry's was right on the lake and had huge windows. Dylan would still be able to watch the rain fall, which would relax him. But there was no way he would be able to relax with that fine specimen of Black man sitting across from him. His mind would be working overtime trying to be cordial while blocking out improper thoughts.

He had been joking about getting two daiquiris. He rarely drank, especially in public, but he had a feeling he would need something stronger than soda to get him through this dinner.

Landon broke the silence. "How often do you come here? It seems like a nice place. As much as I love seafood, I can't believe I've never been here. If the food is good here, this may be my new hangout."

"Well, you'll definitely be back. They fry fish like they fixed suppers at a Baptist church. I come here about once a month, maybe more if we decide to come after church."

"Oh, what church you go to?"

"Greater Bethlehem."

"Really? That's right by my house."

"Yeah, I know. I see your car when I go to church."

"Really? I guess I need to start parking in my garage. I can't be spotted like that."

"Yeah, you really should. You never know who may be snooping." Dylan said as he stretched, his short sleeves revealing a hint of his tattoo.

"Man, you have a tat?" Landon asked, wide-eyed. "I never woulda guessed. You got a lil thug in you huh?"

"Nah man, a student bit me once when I was a teacher, and it left an ugly scar. I decided to cover it with a tattoo."

Dylan lifted his sleeve and revealed an angel tattooed on a very solid bicep. In one instant, Dylan revealed a whole lot more about himself than he realized. Landon now knew that he used to be a teacher, he had enough courage to get a detailed tattoo, and he still worked out.

"Man, that's tight, and not just the tattoo," Landon marveled. His biceps looked like marbles compared to Dylan's. "Look at your guns. How often do you work out?"

"Four or five times a week. I work out at Barry's gym. Alumni get a discount on membership, and a friend of mine is a trainer there."

"Cool. I used to go to Anytime Fitness, but I stopped. Now I just work out at home and play ball with my boys. I might go with you sometime."

"Maybe," Dylan mumbled. He didn't want to be rude, but he did not want Landon as a workout partner. He didn't need to see Landon sweaty or in gym clothes. That would just cause more temptation and struggle for him.

The waiter came to take their orders, giving Dylan something else to focus on. The guy was kind of cute, with a caramel complexion, shoulder-length, reddish-brown dreads, and a basketball player's body – very nice. He tried not to stare too long because he didn't want the guy to notice.

But Landon noticed.

The waiter walked away, and Landon watched Dylan's eyes follow the waiter's butt. Landon had to admit the guy was nice looking, but was Dylan really peeping dude out? Or was he imagining things?

Before long, a waitress came with their drinks. She was phoine! This time, it was Landon who stared and flirted, but Dylan hardly paid her any attention. The waitress was flirting back with Landon when the waiter came back with their orders. Landon stopped talking and watched Dylan as the waitress wrote down her number for him. He saw Dylan look the guy over again. Dylan's demeanor appeared to change, but Landon may have been making inaccurate assumptions.

As they ate, the two men talked about some of the kids at

the home and how they were doing in school. They talked about college—frats, where they pledged, line names, the actual pledge process. The conversation was good. Dylan found that he actually enjoyed Landon's company, but the sooner this ended, the happier he'd be. He couldn't allow himself to get too comfortable with Landon, who was the kind of man Dylan imagined himself being with. If he let himself get too comfortable, he might let his wall down. He couldn't afford to let that happen. He'd worked too hard for too long to build it. He'd been taught all his life that homosexuality was wrong—a sin, as his pastor had said.

He tried to deny his feelings from the very beginning. He couldn't pinpoint exactly when they started, but remembered having them in junior high. So far, he had been able to avoid any compromising positions. He would look at men and silently appreciate their beauty, but he'd never done anything sexual with a man. He never really got close to anyone he found attractive.

No one except Landon. Landon was a threat to Dylan's chastity. Dylan knew that if the opportunity ever presented itself, his twenty-six years of virginity would be out the window. He had to be strong, keep his wall up. There was no way he could let Landon in.

"Man, this fish is good. The cook stuck his foot in it. This is almost as good as my momma's. I'm glad you let me tag along. This definitely won't be my last time here."

Dylan didn't respond, seemingly lost in thought.

Landon looked at him. "Wassup bruh, you a'ight? You all zoned out. What's on your mind like that?"

"Oh, I'm sorry, man. It's nothing really. Just something I need to take care of when I get home."

"You sure? I know we not all that tight, but you cool people. If you need a listening ear, I'm here."

"No, I appreciate it, but I'm straight."

"Cool, but remember I'm here if you need me. Anytime, anything," Landon said, making sure to emphasize *thing*.

Landon's offer of friendship was genuine, but it could be

problematic for Dylan. Dylan never had any friends who made him feel the way Landon did. Would they be able to keep the line clear between friend and lover?

Landon's new girlfriend came back asking if they needed more drinks, and they flirted some more. The waitress giggled and grinned as Landon complimented her. Dylan was finished eating and ready to go.

"Man, I'm done. I'm going to the restroom. After you pay the bill and tip the pretty lady, meet me at the car." He stood and walked away from the table, heading to the front of the restaurant where the restrooms were located.

Chapter 3

It was still raining when they stepped outside, so they ran to the car. The ride home was the complete opposite of the ride to the restaurant. Landon talked non-stop about his newfound sidepiece. He asked Dylan what he thought of her, and Dylan only mumbled.

"Man, what's wrong with you? As fine as she is, I know you had to notice her. Face like Meagan Goode, booty like J. Lo and tits like Beyonce."

"No, I didn't really notice. I had something else on my mind."

"Yeah, like the waiter with the dreads." It was out of his mouth before he realized it. He looked at Dylan and instantly saw his face go from shocked to sad.

"Man, I'm sorry I didn't mean to say that out loud. I didn't really mean anything by it."

"Forget it. I'm just not having a good day. The sooner I get you out of my car, the sooner I can go home, get some sleep, and get up and start over again tomorrow."

"Dylan, I can tell something is bothering you, man. Why don't you just get it off your chest? You can be honest with me. It'll be between me and you."

"*You* are part of my problem. People who say things and don't realize the impact of their words. People who walk around like they've got the world in the palm of their hand and don't give a damn about what their fellow man might be going through. That kind of stuff really gets on my nerves."

Landon took advantage of the opportunity and jumped in feet first. "Man, I know you not tripping off what I said about the waiter. If you dig dudes, ain't nothing wrong with that. If you like dudes, you like dudes. You still cool people."

What the hell, Dylan thought. The most Landon could do

was gossip and if that happened, he'd simply resign and look for a new job. "No, Landon, it *is* a big deal. There *is* something wrong with me liking dudes. Imagine being attracted to men for as long as you can remember and never saying anything about it or never acting on it because all you hear is that it's wrong or that it's a sin. Do you know how hard it is to not tell someone you think they're cute because you're afraid of how they'll respond? Do you know how heart-wrenching it is to sit across the table from someone you find extremely attractive and watch him flirt with someone else the entire time? Or how it feels to be teased about the way you talk or how you do certain things because people feel you're too feminine? I don't think you do, but I can tell you. It hurts like hell, but there's nothing I can do about it. I just have to accept it and keep living like I have the perfect life."

Landon couldn't believe what he'd just heard. Dylan had been holding that in for a long time. No wonder he looked so sad at the restaurant when he was watching the waiter. He looked over and saw tears running down Dylan's face as they pulled in front of his house.

"Look, man, I'm sorry," he said. "I really don't know what to say right now. One thing I do know is that you have a lot you need to get off your chest. Why don't you come in and we can talk about this?"

"Thanks, man, but I think it would be best if I just went home and went to sleep."

Landon was offering just what Dylan needed, but Dylan knew going into Landon's house in his weakened state wasn't wise. Yet, Landon wouldn't take no for an answer.

"Look, Dylan, you need to let this out. You're really not in any condition to be driving right now, especially in this weather."

"Okay, man. Thanks, I appreciate it. I don't mean to be dumping this on you, but I've been holding this in for a while and some things happened today that just triggered all the feelings I thought I had locked away."

They got out of the car and went into Landon's house. Landon told Dylan to make himself comfortable and walked to the back of the house. When he came back, he was dressed in dry clothes and gave Dylan a pair of sweats and a t-shirt. Dylan changed clothes and got comfortable on the couch next to Landon, who handed him a bottle of water.

Landon turned on the television and saw that the Pelicans were beating the brakes off the Lakers. "Right about now I bet Anthony Davis is wishing he was still a Pelican. They're making the Lakers look like amateurs."

"Yep," Dylan replied.

Maybe inviting Dylan in wasn't the best idea. He still didn't seem like he was ready to talk. Landon decided to just tackle it head on rather than ease into the conversation.

"So how long have you been having these feelings?" Landon asked before taking a sip of water. "I never would have guessed that you dealt with anything like that."

Dylan sighed and sipped his water. "I don't know when it really started, but I can remember staring at dudes in junior high, and have been doing it ever since. I've never done anything with a man, but that doesn't mean I didn't want to. I was scared. Like I said before, I had always been told it was a sin and I didn't wanna make God mad. Plus, I mean, how do you approach a dude like that? Suppose I approached the wrong person and he started beating the mess out of me. I mean, he would be justified and that would cause a whole different set of problems. So, it's easier for me to keep it to myself, deny my feelings, and never act on them."

"Man, that's a lot to hold in. You never talked to anybody about it? You never tried to act on your feelings and see whether or not you would even like it?"

"Believe me, I wanted to, but there was never anyone I felt that comfortable with. I've never had a lot of friends. Even after I pledged, I couldn't talk to anybody in the frat about it. You know how they feel about gay men. So, I just kept it to myself. There was no one else I could trust."

"Until now." Landon leaned forward and kissed Dylan. Dylan wanted to push him away, make Landon get off him, but his wall was crumbling. He finally felt like he belonged. Like all was right with the world. He surrendered to what he felt. For the first time in a long time, he let go and went with the flow.

Chapter 5

This may have been Dylan's first sexual experience, but Landon was an expert. He somehow managed to remove both of their clothes as he kissed Dylan and then pulled away and stood up. Dylan couldn't believe what he saw. Landon was as fine as Dylan had imagined, and that bulge in his pants concealed a python, just like he had suspected.

Landon leaned in and kissed Dylan again, and he responded by opening his mouth and letting Landon slip his tongue inside his mouth. It was the sweetest thing he had ever tasted. Landon moved from Dylan's lips to his neck, and then to his ears. Pure ecstasy is the only way to describe what Dylan felt.

Landon stopped. "You wanna go all the way?"

Dylan nodded yes and Landon got up and left the room. Dylan sat up and began to panic, thinking Landon was on his way back with a recording of the whole thing that he would use to blackmail him.

Landon returned a few minutes later and noticed the paranoia on Dylan's face. "What's wrong?"

"When you left, I thought you were going to come back and say this was some type of joke."

"Nah, man. I wouldn't do that to you. The truth is I've been kind of curious, myself. After you made your confession to me, I figured you would be someone safe to share my secret with. But I don't wanna pressure you. If you're not comfortable, we don't have to do this. This is a big step and I'll understand if you change your mind."

"No, I want to do this. I've come this far, so I might as well go all the way."

Landon responded by kissing Dylan again. They lay back on the couch with Landon on top, and Dylan tensed.

"Relax," Landon said. "It will make it easier."

Dylan relaxed and let Landon take control. Before long, they had made a connection that couldn't be retracted. True to his word, Landon made things more comfortable, and they had the time of their lives. It was a new experience for them both.

Chapter 6

Dylan awoke a few hours later feeling a tremendous amount of guilt. As he thought back on what happened, he remembered crossing a line he promised himself and God he would never cross. Realizing the severity of his actions, he began crying uncontrollably.

Landon awoke, startled. "What's wrong? Why are you crying? You okay? Did I hurt you?"

"No, I'm fine. But I shouldn't have done it. I should have never allowed it to happen. I should have dropped you off and gone home. I knew better, but I let my guard down. Now I have to suffer the consequences."

"What are you talking about? Consequences?"

"You and God. I know God is not pleased with me, and I don't know how I'll be able to face you at work. I feel so ashamed."

"You have nothing to be ashamed of. We're both adults and we both enjoyed what we did. It may not have been right by religious standards, but I don't think God is gonna send you to hell for committing a sin. I may not be into church like I should be, but I remember learning that God is a forgiving God. And as far as facing me at work, I should be the one worried. I feel responsible, like I may have pressured you into this."

"No, not at all. We are both responsible for what happened. To be honest, part of me is glad it finally happened. I just hope I don't regret it later."

"I promise you, you'll have nothing to regret. As I told you before, I'm here for you anytime, anything. Especially this."

Landon leaned forward and kissed Dylan on the lips, but this time, Dylan abruptly pulled away.

"Landon, you don't understand. It's more than me just sinning," he said. "It's about me going against the will of God. It's about me breaking a commitment between God and myself. I know that God forgives us for sinning, but that doesn't mean we're free to commit sin and then repent when it is over. He expects us to avoid sin and not put ourselves in situations where we'll be tempted."

Although Dylan wasn't angry, his words seemed filled with venom. The truth was that he was actually angry with himself. Even though he knew God would forgive him if he truly repented, he didn't know if he would ever forgive himself.

"Look, Dylan, there's no reason for you to be so mad," Landon said. "We all fall sometimes. This isn't the end of the world. God will forgive you, and I promise to never compromise you or your values again. I hope we can not only still work together, but actually become good friends and grow from this experience."

Landon extended his hand and when Dylan accepted, Landon pulled him into a tight embrace. They decided they could both benefit from a good night's sleep, so Landon left Dylan on the couch and retreated to his bedroom.

Chapter 7

Dylan awoke the next morning wondering if the previous night had been a dream. When he opened his eyes, he knew part of it was true—this was definitely not his apartment. Since Landon was in his dream, he assumed he was at Landon's house. Did he and Landon really have sex or was it just a fantasy unfolding as he slept?

He tried to stand up, but his leg muscles hurt. *Last night definitely wasn't a dream*, he thought. The pain in his legs reminded him that his body had been bent in strange positions the previous night.

Landon's voice coming from the kitchen confirmed his fears. He had slept with a man. And not just any man, but a co-worker—someone he had to face every day. How could he have messed up like that? Did the daiquiris have a stronger effect than he realized? Did Landon slip something into his drink?

No, he knew exactly what happened. The kiss.

Dylan had been determined not to give in. He knew being alone with Landon could be dangerous, but things had been going well. Landon was easy to talk to. Maybe he could be the male friend Dylan needed. It would be good to talk to another man about what he felt sexually. Landon seemed comfortable with the discussion, so Dylan let it all out. He felt he could trust Landon. He was safe; he was Dylan's safety net.

But when Landon kissed Dylan, something inside him clicked. Like all his pent-up desires had been released. He submitted to the kiss. It felt so perfect. The way their lips felt against each other. The way Landon's goatee tickled Dylan's chin. Dylan never imagined a kiss could be so pleasurable. It felt so good, he just let go, allowing his body to experience what he had been denying himself for so long.

There was no doubt he enjoyed it, but he regretted it for so many reasons. How would this affect his job? He still had to work with Landon. Would this create a tense work environment? Would Landon still respect him as his boss, or would he now expect preferential treatment, or worse try blackmailing him? Was this a one-time thing, or would Landon want to do it again?

Landon seemed to enjoy it too, judging from the kiss he gave Dylan afterwards. But Dylan couldn't allow it to happen again. He couldn't disappoint God like that. He had been praying for deliverance, and although the feelings were still there, he knew God was changing him. How could he have given in so easily? Sitting on Landon's couch, he was consumed by his thoughts. The more he thought about what he had allowed to happen, the harder he cried.

Chapter 8

Landon moved around the kitchen as if he were floating on clouds. He felt great this morning. Better than he had in a long time. Last night was unbelievable. Dylan had let him into his world. He'd always thought Dylan would be a good friend, but he never thought they'd end up sleeping together. The whole night seemed unreal. Going to Landry's, watching Dylan stare at the waiter, he and Dylan talking on the way home, Dylan agreeing to come in, more talking, the kiss, and the sex. Landon did his best to handle Dylan gently.

Kissing Dylan seemed to work, and he took proper precautions to make sure he didn't put Dylan in too much pain. Although it was both their first time, he knew it could be painful. He took his time and proceeded with caution, gauging how tense Dylan's body was before continuing. Once they began, he couldn't believe how it felt. He had been with many women, but none compared to what he felt at that moment. The resistance Dylan's body presented heightened Landon's pleasure. It definitely wasn't the same as being with a woman.

He felt Dylan tense again and kissed him, reminding him to relax and telling him it would feel better soon. Dylan began to relax, and Landon took it as a sign to continue. He moved slow and steady until he could tell Dylan was comfortable. Then he gave Dylan what he knew he needed—a memorable experience. When they finished, Landon kissed Dylan softly on his cheek before falling into a peaceful sleep.

Reminiscing about last night's pleasure made Landon smile and sing out loud. Ledisi's *I Blame You* poured from his lips as if he recorded the song himself. He put the food on their plates and walked back to the living room.

As soon as he reached the living room, Landon saw Dylan pacing.

"Dylan, what's wrong?

"Landon, last night was a mistake," Dylan said. "I keep thinking about what we did. There's no way I should have let it happen."

Landon's face twisted in confusion. Why was Dylan being so hard on himself? Hadn't he sinned before? Everybody sinned at some point.

"Dylan, I can understand why you feel that way, but you shouldn't," Landon replied, setting the plates on the coffee table. "Nothing that happens is a mistake. I may not be in church like I should, but I have some religion in me. I know what the Bible says about what we did. But I also know what Romans eight and twenty-eight says 'all things work together for the good of them who love God, to those who are called according to his purpose.' Now based on that, there was a reason for last night. We may have committed a sin, but don't we always sin? God knows we're gonna sin, but he forgives us for it. So don't feel bad about what happened. Just know there's a reason for it happening."

Dylan knew Landon was right, although he couldn't think of one reason the sex *had* to happen. He would have never guessed that Landon had any type of spiritual knowledge. He seemed like such a thug, like God and church had no part of his life. Dylan appreciated Landon's attempt to comfort him, but Landon had no idea how significant this was for him. Besides, wasn't it Landon's attempt to comfort him that led to the current situation?

"You're right, Landon, and I appreciate what you're saying. But this is something I've been dealing with for a long time."

He looked around for his phone and remembered it was dead because he hadn't charged it last night. Landon, like most people these days, didn't have a house phone because he didn't see one anywhere. Sitting back down on the couch, he let out what seemed like a sigh of relief.

"Landon, I have a lot going on in my head right now and need some time to think. Where's your phone? I'm gonna call in today. As soon as I eat, I'll leave. I know you have to get ready for work."

"My phone's in the kitchen. You can have some privacy in there. You don't have to rush. You can stay here and get your head together and we can talk when I can get home this evening."

"Thanks, man, but I need to go home so I can shower and get clean clothes," Dylan replied as he walked to the kitchen. He needed to be away from Landon and everything that brought him to mind. Staying at his house would not be wise. He dialed his secretary's number and she answered on the first ring. He loved Hailey's efficiency.

"Hi, Hailey," he greeted, hoping she wouldn't ask a million questions. "I've had a personal emergency and won't be in today."

"No problem, Mr. Boyd. We don't have anything major scheduled the next couple of days. Take however long you need. I'll make sure everything runs smoothly while you're out."

"Thanks, Hailey. I appreciate how you always have my back. Call me on my cell if anything comes up. I have my laptop if necessary."

As Dylan finished giving Hailey instructions, Landon walked into the kitchen, placed Dylan's cold breakfast in the microwave and walked back out into the living room. After ending the call with Hailey, Dylan grabbed his plate and walked back to the living room.

He heard water running and assumed Landon was taking a shower. He entertained the thought of joining him but knew it would lead to more problems. Instead, he enjoyed Landon's cooking. After cleaning his plate, he placed it in the sink and walked through the living room and out the front door, not even bothering to say goodbye.

Chapter 9

Dylan was in no condition to drive, but he had to get away from Landon. The tears wouldn't stop flowing and he could barely see, but he was able to make it home without running into or over anyone. He wanted to be left alone so he could meditate and reconnect with God. How could he have allowed himself to fall so easily?

Once he got inside his apartment, he went straight to his shower. He felt dirty and nasty. He scrubbed and scrubbed, trying to wash away his guilt, but as much as he couldn't wash away his sins, he couldn't get rid of the dirty feeling that enveloped his body. As he continued to scrub and wash, a scripture he had heard repeatedly as a child began to repeat itself in his mind: *thou shalt not lie with mankind, as with womankind; it is an abomination.*

Each word rang loudly in his head. He finally realized there was only one thing that would bring him relief, and immediately fell on his knees as the water beat his neck and back.

"Father, in the name of Jesus, I come before you now acknowledging my sin. Father, I gave in to the flesh. Not only did I drink, but I let down my guard and had sex with a man. I let myself down, but most of all, I let you down. I feel so guilty, I don't know if I can ever move beyond this. I am asking you for strength. Please forgive me for giving in to my desires. Help me to move on from here and not do it again. Help me to forgive myself and rededicate myself to you and your will. In your name I pray, amen."

Usually, a heartfelt conversation with God helped Dylan feel better, but today it didn't seem to do any good. After he finished praying, he stayed on his knees in the shower and continued crying. After what seemed like an hour, Dylan turned off the water, went to his room, and fell across his bed.

When he opened his eyes again the sun had set, and he realized he'd slept the day away. As he sat up, he remembered he'd dreamed about grandfather, something he never did. Pop-Pop was teaching a Bible study lesson about the woman caught in adultery, Dylan's favorite Bible story. Even though her accusers wanted her to be punished for her sins, Jesus saw fit to forgive her. If Jesus could forgive the woman caught in adultery, couldn't he forgive Dylan for sleeping with Landon? Just as Jesus told the woman to go and sin no more, Dylan could move forward and sin no more.

He still felt bad about giving in to his urges, but he had been reassured God would forgive him. However, with that forgiveness, he knew God expected him to avoid falling into sin again. He wiped the tears from his eyes and began praising God for all that He had done in his life. This incident with Landon was just a setback and would not distract him from following God's plan for his life. It was simply a mistake that would be learned from, but not repeated. He said another quick prayer and went back to bed. How good it is to serve a merciful and forgiving God!

Chapter 10

Landon heard the front door close as he stepped out of the shower. When he walked into the living room, Dylan was gone. Landon was surprised he'd left like that. Weren't they on a different level now, like they were friends and could talk about anything? He understood Dylan had a lot on his mind, but didn't Dylan realize he did, too?

Last night was also Landon's first time with a man. He couldn't say he was actually attracted to men, but he was curious about what sex with a man was like. He'd heard a teammate talk about how different a man felt and how much more he enjoyed being with a man than a woman. Landon's cousin also preferred male partners to women after an extended stay in the county jail. Curiosity got the best of Landon, and he took the plunge the moment an opportunity came. He only knew what to do because he had watched a few videos, but he was nervous, too. And now that he'd done it, what did it mean? Is he gay? Bi? Will he ever do it again?

Then the religion thing came to mind. He surprised himself with the words of comfort he gave Dylan. He had been out of church for a while and was recently considering going back and doing better. He wasn't skateboarding to hell, but he knew he wasn't a saint, either. He wished Dylan had stayed a little longer so they could talk some more. Hopefully, he'd call later.

Landon decided not to let Dylan's behavior ruin his day. He grabbed his bag and headed to the gym. He used the drive time to think about how things had played out the last hour or so. He'd lived most of his life with few friends or associates and didn't care if he had any. If Dylan wanted to act like a religious lunatic, he could do that by himself. Landon didn't tolerate drama from women, and certainly wasn't about to deal with a drama queen of a man. They were both grown men and should act as such. After a good workout and hot shower, he'd go to work and let the chips fall where they may.

***

Landon didn't remember Dylan ever missing a day of work. Was he really tripping that hard? So what? They crossed a line. Did it mean they couldn't still work together and be cordial? Maybe hanging out outside of work wasn't for the best. Maybe there was too much temptation. Yes, Dylan was a good-looking dude, but it's not like Landon was trying to be in a relationship with him. Honestly, they'd both taken advantage of the opportunity. They were both curious and felt comfortable with each other. Why not go for it?

Now that he'd experienced it, Landon still wasn't exactly sure being with a man was for him. He definitely enjoyed his night with Dylan. Yet, despite the pleasure of it all, it still wasn't the same as being with a woman.

The more he thought about it, Landon realized he wasn't bi after all. He wasn't really attracted to guys at all. Yeah, he thought some guys were good looking and had nice bodies, but maybe it was more of an admiration than an attraction. Two things were certain: if he never hooked up with another man, that would be cool, and he and Dylan needed to talk ASAP.

He hoped Dylan would get it together soon. He really was a cool dude and Landon thought it would be good to hang out with him. He'd be a great workout partner, and Dylan could teach him more about the social work side of their job and help him work with the kids better. Dylan just needed to get the stick out of his behind and relax and enjoy life. Learn to roll with the punches and just live.

Once things settled and the kids were all at school, he planned to have a man-to-man, heart-to-heart talk with Dylan. They could put what happened behind them and build a brotherhood that would benefit them both.

Chapter 11

Taking yesterday off was exactly what Dylan needed. After praying, he fell asleep on the couch and stayed there most of the day. Surprisingly, his thoughts didn't consume him. Once he'd repented, the guilt seemed to leave his body and he was able to relax. It was the best day off he'd had in a long time.

He actually sang as he entered his office the next morning. Stokley's *She* rang from his lips as though he'd recorded it himself. Having never heard him sing anything other gospel or Christmas carols, his secretary gasped loudly as he walked past her desk. "Is everything okay, Mr. Boyd?"

"Everything's fine, Hailey. Why don't you run to Starbucks and grab some goodies for the staff?" Dylan suggested, handing her his debit card instead of the normal laundry list of morning tasks.

Hailey slipped the card in her purse and was out of the office before he had a chance to change his mind.

His good mood lasted about an hour. He pulled up his work calendar and felt like he'd been sucker punched. Dylan had forgotten that he and Landon were supposed to go to San Francisco together for a conference. There was no way he could skip the trip. He was a presenter, and not showing up would be career suicide.

Never crap where you eat.

The old saying he used to hear Pop-Pop say never made sense until now. Office romances and hookups could be very ugly and messy and usually didn't end well. How had he allowed himself to get entangled in one? He made a silent vow to never touch a drop of liquor ever again in life. Didn't Jaime Foxx say *blame it on the alcohol?* Not this time. He was in control throughout the night's shenanigans and though he had second thoughts now, he enjoyed it in the moment. He might not ever drink again, but it was more about his commitment to God than releasing his inhibitions.

***

As Landon came out of the break room, he was surprised and glad to hear music coming from Dylan's office. Music meant Dylan had come in that morning, but it wasn't his usual gospel music. It sounded like early 2000s pop, something Landon would never admit he enjoyed. Hearing something different come from Dylan's office brought a smile to Landon's face. Maybe he was in a better mood, and they'd be able to have that brother-to-brother conversation they needed to have.

Landon didn't want to create any problems at work. Besides earning a pretty good salary, he enjoyed what he did, and didn't want to risk losing this blessing. Especially not over an evening of pleasure. Knowing Dylan was always the last one to leave, Landon decided he'd wait until the kids had eaten dinner and returned to the residence hall. He knew Dylan wouldn't act a fool at work, so they'd be able to have a civilized conversation and hash out this situation.

After he saw the last kid leave the dining hall and the custodian lock the door, Landon headed upstairs to Dylan's office. The door was open, so he cleared his throat to get Dylan's attention. The sour look on Dylan's face showed he wasn't expecting Landon to be standing there.

"Look, I'm not gonna trip about what happened the other night," Landon said. "I know it was major for you, but we're on two different pages with it. I know you need to figure some things out, but I'm going to be your friend. I always thought you were a decent guy, but after that night I see you're really cool. I could use a friend like you, and something tells me you could use a friend, period."

"You're right, I did overreact, and I apologize," Dylan replied. "There was no reason for me to disrespect you the way

I did. Thank you for your hospitality and your friendship. Having male friends is new to me. I appreciate you extending yourself the way you did."

"You're good, man," Landon said. "What happened that night was uncharted territory for us both. It makes sense that you would freak out a little, but I didn't expect you to be skipping work and ignoring calls and stuff. I'll let you make it this time. Friends?"

Landon extended his hand and then pulled Dylan into a brother-man hug. Dylan didn't resist. The hug was warm and comforting, just what he needed. Landon was right. Dylan didn't have anyone he could truly consider a friend. Having Landon in his corner wouldn't be the worst thing in the world.

Chapter 12

Grind it out, big dawg. You got this! Yeah, one more set!" Landon yelled as Dylan dropped the trap bar onto the gym floor with a loud thud.

Nearly a month had passed since the "incident." Dylan and Landon had progressed from colleagues to friends. They found themselves working out together at least twice a week. Since he realized his spiritual life needed some work, Landon asked Dylan if they could start going to Bible study together. If they missed it at the church, they'd meet up after work and review the Sunday School lesson.

Being Landon's friend wasn't as problematic as Dylan had expected. Landon respected Dylan's personal space and was careful, most times, about what he said when Dylan was around. For the first time in a long time, Dylan began to feel comfortable spending time with a man who wasn't a relative. His brain and other body parts may not have always done what he wanted them to, but he found himself more comfortable with Landon than he'd expected. No lines had been crossed. No slip ups had occurred. They had become friends and accountability partners. Dylan kept Landon on his spiritual toes and Landon never let Dylan get caught skimping with his fitness.

"Let's go, bruh. Stop daydreaming and get it in gear. Last set."

At Landon's command, Dylan picked up the trap bar and began his trek across the gym. The sooner he finished, the sooner he could leave.

"Yeah, dawg, I know you have it in you. Get your head out of your butt and focus."

"Getting my head out of my behind is not the problem," Dylan remarked. "You keeping your snake in the cage is. You know you can't wear those tights, especially white ones, without something over them."

"I can't help it if God blessed me abundantly. Keep your eyes above the waist and do what you came here to do."

"Some things are hard to ignore, especially when they're purposely put on display. Now quit yapping and finish your workout," Dylan snapped, relishing the opportunity to boss Landon around.

Once Landon finished his deadlifts, they showered and headed to work. Landon's anaconda had been properly restrained and wouldn't be distracting, or tempting, Dylan for the rest of the day.

Chapter 13

One of the things Dylan loved about his job was that it afforded him the opportunity to travel on the company's dime. Several times a year, he traveled somewhere nice for professional development. The National Association of Black Social Workers conference in San Francisco was one of those opportunities.

San Francisco was on his bucket list, so this conference would kill two birds with one stone. He was excited about finally getting to visit San Francisco even though Landon would be attending, too. There hadn't been any slip ups or close encounters since the first time, but Dylan didn't want to take any chances. Landon seemed to have moved on from it. He was dating a woman and they seemed pretty serious.

Trainings and professional development trips were typically covered as a work-related expense, but Dylan decided to book and pay for his own room at the conference site, the Marriott Marquis, for convenience and assurance. He planned to not even mention that he had separate accommodations until they landed in San Francisco.

The six-hour flight was restful. Because they were flying early in the morning, they were able to get a direct flight from Miami with no layovers. This was only Landon's second flight in his entire life, so he was extremely chatty the first hour or so. Eventually he dozed off, which gave Dylan the silence he hoped he'd get on the flight. Before long, he had drifted into a peaceful sleep and awakened just in time to feel the plane's impact as it reconnected with the earth.

After retrieving their luggage, Landon and Dylan headed to the rental kiosk to pick up their transportation for the week.

"Man, I hope they give us a decent ride. I know the job be trying to penny pinch and catch a deal whenever they can," Landon grumbled.

"Obviously, you still don't know me very well," Dylan replied. "You should know by now that I do inexpensive, not cheap. We're riding in semi-luxury. As for your accommodations, I reserved a room for you at the Hilton. I will be staying at the conference headquarters."

"You must be the most bougie mofo I know," Landon said with a laugh. "Why you couldn't just get us both rooms at a Hampton Inn and spend the extra money on something fun? We ain't gotta just sit in our rooms waiting on the next session. And why we staying at two different hotels? You ain't that special, Mr. Keynote Speaker. We could have shared your room at the Marriott. They probably put you up in a suite and everything."

"They didn't. I made and paid for my own reservations. I'm not a keynote speaker, just leading a session. I wanted my own space and didn't want to feel like I was crowding someone else or imposing on them. With me having to do this presentation, I'll be staying up late and waking up early. Sharing a room, or even a suite, with you or anyone else wouldn't work."

"You probably got separate rooms 'cause you scared you gone give it up to Big Daddy again," Landon remarked. "You think I don't notice how you act when we're alone? I pay attention, but I wasn't gone call you out on it. I know it's not easy for you. I don't know your feelings or thoughts, but I know it's a battle. Always remember this, though: you're my boy. I'm not going to force you to do anything you don't want to or allow you to do anything you may regret later. I got your back more than you realize."

"Sir, quit hallucinating. You must be the most arrogant mofo I know. Ain't nobody thinking about you or that thing between your legs. You are not God's gift."

"The lies you tell. It's all good, though. I'll let you save face this time."

Landon didn't know how true his words were. Dylan did put distance between them to avoid temptation. He also didn't want to explain his whereabouts if he decided to explore the Castro District, which was famous for embracing members of the LGBTQ community.

"Shut up, clown. Grab your bags and let's go. I'll drop you off at your hotel and come back for you later and treat you to a nice dinner."

***

Dylan chose the Waterbar for dinner. *Definitely the type of place he prefers*, Landon thought. *What's up with this dude and water and seafood restaurants?*

"Being here is almost like déjà vu," Landon said. "The first time we ever hung together outside of work was at a seafood restaurant on the water. This waiter even has dreads like the guy did at Landry's. That's crazy!"

"Most of this is coincidental," Dylan replied. "I love seafood, so I always look for restaurants to try whenever I visit new cities. When I saw that this place had a beautiful view of the bay, it was a no brainer. I have no control over the weather or who these people hire. I actually hadn't paid attention to the waiter or his hair."

Landon didn't believe him. He'd caught Dylan sneaking glances at the waiter, but decided not to give him a hard time. He just wanted his boy to be happy.

Dylan actually seemed to be in a good mood this time. But there would be no fooling around tonight. Even though he'd given Dylan a hard time earlier, Landon had no intention of ever going there with him again. He'd come to consider Dylan a friend and brother, and brothers definitely didn't cross that line. Besides, seeing how Dylan beat himself up afterward tugged at his heart. He never wanted to see his friend hurt like that again, let alone contribute to the pain. He'd decided to be on his best behavior whenever he was alone with Dylan and to always respect his boundaries, even if Dylan crossed them, himself.

Just like at Landry's, the food was delicious. A deaconess from Greater Bethlehem must have been slinging pots back there.

"Let's split some carrot cake. Today can be our cheat day," Landon suggested.

"I'm not falling for your trap. Carrot cake today will mean extra burpees tomorrow. No thanks!"

"I wouldn't do you like that, no cap. We're sort of on vacation. Treat yourself. You been putting in work in the gym. You earned it."

When the waiter walked past, Landon ordered a slice of carrot cake and asked for two forks. As the waiter walked away, Landon could have sworn he saw him wink and smile at Dylan. "Somebody has an admirer, I see. You pullin' 'em even in Cali. I see you, Dyl!"

"What did I tell you about that? My name is Dylan, not Dyl. I am not a pickle. Secondly, nobody is pulling anyone or anything, I don't know what you think you saw, but I am not flirting with anyone, male or female."

Chapter 14

The conference went well. Landon was impressed. NABSW knew how to do things. The sessions weren't long and drawn out. There was food and snacks in between each session. Random prize drawings were held for attendees, and the prizes were nice. The presenters were knowledgeable and engaging. On Day 3, Landon had the privilege of witnessing one of the greatest moments of the conference—watching Dylan shine on stage.

***

Dylan couldn't believe how many people had attended his session. Not only was every seat taken, but people stood along the wall. This wasn't his first time speaking in front of a large group, but this was the largest.

As the commentator read his introduction, he almost didn't recognize himself. While most of the statements were true, the verbiage wasn't what he had submitted. Someone had taken the liberty to jazz up his simple dossier.

After the introduction, Dylan stepped on stage like he owned the place. The words glided from his lips effortlessly. Confidence he didn't know he possessed exuded from him. He didn't stumble over any words, hadn't forgotten any points, and answered every question. He couldn't believe the standing ovation he received when he finished and was shocked at the crowd waiting as he exited the stage.

Thirty minutes later, a facilitator dispersed the crowd, and he was finally able to leave. He had hoped to run into Landon but didn't see him. Since he had the evening free, he decided to head to the Castro District to see what they had to offer.

He was surprised to see Landon walk into a small boutique. He started to keep walking and mind his business, but decided to go in and speak to his friend.

"Never in a million years would I expect to find you down here," Dylan said as he approached Landon.

Landon turned around holding up a pair of rainbow bikini-style trunks. "I decided to buy a gift to congratulate a friend on a fantastic presentation. I think he'd love these, and they're just his size."

Smiling, Dylan snatched the trunks from Landon. "You've never been in a room with sense! Just silly all the time. I'm surprised you're so comfortable down here."

"You act like we're in the hood or something. This is a nice shopping area. Kind of reminds me of the French Quarter in New Orleans."

"It is very similar to the French Quarter, but there's more than shopping here. We're in the Castro District, San Francisco's most prominent gay community."

"No wonder you're surprised to see me here. I damned sure didn't know that when I wandered down here. It's cool, though. I like the area. Long as don't nobody come at me sideways, we straight."

"You don't have to worry about that. I'll keep them off you. Let's go to a few more stores and grab a bite to eat before we head in for the night."

Landon paid for the swimming trunks while Dylan looked around. He had the cashier gift wrap them in purple paper, knowing Dylan's favorite color, and then hid the box inside a bag.

They enjoyed hours of shopping, laughing, and sightseeing. No one flirted with Landon, so it was a peaceful evening, but he did try to get Dylan to flirt with a few nice-looking men.

After dinner, Landon asked Dylan to come back to his room. Once they were back at the Hilton, they laughed and cut up like the frat boys they were.

Chapter 15

When Dylan woke up the next morning, he felt off kilter. He stood and stretched before realizing he wasn't in his own room. He started to panic, but noticing Landon lying in bed half-dressed calmed him a little. Then his mind began to race. Why was he in Landon's room? Why didn't Landon have on pants?

A million questions rushed his mind. Just before he had a full-on anxiety attack, Landon stirred in the bed.

"Good morning, Sleepyhead," Landon said, and then scrunched his eyebrows. "Dude, what's up with your face? You look like you're about to flash out or something."

"I am! Why am I here? Why don't you have on pajamas? I really hope we didn't mess around again." Dylan began looking around the room for his shoes. As he made a mad dash for the door, Landon grabbed him by the arm.

"Stop! Take a deep breath. Yesterday, you told hundreds of people how to deal with kids in crisis. I need you to follow your own instructions."

Dylan took several deep breaths to calm himself. Once he was calmer, Landon walked him over to the couch and sat him down.

"First off, I need you to realize that you're safe. There isn't anyone or anything here that can or will harm you."

Dylan was somewhat stunned to hear his own words being spoken to him, and by Landon of all people. He relaxed a little, but still had questions that needed answering.

"Now that you're calmer, give me a minute to get dressed and make some coffee," Landon stated. I'll tell you what happened last night and answer your questions."

Dylan was amazed at how calm Landon was and how he employed techniques they typically used with their residents.

From the kitchen area, Landon began to explain. "To give you peace of mind, let me go ahead and tell you nothing sexual happened last night. I told you before I wouldn't cross that line with you unless you wanted to. Both of us know if we had, you wouldn't have to wonder. We talked and clowned for a while last night. I hadn't seen you unwind like that before. You even stopped sounding like an English professor and used some slang and Ebonics."

Dylan did remember laughing a lot and sounding like a 'hood' version of himself but thought he had been dreaming. Why was everything so foggy?

Landon continued. "Before we knew it, it was after midnight. Apparently, the adrenaline from giving your presentation had finally worn off, and I could tell you were getting sleepy. I offered to let you stay here and you agreed on one condition: that I behave myself. I agreed and you got in the bed under the covers. I went to shower and when I came out you were comatose. I climbed in the bed with you and fell asleep."

"Okay, everything you're saying makes sense," Dylan said. "I guess I was more tired than I realized. I surely can't blame it on the alcohol since I only had water last night. That doesn't explain why you only have on underwear, and it looked like you were hugging me."

Dylan still looked confused as Landon continued to explain. "Well, you don't know this, but I typically only sleep in my underwear, even when it's cold outside. I started to put on a pair of shorts, but I figured we were cool enough that you wouldn't care."

Dylan nodded. Landon's explanation made sense. He slept the same way.

Landon continued. "You're right. I was hugging you. One of the things we talked about was being more intimate with our friends, especially Black men, without it being sexual. Embracing can provoke feelings of comfort, safety, and love. Last night, I wanted to make sure you felt all those things with no strings attached. You must have really been wiped out if you don't remember any of that."

As Landon finished speaking, things became clearer for Dylan. He was more alert after drinking some coffee. "I apologize, man. You're right. We're in a different place now and I should know that I can trust you. Having male friends is new to me. You had my back and you respected me. I appreciate that more than you know."

"It's all good. Just remember, we transcended—I think that's the word you would use—to a basic level of friendship and are developing something deeper. If I can't help you, I definitely won't harm you. Plus, I'm not trying to make God mad by mistreating one of his good boys. I have enough sins to repent for already."

Landon smiled and winked and then handed Dylan his gift.

"Are you ever serious?"

"Only when I'm in church, choir boy," Landon joked as he pulled Dylan in for a hug.

Searching For What She Needs

By Keesha Dancy

Chapter 1

Alexis rolled over to hit her snooze button a few times before finally deciding to get out of bed. Still in her birthday suit, she rose and opened her blinds, standing in amazement as the sun shined through her ceiling-to-floor windows and warmed her chocolate skin. She still couldn't believe she'd finally purchased the home of her dreams. Her retirement gift to herself.

She turned away from the window and walked to the bathroom, admiring her skin as she passed her full-length mirror.

"Hmph," she said with a chuckle. "I can't let this chocolate go to waste. They say chocolate melts in your mouth and not in your hand."

After freshening up, she went to the kitchen and prepared a big breakfast of toast, her favorite crispy applewood bacon, scrambled eggs with cheese, and Belgian waffles with fruit on top. After spreading her breakfast on her fancy dishes, she placed it on a Moroccan wicker table tray and retreated to the living room. As she ate, she turned on the TV just as a news ticker flashed across the screen. Another young black king had died at the hands of the police.

"Our modern-day enemy," she mumbled as her cell phone rang. She picked up the phone, saw Jordan's name on the screen, and cradled it between her shoulder and ear so she could finish eating.

"Hola," she greeted her with a smile.

"Girl, if you *hola* me one more time…" Jordan threatened. "As a matter of fact, when are you going to learn more words than *hola*? When are we going to Mexico, Colombia, or Spain? Heck, when are we going *anywhere*?"

Before Alexis could respond, Jordan snapped, "As a matter of fact, I'm around the corner. I'm stopping over."

"OMG, really?" Alexis exclaimed. It had been a minute since they'd had an opportunity to see each other for an extended period outside of social media and occasional zoom chats. The pandemic had everyone on edge, and it didn't appear to be letting up anytime soon. However, she blamed their separation on Jordan's controlling husband.

The two women had known each other since high school, almost thirty years. They had even joined the military after graduation. However, Alexis retired after twenty years, while Jordan served ten, leaving at the height of her career. Due to multiple deployments, Jordan's husband Devaris convinced her that the dual military life didn't have a place in their home. Instead, he felt Jordan should focus on being a mother to her daughter Ciara and Devaris' son DJ and daughter Daija. They had no children together, but Devaris hoped to change that.

Devaris also never trusted Alexis because he was convinced that she'd tried to break them up. When Devaris first proposed, he gave Jordan an ultimatum to either stay in the military or get married, but she couldn't do both. Alexis told her to think about her career and not throw it away, but Jordan chose what she thought was love at that time. She left her ten-year career, believing they would be fine since Devaris was a higher rank. Five years later, Jordan regretted her decision, unprepared for life after the 'honeymoon phase'. She tried working full time, but her hours didn't work with the kids' schooling and activities and Devaris' many deployments and training. As a travel consultant, she had seen a steady stream of clients, but the pandemic affected work due to lack of travel.

***

Jordan rang the doorbell a few minutes later. Alexis opened that door and Jordan waltzed in with a bottle of Cabernet Sauvignon wine and a bouquet of sunflowers. After hugging and giving their "hey girl hey" hellos, Alexis looked for a vase for her favorite flowers, while Jordan searched the cabinets for two wine glasses and a bottle opener.

"Where's your bottle opener?" Jordan yelled to Alexis from the kitchen.

"Look on the patio table," Alexis replied.

"What were you doing?" Jordan asked, smirking. "Having a nightcap under the stars? With whom?"

"You know I enjoy watching sunsets and sunrises. My patio and pool are my sanctuaries," Alexis replied as she walked to the patio door. She retrieved the bottle opener from the patio table and headed back into the living room. "Wow, it's been six months since we've sat and chilled like old times."

"You know where my sanctuary is: right here," Jordan proclaimed as she twirled around with her arms spread wide. "I feel more at peace in your home than I do in my own. Sometimes I feel so bitter when I'm home. I mean, Ciara is my world. I love my husband, and I adore his kids, but Devaris just irks me. After all these years, I don't think I'm over my decision to leave the Army."

The two friends plopped on the couch with their full wine glasses and caught up on their lives as the news played in the background. Throughout their conversation, they discussed the news and their disdain for everything that was going on in the world, including the president and his antics, police brutality, racial injustices, Black brothers and sisters dying at the hands of the racist police, and the deadly virus that seemed to come out of nowhere.

"Girl," Alexis compassionately groaned, "these cops are getting out of hand. I feel sad for the families. I couldn't imagine having to deal with these situations. You would think the police would be a little more proactive versus reactive, especially after the last incident made national news."

"I just don't understand. Enough is enough."

"I can only imagine how you must feel having a son," Alexis said. "As much as I hate this whole virus thing, the one good thing is not too many people are on the streets. I know we shouldn't think this way, but we're a lot less likely to be confronted with violence or death."

"I feel trapped in my own home, and this pandemic doesn't help any," Jordan said after sipping her wine. "As bitter as I am, I have slight anxiety every time Devaris or DJ leaves the house. Well, any of the kids for that matter. It's always in the back of my mind, what if...."

Jordan shook her head as if trying to erase the thought. "I don't even want to talk about this virus. It's like it came out of nowhere and turned our lives upside down. We rarely get out these days. We just started letting the kids participate in school activities; we're a lot more cautious. I miss my girls. We need a girls' spa day!"

'We'll never have a 'normal' routine as we once knew," Alexis said, her eyes glued to the TV. "Yes, we all need to get together soon. I spoke to Denice and Kendall the other day. They're both doing good, considering what we're all dealing with. Kendall says she needs a mommy break."

They both chuckled before a moment of silence.

"I need a break," they said almost simultaneously.

Jordan stared at Alexis. "Why do *you* need a break? I'm the one with a house full of kids and a lousy ass husband. You live alone and can come and go as you please with no one to mess up or answer to. Girl, give me your shoes!"

Alexis sat up with a sad look on her face. "Baby girl, everything ain't always what it seems. I am mentally and physically drained. I'm tired of hearing and seeing our people being killed in cold blood. I'm tired of your shit show president. I'm tired of being stuck in this house due to this stupid ass virus. Most importantly, I'm kind of tired of being single."

She flopped back, bumping her head softly on the back couch cushion. Another moment of silence passed, each woman seemingly lost in her own thoughts. *I wonder what kind of wife or mother I would be,* Alexis thought. *Jordan has it made, sadly with the wrong husband.*

"Now, what were you saying on the phone?" Alexis asked, trying to change the subject. "What do you mean when and where are *we* going? Your ass ain't going nowhere. You have to get permission just to go to the grocery store and hair salon. Chile, please, ain't nobody got time for that."

Jordan chuckled. "I never knew you felt that way."

Deep down, Jordan felt a sting because she knew everything Alexis said was true. Although she didn't technically have to ask to go some places, she felt the guilt trip before she walked out the door, and even days after she returned, even if she was only gone for an hour. Devaris would always find a way to make Jordan feel guilty by becoming the victim.

Jordan was happy about having a family, but hopeless about her marriage and her future. She was protective of her family, but pained about her life. She adored her children, but despised their father. It was like she lived a double life—the one that family, friends, and church members saw, and the one she experienced.

"I really need a break, a weekend getaway," Jordan admitted. "It has been several years since I've had some real me time. I'm home most days cleaning up after and catering to three—no, four—kids, if you count Devaris. My concern was always Ciara. She's almost thirteen years old now. She's old enough to fend for herself and say what's bothering her, so I feel comfortable taking a short break."

"It seems like just yesterday that you were pregnant with Ciara," Alexis said with a smile. "I remember speeding down the Autobahn in my pumpkin, following you and old boy to the hospital."

They laughed out loud, and then Jordan said, "That was the ugliest orange Mercedes I had ever seen in my life till this day."

"Yeah, but I bet you it got us everywhere we wanted to go. I can't believe I had the nerve to try to ship it back to the States," Alexis said as she crossed her arms behind her head and sighed. "Those were fun times."

"Yes, indeed. Pumpkin took us everywhere." Jordan smiled as she reminisced about their time in Germany. "I'm ready to go somewhere sunny, now. I want to put my toes in the sand, wade in pristine waters, sip on mai tais, watch the sunset and sunrise, and just relax."

The chimes on the grandfather clock began to play a melody, followed by two gongs. Jordan looked at her watch. "Oh my! Time flew by quick. It's already two o'clock. I have to head home and get dinner prepared."

"Same here, but thank goodness for old faithful," Alexis said as she pointed to her crockpot. "Time sure does move quick when you're having fun. It was so great to see you in person for a change. Hopefully old boy will let you out the house again soon."

"One day, I'm going to show your ass," Jordan proclaimed, rising from the couch and sashaying to the door, her long curly hair flowing. "I'm grown."

"Yeah, yeah," Alexis said with a laugh as she walked Jordan to the door. "I miss our outings. Hopefully things can get back to normal soon so we can get back to our girls' trips. Our last trip to Jamaica was canceled. Maybe we can plan for that."

"Sounds like a plan," Jordan said as they hugged. She walked off, waving goodbye as Alexis locked her door.

Alone again, Alexis walked into the kitchen and poured another glass of wine. She then walked out back and stretched out by the pool while enjoying the afternoon breeze. She despised feeling like a prisoner in her own home, aka the USA. Each time she left her home, she felt like she narrowly escaped being a victim of police brutality, racial injustice, and prejudices. Although she had not directly experienced anything, it still took a toll on her mentally. She was always on edge, especially when police were around. As much as she enjoyed the outdoors, she no longer felt comfortable.

Alexis had other concerns, too. She felt she was too dark to fit in with most of the non-Black society and not Black enough to fit in with her own people. Due to her military experience, upbringing, and self-awareness, she was great at code-switching. She knew when to be professional and when to be down. She knew when to adapt. The one thing she was not good at was relationships.

For the most part, Alexis enjoyed her newly retired life, but longed for a meaningful relationship. It had been more than five years since Alexis was in a serious relationship, and that turned out to be a disaster. For the last few years, she'd been in a back-and-forth situationship with another ex. She'd grown tired of it, but she was comfortable and knew he would always be there for her. Although he refused to commit, she was afraid of the unknown world of meeting new people.

Chapter 2

Over the course of the next month, Alexis and Jordan mapped out the details of a four-day girls' trip to Martha's Vineyard with their friends, the newly divorced Denice and Kendall, a single mother to five-year-old Kyle. Martha's Vineyard wasn't too far away. It was big enough to isolate and plan a few outdoor activities, and would be a different experience for all of them. All Jordan had to do was convince Devaris that she needed a break.

One evening, while lounging on the sofa, Jordan decided to try. "Babe, we need to talk."

"What's up, Boo?"

"You know it's been a few years since the girls and I have been on a trip. Our annual girls' trip was three years ago. Alexis, Denice, Kendall, and I are long overdue, and this pandemic hasn't made it any better."

"So, what are you saying? You don't like our family vacations?" Devaris asked as he pulled her close to his chest.

"I love our time together, but I also enjoy and miss time with my girls," she said as she kissed him on the cheek. "You know what I mean."

Devaris placed his hands on Jordan's face to look into her eyes. "Babe, I understand. You've been working from home, everyone is pretty much isolated, you've not had a break. Although I go to work every day, I get a little break, albeit going to the field. If you really need a break, take it. I support you, but I want to know your plans."

Jordan smiled at Devaris and hugged him. "It will be a short getaway. I promise. You know I can't stay away from you and the kids too long. We looked at a couple of options. I'll let the ladies know it's a go and we can lock everything in place. I love you."

"I love you more," he replied. He then chuckled and popped Jordan on her butt. "And I'm watching that Alexis."

She laughed, but couldn't mask her concern. "Babe, you still never explained why you dislike her. What do you have against her? We've been married over ten years now and you've still never explained why you disliked her."

"I know Alexis didn't want you to marry me," Devaris quipped. "Plus, she's still single and I know she doesn't like me. She thinks I'm not good enough for you."

Jordan placed her hands on her hips. "First of all, my friend never said she dislikes you. I'm sure if that was the case, she would have never 'approved' the wedding or been my maid of honor. Like a sister, she showed genuine concern for my decision to end my military career so abruptly. One I worked so hard for, sacrificed for, and enjoyed."

Devaris sat up with a serious look in his eyes. "How do you feel? Do you feel like you made a mistake?"

"Sometimes I regret getting out of the military, but I'm glad I was able to be there for Ciara's milestones and moments that I may have otherwise missed. Making the military a career was a dream of mine since high school. Alexis and I had similar aspirations, and we encouraged and supported each other. We were also able to talk to each other about anything. Since our marriage, it feels like she and I are growing further apart."

Jordan dared not tell Devaris that her upcoming trip would only be her and Alexis. While having brunch to solidify their travel plans for Martha's Vineyard, Kendall and Denice opted not to travel until they could go to Jamaica. The four friends had originally planned to go to Jamaica prior to COVID. Waiting for the trip they really wanted would give Denice and Kendall more time to plan.

However, Jordan and Alexis needed a break now! Who's to say Devaris wouldn't change his mind? Who's to say this pandemic wouldn't get any better? Waiting wouldn't work, so they decided to take a quick mini getaway for now and move Jamaica six months down the road.

Jordan figured by the time the six-month mark came, she'd be able to convince Devaris that she needed another break.

Unfortunately, two days before the trip to Martha's Vineyard, Devaris made an announcement.

He walked into the house, took off his boots and uniform jacket in the laundry room as usual, and gave Jordan a wet kiss as she set the table for two.

"Hey sweetie, how was your day?" he greeted.

"Babe, the girls are at the library working on a project and DJ has late practice, so we'll be eating dinner alone and will pick up the kids later," Jordan announced as she continued preparing dinner.

"Woah, I'm glad you let me know," he replied, walking toward the bathroom. "I was about to shower and kick up my feet. This has been a long day. We have a lot of Soldiers out, and not enough to cover down. Double duty has been killing everybody."

"Sounds tough," Jordan called after him.

"What time does DJ's practice end?" he yelled back. "We're picking up all the kids at the same time. I am not going back out the door when we get back. About to take a quick shower."

Jordan heard the bathroom door close, but she yelled a response anyway. "Fair enough. I told him to call thirty minutes before it ends."

She fixed two plates for her and Devaris and placed the kids' food in the microwave on paper plates. She turned on some music and cleaned the kitchen while waiting for Devaris to eat.

He returned to the kitchen a few minutes later and sat in front of his plate. While eating dinner, he announced that he volunteered to work someone else's weekend duty since Jordan would be on vacation.

Jordan gave him a hard stare. "You did what? How could you do this? Who's going to watch the kids?"

"The girls are teenagers. They can stay at home by themselves for a few hours at night and DJ can stay with his friend," Devaris assured her.

Oh, that makes it even worse, Jordan thought. *Leave two teenaged girls alone at night while their overprotective, yet gullible brother hangs out with his friends doing who knows what.*

"Devaris, I'm not comfortable with this idea." Jordan's voice cracked as she continued. "We've never left Ciara alone for overnighters. We know DJ is very protective when it comes to his sisters, but he has no brain of his own. He's easily manipulated by his so-called friends and thinks he has to conform just to fit in."

"Babe, I'll come home to make sure the kids eat dinner, homework is done, and they are in bed," Devaris replied. "I've been talking with DJ, and you have to admit he's doing much better since he stopped hanging with a select few."

"You're right," Jordan relented. "I'm proud of him. However, I don't think he's ready for this type of responsibility."

After dinner, Jordan sat silently, torn between canceling her trip and letting her husband win, or going on the trip and not having a good time because she'd be too busy worrying about her family. Unwilling to spoil the trip for Alexis, she prayed, pondered, and prayed some more.

The telephone broke her thoughts. She pulled her cell from her pocket and pressed TALK. "Hello, DJ."

"Momma J," he greeted, "practice will be over soon."

"Ok, Sweetie," she replied. "Call your sisters and let them know we're on our way."

Jordan hung up the phone and looked over at Devaris. She immediately turned away and stood up from the table.

"Babe, why don't you stay here?" he suggested. "I'll get the kids."

Jordan took a deep breath and screamed at Devaris with tears in her eyes. "Why did you do this? Why did you really volunteer to work the weekend I would be gone? Out of all the weekends!”

“Babe, we need the money,” he replied. “Times are getting hard. I mean your work hours were cut way down due to this virus, clients aren’t coming through as usual, and remember, we lost an extra two thousand dollars per month when we decided to come back to the States.”

“What do you mean when *we* decided to come back to the States, Devaris? That was *your* decision!”

Devaris sighed. “Babe, ever since we returned from Germany, things have been unstable, unpredictable. Sometimes, I wish we would have stayed in Germany. We didn’t have to see all of this mess on television, we didn’t have to worry about the kids getting encountered by the police. I mean, we were in a foreign country known for its prejudices, but we didn’t have to worry about *us*. We were at peace, living life, able to pack up and expose the kids to other countries and cultures on our long weekends. Life was so simple for us, but we had to come back.”

“Wait a minute,” Jordan interjected, “are you blaming me for our financial situation, or are you blaming me because we came back home? Devaris, you gave me an ultimatum to get married now and come back to the United States, or stay in Germany and get married when our tours ended. What kind of—never mind.”

She walked away from the table, but before leaving the room, she turned and shouted, “With everything that’s happened in the past five years, I should have said no, stayed in Germany and continued living my happy life!”

With that, she stormed into their bedroom, slamming the door behind her, and cried on their bed. The past five years raced across her mind. They’d almost lost their home and had to file for bankruptcy due to the mounting medical bills. They’d tried for several years to conceive. After multiple attempts, doctor visits, testing, counseling, and researching, they decided to look into IVF. After two failed attempts,

Jordan gave up. It was too much of a toll on her mentally and physically, and it put a strain in their marriage.

She thought about what Alexis and Denice said. She thought about what her family said. She thought about Ciara and the many *what ifs* that crossed her mind. They all had a genuine concern for her and only wanted the best for her. When she told them about her plans to get out of the military, they reminded her about her military aspirations and her desire to get her PhD and open a boarding school.

Devaris came into the bedroom and kissed her on her forehead.

"I love you," he whispered into her ear before grabbing his jacket and keys to head to work.

Chapter 3

The next morning, Jordan reached for her phone to call Alexis. She had some soul searching to do and needed a clear head to contemplate some life-changing decisions. Just as she started to dial, the phone rang.

"Hola chic," Alexis greeted, giggling in excitement. "I was checking to see how your packing is going. I got the liquor. Don't forget your sunscreen. You know Black people need sunscreen, too. I'm about to let this sun kiss all over my body, baby!"

Without taking a breath, Alexis continued, "I bought us these cute little hats. I so wish Denice and Kendall were joining us. It has been a looooong time since the four of us have taken a girls' trip together."

Jordan sat mute, sadly listening to her friend.

"Jordan, are you there?"

"I'm here," she responded.

"What's going on with you? Why does it sound like I'm the only one excited?" She paused. "Hold the hell up. Don't tell me—"

"I can't go!" Jordan blurted. "It's not what you think."

"Well, when the hell were you going to let me know, J?"

"I picked up my phone to call you, but you were on the other end calling *me*. The decision was made this morning. I barely slept last night. You just happened to call me before I could call you." Tears rolled down her cheeks.

"So, what the hell happened *this* time?" Alexis asked. "You need to—you know what? Never mind, I'm not surprised. I should've known."

"It wasn't Devaris's decision. It was mine," Jordan insisted.

"Oh, now, you're lying for him. This man has had you brainwashed since day one, and you still can't see it," Alexis snapped before hanging up.

***

Alexis poured herself a glass of wine and kicked up her feet on her round plush ottoman while listening to some music. *Geez, maybe I should rethink married life*, she thought. *One friend brainwashed, another friend recently divorced. Oh wait, I do know other happy couples. Now, I wonder if it's all a facade. Are they truly happy?*

"Hmph," she grunted aloud as she sipped her wine.

All I want is someone to make me happier than I make myself, love me just as much—if not more than—I love myself. Someone to be there for me, treat me like a queen, share my life, experience things with, and, most importantly, someone who is not already married!

She thought she'd found all of that in Allen. They were happy for two years until she found out he had a whole family. She often wondered what life would have been like had she not been persistent about marriage and let him continue stringing her along. What if she had not become suspicious of his sudden change in behavior?

Alexis felt like she had lived a lie for two years. When she confronted Allen with this new discovery, he had a lot of excuses. He asked her to wait until the divorce was final so they could build a life together. She was not having any part of that. She loved that man, but not enough to marry him after his divorce. Alexis wanted her own man, on her own terms, with honesty from the beginning, and not after an avoidable "disaster."

"I'm not going to stress; it will all come together," she told herself as she poured another glass of wine, turned on Ledisi, and sat out on the patio. She just needed a plan B.

The next morning, Alexis canceled her flight, hotel reservation, the excursions, and their in-home chef. She was disappointed in herself, but still felt bad. She called Jordan to apologize.

"Hello, what's up?" Jordan answered quickly.

"Hey, Jordan," Alexis mumbled.

"Hello, wow. What happened to your infamous hola?" Jordan replied with a chuckle.

"You caught that?" Alexis replied. "I'm not in an hola type of mood. I feel bad and wanted to call to apologize for how I talked to you. I should not have responded that way. I should have been a more supportive friend. I was excited that we would be taking a girls' getaway and disappointed when you canceled. Please accept my apology. How are you doing?"

"I appreciate that," Jordan replied. "I can't complain. It's the same old thing. The kids have busy schedules outside of school. Devaris will be deploying soon, and I'm thinking about going back to school."

"That sounds great!" Alexis said. "Let me know if you need anything. I know we both have a lot going on and our priorities may be different, but just know that I'm here for you."

"Thanks friend," Jordan replied. "I appreciate you and love you."

Alexis smiled. "Now that our girlfriends' getaway is nixed, I need a plan B."

"If you really need to get away, why don't you take a solo trip? It's not like you hadn't already."

Alexis pondered the thought. *Screw it*, she thought. *I'm going somewhere. I don't know where, but today or tomorrow I will be on someone's beach.* "You know what? I just might do that. I've heard of people going on a blind trip."

"A blind trip?"

"Yeah, it's called surprise tripping. It's when people buy a ticket to anywhere leaving in the next twenty-four hours," Alexis explained. "I've always wanted to try it, and this feels like the perfect time."

"Well, that's adventurous," Jordan said. "I could never."

"We'll chat later," Alexis said, feeling excited. "I have some planning to do. Again, I apologize. Love you, girlie."

Alexis hung up the phone and went right to work. She decided to pack a bag and find the cheapest flights leaving within the next twenty-four hours. She found that Freedom Airlines had more options for short last-minute getaways to COVID-friendly places. It didn't matter where she went, as long as it wasn't home. This would be her opportunity to do something out of the ordinary, take a chance, and live an adventurous and unconventional life. She was open to go anywhere, as long as a beach and warm weather were involved. It would be a unique experience: show up at the airport, book a ticket, board a flight, and enjoy the vacation.

The next morning, she repacked her luggage, checked her email, set her home alarm and headed off to the airport. As she drove, she called her parents.

"Hey, Mom, how are you? What are you doing?" she asked once her mother answered.

"Your dad and I are sitting out back enjoying the nice breeze. What are you up to? Sounds like you're driving."

"I am, put dad on the speaker phone."

"Alexis, what's going on? Is everything okay?"

"Yes, Mom, everything's good," Alexis replied with a laugh. "Why did you ask me that?"

"Just wondering. Here's Dad."

"Hey, Dad, how are you?" Alexis greeted.

"Hey, baby girl," her father greeted.

Alexis hesitated and then started talking quickly. "I'm driving to the airport. I'm taking a minibreak. I'll be back in four days."

"Okay, what's new?" her dad remarked with a laugh.

"Where are you going this time?" her mother asked.

"I have no idea," Alexis admitted. "I'll know when I get to the airport."

"What do you mean, you have no idea?" her parents asked almost simultaneously.

"I don't know. I'm trying something new," Alexis explained. "I know a few people who have done this before. It's called surprise tripping."

"Alexis, please don't do anything crazy or go anywhere we can't get ahold of you like that one place you went," her mother pleaded. "We didn't talk to you for two days before we knew you were okay."

"Mom, that was Cuba. I told you and Dad about the wifi situation before I left. I invited you two, but you were adamant about not going. Dad was all for it."

"Just be careful, baby girl," her dad said. "Can you call or email us to let us know that you're okay and let us know your whereabouts?"

"Yes, Dad," Alexis assured him. "Mom, I will be sure to check in every day. I might even video call you, so please make sure your WhatsApp is working. I gotta go. I love you. Talk to you later."

They simultaneously replied, "We love you, too."

After hanging up with her parents, she left her sister a voicemail. "Hey, Sis! I'm taking a short sabbatical. I don't know where I'm going, but I'll call whenever I get there. I wanted to tell you first, but I see you're busy, and I already talked to Mom and Dad. Like most of my trips, they had a lot of questions. I agreed to call them every day."

Next, she called Denice.

"Hey D, how are ya? What are you doing?" Alexis yelled through the Bluetooth speaker.

"I'm chilling, about to make myself a light lunch. What's going on?" Denice responded.

"Oh, nothing. Hold on a minute," Alexis pushed Kendall's speed dial button before Denice could respond. "Ok, I'm back."

"Hey, lady," Kendall greeted.

Alexis quickly announced, "Hey Kendall, Denice is on, too."

"Uh, what's going on here?" Denice asked.

"I'm just as confused," Kendall said with a chuckle.

"Calm down, I'm about to tell you two. Remember I kept saying I really needed a vacation? Well, I'm headed to the airport."

"So, what's new about that?" Denice asked.

"Wait, let me finish," Alexis insisted. "I have no clue where I'm going. I just decided yesterday that I would pack a bag and show up to the airport. I told Jordan yesterday. Remember we discussed doing a blind trip one day? Well, I'm doing one *today*!"

There was a moment of silence.

"What brought this on? I thought we were taking a trip in October?" Kendall asked.

"We are, but I needed a quick break," Alexis said. "We're still planning for Jamaica if the pandemic doesn't get out of hand. Once I get settled, I'll call you all on WhatsApp."

"Well, what a way to break some good news. I'm going to be like you when I grow up," Denice responded.

"Heck, I'm going to be like her when *Kylie* grows up," Kendall chimed in.

They all laughed.

"Okay, I just wanted to let you two know that I'll be out for a bit," Alexis said as she drove onto the highway. "Love you. Smooches!"

With that, she ended the call, turned up her music, dropped her top, and cruised along Highway 1 while Lizzo played over the speakers.

Chapter 4

Alexis's made it to the airport an hour later and parked her car in the short-term parking garage, taking a picture of the level and row to remind herself where she parked.

After grabbing her backpack and purse, she donned her blue cloth face mask and marched to the Freedom Airlines ticketing counter with a mission. Nervously placing her passport on the ticketing counter, she smiled at the gentleman through her mask. He had the most gorgeous chestnut-colored eyes.

"Good afternoon, Terrell," she greeted. "Can you please tell me which flights you have that leave within the next 24 hours, heading anywhere with tropical islands and beautiful beaches, no visa requirements, and accepts COVID testing within forty-eight hours of departure?"

The tall, young-looking, dark chocolate specimen of a man looked into Alexis' eyes and with a raspy accented voice said, "Good afternoon. My apology, I am not good with faces. I believe I forgot your name. I am so embarrassed. How can I forget a beautiful lady such as yourself?"

Alexis chuckled. "I don't believe we've met before."

Now looking confused, he asked, "So, how do you know my name"?

"Your shirt," she replied, pointing to his badge with a childish grin.

Terrell looked down at his badge, shook his head, chuckled, and said, "Wow. I didn't pay that much attention. Now, I'm really embarrassed."

He then smiled and whispered, "I was too busy admiring your beauty through your mask when you walked through the door and hoped that you would get in my line."

Too eager to assist Alexis, Terrell forgot about his badge and looked at Alexis's passport. He asked her to remove her mask and compared the picture with her face.

"You're even more beautiful with a smile," he said with a wink.

Alexis felt his flirtatious vibe and figured she'd play along. For a minute, she forgot all of her troubles and what led her to the airport in the first place.

"Five days. No, seven days," Terrell said, interrupting her thoughts.

If only you knew, she thought. "Okay, I'll go with five. You're the expert."

Terrell smiled. "Five would be perfect. It will give you exactly what you're searching for and a little of what you need. Every so often, we get a small group wanting to purchase flights to anywhere, the day of. Interesting. I like the concept."

Alexis smiled in response, not wanting to tell him this was her first time doing something like this.

"Great, it's two o'clock," Terrell stated. "Your flight leaves at ten. You have a short layover, and then you will arrive at your destination at eight a.m."

"Just curious, how do you know what I need?" Alexis asked flirtatiously as she handed Terrell her credit card.

He printed the boarding pass and receipt and stuck them into her passport. As he handed them back to her, he winked and replied, "Gate A4. I'll see you later. Take care."

Alexis purposefully touched his hand as she took her documents, and then adjusted her backpack as she walked to TSA Precheck, laughing out loud as she fought the urge to look at the ticket. *Oh my, I can't believe I just did it. Oh shit, I have no clue where I'm going. I mean, I told myself I wanted to do this one day, but had no clue this would be that day. What if I packed the wrong clothes? What if I forgot something? What if I've already been to this destination? What if I don't like this place? Wait, what is there not to like on any island?*

"Ma'am, next. Next!"

The lady behind Alexis tapped her on the shoulder. "Ma'am, he's calling you."

"I'm sorry," Alexis whispered as she walked up to the TSA agent.

"Pull your mask down, please," he requested, barely looking at her.

Alexis stared at the agent as she pulled down her mask and he stamped her boarding pass.

Man, I will be glad when we no longer have to wear these stupid masks, she thought as she proceeded through security. *Whatever this virus is needs to go away quickly!*

Alexis placed her bags on the conveyor belt, walked through the scanner, and waited patiently for her bags. After a few minutes, her bags were flagged for inspection, and she suddenly remembered her can of Lysol she accidentally packed in her backpack. There was no way she would lose that can. Lysol was too hard to come by these days!

"Sir, please don't make me get rid of my Lysol," she pleaded. "I forgot it was in my bag. I know it's over three ounces, but I honestly forgot. If I need to check my bag in, I'll go back to the ticketing counter. My flight doesn't leave for another few hours."

Another agent heard Alexis's pleas and approached the inspection area. "She's good at 3.2 ounces. The rules recently changed; anything under 3.5 ounces is allowed."

"Thank you, thank you, thank you," Alexis said, repacking her bag. "I think I would have had to cancel this trip. I need a vacation, but I need my health more."

Alexis thanked them again as she walked to her gate, anxious to see where she was going. She decided to hang out in Freedom Airlines' lounge and relax with a cocktail and snack since she had six hours before she had to board the plane. Going back home wasn't an option. If she left, she may not have returned. *Thank goodness for airport lounge access*, she thought.

The events from the past week replayed in her head. Alexis was filled with anger, disappointment, determination, excitement, nervousness, and accomplishment. She even felt a little flirtatious and bold. Downing her cocktail, she set an alarm on her phone, and then pulled out her laptop and worked a little. She eventually took a quick power nap in one of the leather recliners, still having no clue what was in store for her.

Chapter 5

The alarm went off about an hour before her flight, so Alexis stood up and went to the washroom to freshen up. She then grabbed a bottle of the complimentary wine and water, a bag of chips, and a fruit, and then scurried to her gate to wait for her section to be called. As she scanned the area to check the demographics, she finally decided to look at her boarding pass.

Oh no, not again, Alexis thought. *I guess I should've been specific.*

She was going back to The Maldives. Although she loved everything about The Maldives, she knew she wouldn't be sipping on mai tais, as it was a Muslim dry country. No legally free-flowing alcohol. Alexis also knew that although the beaches were beautiful, her chance of meeting a nice suitor was almost nonexistent, as most people who traveled there were already boo'd up. There was also no chance of meeting a local, as most were too young, or third-country nationals working in hospitality. *The men in The Maldives are gorgeous though, and their hair—*

OMG!

Alexis remembered the *friend* she met there on her last trip more than four years ago. She smiled, wondering if Raul was still there. Was he still in the same place? Was he married with children? Of course, she wondered all of that when they first met, but it didn't stop there. They kept in touch for two years, but then they lost touch.

She shook off the thought. No distractions this go round. She needed to secure accommodations and transportation as soon as possible. Internet service wasn't consistent in The Maldives, and accommodations weren't aplenty. Something had to be locked in before she landed. At worst, she would spend one or two nights on the mainland before going to an island. As she stood in line, she surfed the hotels on Booking.com and decided on an all-inclusive resort.

After booking, she looked up and saw a familiar face at the gate—Terrell. Mister Raspy Voice, himself. Could he see the big smile on her face?

"Oh my," she mumbled.

"Told you I'd see you later," he said with a wink.

Alexis handed her boarding pass to the ticket clerk and grinned through her mask as she walked through the jet bridge onto the plane. Once she reached her seat, she thoroughly wiped the seats and trays down with her Lysol wipes, and then stowed her backpack and placed her purse in the middle seat, praying no one sat beside her. As she settled into her seat, her mind drifted to Mr. Raspy.

OMG! What if he's on this plane? she wondered. *I don't know what I'm going to do. I may lose my mind. Heck, I may lose more than my mind.*

"Ladies and gentlemen, I am your captain, Peter," a voice announced overhead. "The doors are now closing. Please get to your seats and ensure your luggage is stored away securely. Our flight crew will give instructions, go over the safety brief, and ensure you have a comfortable and safe flight."

A woman's voice came next. "Ladies and gentlemen, I am Sarah. I, as well as Fernando and Mark, will be servicing you all tonight as we make our way to the Maldives. We will begin our safety briefing. Please follow along on the safety card in the pocket in front of you, the overhead monitors, or please watch our demonstration..."

The last thing Alexis remembered hearing was the flight crew. She watched Mark as he demonstrated the safety instructions. Although her eyes were fixated on his every move, her mind was on Terrell.

Twenty minutes into the flight, Alexis saw him. He no longer had on his badge and had changed clothes. *OMG, OMG, he's walking toward me,* she thought, giddy as a schoolgirl. *Is he looking at me? Can he see me? I can pretend like I'm not looking at him. Oh silly, he knows where you're sitting. Remember, he booked your flight earlier.*

As Alexis finished rambling to herself, Terrell stood over her and leaned in. "It would be my pleasure if I could chat with you later or maybe see you tomorrow once you get settled in. My vacation has officially started, and the Maldives is one of my happy places."

For once, Alexis was at a loss for words. She nodded and gave a wink that told him *yes, you can see me now, you can see me later, you can see me whenever you want.* Those exact words could never come out of her mouth.

After a couple of hours, dinner and spirits were served. Soon, the lights were dimmed, and most passengers had gone to sleep or were watching movies. *Here comes Mr. Raspy*, she thought as she watched Terrell approach her. *He knew what he was doing by putting me on this flight. He even gave me a whole row to myself.*

Terrell stood over her again and properly introduced himself. "Good evening. My name is Terrell, and it is a pleasure meeting you."

After a quick fist bump, Alexis obliged with her own introduction. "Hello, Terrell. My name is Alexis. Nice to meet you.

"May I?" he asked, gesturing to the empty seat next to her.

Alexis pointed to the seat, and he sat down.

"Now that we've introduced ourselves, I would like to know more about you," Terrell said. "Ladies first."

"I'm good, you can go first," Alexis pointed in Terrell's direction.

"Well, let's see, what do you want to know? Where should I start?" he asked.

"How about you start from the beginning?"

They both chuckled.

"I was born in a little town—" he began.

Alexis cut him off quickly with a straight face. "How about your marital status? Do you have a girlfriend, boyfriend, significant other? Can anyone claim you to be their husband, boyfriend, significant other, or similar term of endearment?"

"No to all of the above, but someone can claim me to be an ex-husband and a father. Is that okay with you, Ms., Ma'am or Mrs.?" He smiled as he waited for her answer.

"How long since your divorce? How many children? How old?

"I've been divorced for a year and half. I have two children, a boy and girl. TJ is ten and Tyler is thirteen. They are my pride and joy." Terrell's smile brightened as he pulled out his phone to show Alexis their pictures. "What about you?"

"Beautiful children. I'm not married, no children, and I'm in a situationship of some sort."

"Thank you, they are my pride and joy. So, what's up with this situationship? What is that like?"

"I'm not in a committed relationship. I'm kind of dating my ex; it's not sexual. More platonic."

"Interesting, how does that work again?" he asked, looking confused.

"We hang out, maybe go to the movies, dinner. If I need something fixed, he'll help out."

"Interesting," he mumbled.

They continued talking until Alexis finally dozed off. Terrell, put a blanket over her and went back to his seat. She woke up to the sight of the sun rising above the horizon. The orange and red hues protruding from the dark clouds in the foreground was always a beautiful sight. Alexis enjoyed watching sunrises and sunsets, especially while flying or above the waters, so she couldn't help reaching for her phone and taking a picture. She would ensure she captured every sunrise and sunset, no matter where she was in the world.

The plane would be landing after breakfast. Alexis was excited, not only because she was going to one of the most beautiful islands in the world, but also because she would be spending the day with Terrell.

Once the plane landed, Alexis went through Customs and patiently waited for Terrell to meet her at the airport lounge.

So many thoughts went through her head. *If only Jordan, Kendall, and Denise could experience this small piece of paradise.* She smiled, and for the first time in a very long time, she did not have to wear her mask. She knew this place would give her what she needed. By the time her vacation ended, Alexis would be renewed, refreshed, and revived.

Piper's Wings

By LaRita Dalton

Suddenly

As I rest comfortably in my mother's arms, I feel the warmth of her breath on my forehead, each one providing a sense of love and protection. Little does she know when my father removes me from her arms and cradles me close to his chest, that would be the last contact we would ever have with one another. My father places me in my crib and whispers, "I love you" while ensuring I am as comfortable as he thought I should be, and creeps away to not wake me. During the night, I stir in my sleep. I roll over, getting my head caught in the neck pillow. I struggle to lift my head but am unable to do so. I try to catch a breath, another breath, and then another. I want to breathe. It becomes more difficult the more I try. My nose starts to bleed. I no longer have the strength to fight. Finally, I succumb to suffocation, passing away suddenly and unexpectedly on June 7, 2021.

Dad

This has to be the most devastating day of my life. I have experienced a lot of traumas in my life, but this one hit me differently. I woke up early as I always do to help my wife prepare the children for daycare. I was a little surprised that Piper hadn't made a sound throughout the night. It was only a quick thought I made to myself before going back to helping my oldest girls get ready for school. After the girls got dressed and went downstairs to their mom, who was busy preparing breakfast, I went into Piper's room to wake her, change her diaper, and give her a morning bottle.

As I walked to her crib, I noticed that she had turned over. I thought to myself that this little girl is growing up too fast. I went to her changing table to get the wipes, a diaper, and a onesie. I called her name in song, saying good morning to my baby girl.

No response.

As I got to her crib, I noticed that she was face down over the neck pillow. I chuckled, thinking this girl is going to be a wild sleeper. I reached down to pick her up, and to my horror, my daughter didn't respond to my touch. I turned her over to face me and all I can recall is screaming to my wife to come upstairs. There was dried blood on her nose and sheets. Her lips looked black. Her body was stiff. I yelled to my wife to call 911 and fell to the floor to perform CPR. I couldn't get her mouth to open wide enough to blow air into her.

I called her name, begging God to not let this be happening and to help me. I pleaded for my daughter's life as I blew as much as I could into her mouth and nose. She wasn't responding to anything. I pulled her to my chest, screaming, yelling, crying that my daughter couldn't be dead. She was just a baby.

I lost all control when my wife entered the room. The look on her face and the sound from her voice is one I never want to hear again and one I can't forget. I couldn't bear looking at my two daughters, who were in tow with their mother, crying, trying to process the confusion. She tried to provide them a sense of security while all of this was happening. As a father, I was devastated. As a husband, I was a failure. As a man, I was defeated. I, for the life of me, could not comprehend or accept what was going on.

Mom

As I made the girls breakfast, I heard them running down the stairs like a pack of wolves. You would think it was a herd, but it was only two of them. I yelled out to them to stop running down the stairs and walk before someone falls. I heard them giggling like what I was saying was funny, but they knew I wasn't playing with them.

I turned to them as they entered the kitchen, giving them both the side-eye for running down the stairs and beckoning them over for the "good morning" routine of hugs and kisses. My girls are beautiful, and they keep me smiling, but I never understood how they could always be so hyper. It's tiring, but I love it.

As they sat down at the breakfast table, I heard this awful scream from upstairs that scared me to the point that I froze. I realized my husband was yelling for me to come to him and to call 911. I rushed upstairs, following his voice to see what the problem was. As I arrived at Piper's room, I saw my husband on his knees cradling her, crying, and saying she wasn't breathing.

At that point, I lost it. I grabbed my daughter from my husband, not believing I held my dead daughter in my arms. As a nurse, I began CPR and told my husband to call 911. In all my efforts, I couldn't resuscitate my daughter. I tried and tried again, knowing she was no longer here. I begged and pleaded for her life, crying out for help.

Nothing.

No response.

EMS and my husband had to forcefully take my daughter from my arms. I felt helpless as I watched them attempt the same lifesaving measures I had seen performed numerous times before. My husband held me in a corner as I watched every moment with pain and disbelief. EMS took my daughter and husband away. Frantically, I tried to get myself and my children together to go to the hospital. My neighbor, a good friend, took over as I lost all sense of time and self.

Ava

It scared me so bad when I heard my mom and dad yelling and crying. I went upstairs to see what was going on and found my mom holding Piper and crying. She was holding my sister in her arms and crying "Please God" over and over again. My father was standing over her on the phone telling someone that his daughter wasn't breathing, and she was stiff. I didn't understand what was going on. I looked at Piper. She wasn't moving in my mom's arms or anything. I asked my mom and dad what was going on and neither one of them said anything to me. My sister Zhuri stood by me, and I took her hand. She cried, and seeing her cry made me start to cry. I didn't know what to say or do.

A few minutes later, these people rushed into my sister's room and pushed us into the hallway. All I could see was them pressing on my sister's chest, holding her face, blowing into her mouth, removing all kinds of stuff from big bags, and putting stuff on my sister. Stuff was everywhere. It was loud and I couldn't make out what people were saying. I peeked in a little further and saw my mom and dad standing in the corner looking at everything going on. I had never seen the look my parents had on their faces before. All I could do was stand there, watch my parents cry, try to make out what those people were doing with Piper, and hold my sister's hand.

Zhuri

I grabbed my sister's hand. I was so scared that at some point, I peed on myself, and I don't even remember doing it. My dad was on the phone yelling, "I think she's dead, Ma'am.

He was crying and walking back and forth. My mom was on the floor holding Piper and crying. She was saying something, but I couldn't make it out. Ava and I were pushed out of the way, and all these people were in the room making a mess and talking loudly. I stood behind my sister, trying to look around her to see what was going on. I saw Piper lying on the floor with no clothes on with stuff on her chest and a plastic thing on her face. I asked Ava what they were doing to her, but she didn't answer me. My sister moved further inside of the bedroom door, and I could see my parents hugging and then my mother held her face in her hands. The look in my dad's eyes made me feel that whatever was going on, things would never be the same. I didn't like how I was feeling, and noticed I peed in my clothes.

Piper's Girls' Time

My sisters love me to death. They were always kissing, talking, and trying to play with me. I loved seeing the smiles on their faces when I woke up or they were coming home from daycare. It seemed like they always looked for me first, no matter what was going on. They had so much fun with me, and I enjoyed spending time with them, too. I especially liked it when they thought I was laughing and talking back at them. There was nothing they wouldn't do for me. They were always trying to feed me, change my diaper, or change my clothes because I slobbered a lot.

I remember the last evening we all spent together. Momma allowed me to play on the floor with them for what she says was tummy time. We were on the floor for hours just playing, laughing, talking, sharing toys and games. We were so happy. Never for a second thought did we think that would be one of our final moments together. I'm going to miss girls' time. I'm happy that we all got to bond with one another as sisters. I know we would have been the best of friends if given the opportunity to grow up together.

Believe it or not, my middle sister Zhuri was the boss. She wanted to control everything I did and what others did with me. She was such a busy body, and she was so bossy. She was always telling people what to do. She called me her baby, and no one could tell her any different.

Zhuri was also loving and was the life of everything. She was an artsy/crafty person, always doing something with her hands, making something, playing with something, and at times, breaking something. She was very creative, and I loved watching her do things. Even though I wasn't able to hold things, she was always trying to give me something as if I could play a part in whatever she was doing. My sister also liked to draw, paint, and color. Everything she did was so bright and vibrant and matched her spirit perfectly. I enjoy seeing her works. She was always proud of herself and what she had done. I was proud of her, too.

My oldest sister Ava was so nice and gentle with me. She was smart and always wanted to be in the know, always asking questions and learning new things. She was always looking at something and sharing what she learned with others. I liked hearing her voice and was always looking for her.

She liked to read her storybook to me and show me the pictures. She loved to read, and would read to me all of the time. I think that was her favorite pastime with me as well because that's how she mainly spent her time with me. There were so many books in her room. They were all over the place, even though she had a bookshelf by the window to store them all. Some of the books had pop-outs, lights, and sounds, and others had activities that you could complete.

I know Ava is going to miss me. She told my mother that she saw me in a dream one night. She said she saw me sitting by the window, on top of the bookshelf reading a book. My mother cried.

I remember the night I appeared to my sister in her dream. I was sitting in the window just as Ava said, silently looking at my sister's favorite storybook. She turned over and looked over in my direction. Her eyes widened like she was surprised to see me. As she stared at me, I smiled at her.

"Hey, that's the book I like to read to you, and I'm glad you liked it, too," Ava told me. She told me that she loved me and missed me a lot, and then laid back down and placed the covers under her chin with a smile on her face. It feels good to know that even though my sister may be sad that I'm no longer there, I will always have a special place in her heart. I want her to know that my death was not to cause hurt or pain, but it was planted on earth so that my life could continue to bloom in Heaven.

My death was also hard on Zhuri. One evening, when she was in her room doing one of her favorite things, crafting, she was putting the finishing touches on a picture she had been working on. She walked past my room. Since my death, my bedroom door was kept closed, but for some reason, the door was open. As she started to close the door, my crib mobile activated.

The sound startled her, so she entered the room to see what she was hearing. The sound and lights from the mobile attracted her attention to my crib. The look on her face was confused and I know she wondered why the mobile was on. She looked around my room for a few minutes before turning from my bed to leave my room. On her way out, she picked up a stuffed bear that my grandmother had made for me. She hugged and kissed it.

"I miss you, Piper, and I will always love you," she said before closing the door and running downstairs to tell my mom and dad that I was in my room playing with my crib mobile.

Grief and Loss (Mom)

We're sitting in this hospital room waiting for someone to come out and speak with us, provide an update, hell, just say something. Neither of us knows what to say or do. My husband calls his mother and tells her what's happening. Once he finishes the call with his mother, I muster up the energy to call my own mother. When she answers the phone, I can't say a word and just begin crying hysterically. My husband takes the phone and tells my mother that Piper died.

I hate him at that moment for saying that. Even though I know she passed away, I don't want to hear it from his mouth. The reality of it all is happening way too fast for me. I know my mother wants me to take the phone back so she can comfort me, but I can't bear to talk to anyone. My husband gives his quiet apologies and states he would have me call later. I turn away from my husband and cry.

I feel a hand on my shoulder. A woman speaks my name, stating that the police want to speak with us. The physician walks in with another woman and provides the condolence speech, one that I had heard so many times before, but would have never guessed I would be hearing for my daughter. Piper was five days shy of turning three months old.

Investigation (Dad)

I am becoming angrier and frustrated the more they ask questions. It's invasive and at times feels accusatory. They question everything we did. They question everything we say. They ask about our other children, our relationship, parenting, employment, finances, legal issues, and substance and alcohol use. It goes on and on. I get nervous when I'm informed that the Georgia Bureau of Investigations is being notified.

When asked about the day and the last contact with our daughter, the pressure hits me. My wife gives details of the day at home with Piper, interactions with our other daughters, and doing her daily routine at home. I listen to my wife talk about her day. Nothing seems out of the ordinary. It was just like any other day. My heart aches for my wife because I know she was probably thinking she did something wrong or didn't pay attention to something, but neither of the investigators appear to show that anything she was saying or did that day was a problem.

Memories (Mom)

Getting pregnant at the time we did was planned. My husband and I had just closed on our first home, and we were looking forward to expanding our family. I had a great pregnancy, with no issues or concerns. Every visit was positive, and I was looking forward to giving birth. I was excited when we found out that we were having another girl. I know my husband was hoping for a boy, but his face lit up when he saw the ultrasound that revealed it was a girl. I believe he was prepared either way because when we started discussing names, he only had one name in mind. He said he wanted our child's name to be Piper, whether it was a girl or boy.

Our entire family, his and mine, was excited about our pending birth. Preparation wasn't stressful for either of us because our families collectively did everything. Piper's birth was a celebration. I had a smooth labor and birth with no complications. She was born seven pounds, nine ounces, with a head full of hair. She was so beautiful. She was a joy and did everything my other children did when they were born.

At first examination, she didn't have any issues or concerns, and was healthy, according to all the newborn tests and exams. We left the hospital within forty-eight hours. Our family was complete. Piper was another blessing, an angel in our lives for almost three months (eighty-five days), and then she was gone. Without warning, without explanation.

Looking Back (Dad)

During the week, I usually get home from work around twelve-thirty in the morning. As I do every time I get home, I make sure the house is secure, check on the girls, put Piper in her crib, and take a shower.

My wife wanted to keep Piper in our room with her until I came home. That morning, I kissed my wife on her forehead to let her know I was home, picked up Piper, and placed her in her crib. I laid her on her back on top of a neck pillow that we used to prop her up during the day so her head wouldn't flop side to side, especially if she fell asleep in the rocker or swing. I checked her and she was dry, so there was no need to change her diaper. I turned on the child monitor and returned to my room.

Usually, one of us would hear Piper and get up to see what she needed and put her back to sleep. It never crossed my mind that morning that there was a problem. I figured she was getting her sleep habits understood and was starting to get to a place where she would sleep through the night. I never expected anything to be any different than it had always been. That morning, I dressed the girls for daycare and sent them downstairs to their mother. I then went into Piper's room and found her stiff with dried blood on her face and sheet and lost it. I tried to revive her, but she never took a breath. I knew she was dead.

We have been at the hospital with Piper for almost four hours. Family members and friends start coming in and out of the hospital room along with visiting family. The hospital provides support, and everyone is attentive to our needs. I appreciate our church pastor and his wife visiting because it gives us some relief for a little bit.

The detectives continue going through their process and procedures, asking more questions. I find out my daughter's body was checked for signs of abuse, which upset us both.

The following day, CSI is at the house for most of the day taking pictures of the house and her room. A couple of days later, our daughter is released for autopsy and to GBI for further investigation. Shortly afterward, we are contacted by social service professionals, a team designed to provide resources and support in cases of infant and child deaths.

Homegoing (Piper)

It is a beautiful Saturday morning the day of my funeral, or should I say homegoing. It's outside, and it is like a day that my mother would let us go outside and play in the backyard. Everyone is emotional, I guess more so for my mom and dad because everyone focuses on them.

I'm dressed in my white christening gown and ruffle socks, with a small white and blue tiara with pearls and matching earrings, and a small bracelet that my mom made from a pearl necklace she had. Everyone says I am beautiful and look like an angel laying on a white cloud. As my family and other guests arrive to view me and comfort my parents, I wonder how my life touched so many people. I know they are all relatives or friends of the family, but I cannot put the two together.

It is a beautiful ceremony. A relative put together a presentation that played on the screen. A woman with a beautiful voice sings *"His Eye is on The Sparrow,"* one of my mom's favorite songs. And I can't forget the flowers, balloons, and stuffies that decorate the church. My pastor, who also christened me, gives words of encouragement that makes the church feel like it's Sunday service.

My mom writes three things on my obituary that she would later share with my dad: first, *But Jesus said, "Let the little children come to me and do not hinder them, for to such belongs the kingdom of heaven."* (Matthew 19:14), second, *The LORD is near to the brokenhearted and saves the crushed in spirit* (Psalm 34: 18), and third, *"Fear not, for I am with you; be not dismayed, for I am your God; I will strengthen you, I will help you, I will uphold you with my righteous right hand"* (Isaiah 41.10).

I'm not sure why my pastor spoke these words, but as my mom writes each word, I can see pain and anguish leave her face and be replaced with joy and acceptance. In her next breath, she raises her head, looks at my casket, and whispers, "I love you, angel." I wish she could see the smile on my face and feel me reaching out to wipe away a tear. Even though my family has so many people there to support them during this time, I'm happy that my mother found the strength she needs to help my dad and sisters heal.

Healing

The support team is there for my family. Even though everyone knows an investigation is still going on, the team ensures that my family comes first and foremost. My wife and I speak to a social worker who offers grief and loss therapy for my family. Without hesitancy, my wife accepts, and I follow her lead. A few days later, we begin therapy with a well-known counseling agency in the area.

Losing a child has been the most devastating thing my wife and I have ever been through. As a father, I feel responsible for taking care of my family and their well-being. When this feeling is lost, it is beyond stressful, and I personally experienced challenges physically, mentally, emotionally, spiritually, and socially. At one point, I found it a little difficult to move on. Working with the therapist helped me find acceptance, meaning and a purpose to live.

Therapy provides a sense of relief for me. It really helps me a lot as we go through the various stages of grief. I'm happy that we agreed to therapy because it helped us through some difficult times. One of the hardest things for me was getting up every day and figuring out how to parent my girls. Our goal as a family is to not let Piper's death tear us apart, but to bring us closer together. One thing the therapist wants for my family is to not make therapy a troubling experience, but an empowering experience. As a family, we welcome the social worker's support and resources, and remain in therapy for the next twelve weeks.

Ava/Zhuri

Mom told Zhuri and me we were going to talk to a lady about Piper. She told us that we could talk about our feelings and that she would help us understand why Piper died. We don't know what to expect, but we like her office. She has toys, games, a sand table and books that she shares with us when we visit her office. We like going to see her. She helps my sister and me understand that Piper isn't sleeping, and she won't be able to do the things she used to do. We talk about being sad and that it's okay to cry because we miss her.

At the end of therapy, we create a memory box with Piper's name engraved on it. Underneath her name were the words "Sweet Angel." We write a letter to her and place items that were special to us in the box and explain why. It's fun making the box because we are all doing something just for Piper. It helps us understand her death better. For my parents, I believe it lets them take the first step in getting used to not having Piper around, and feeling better too.

Feeling My Presence (Piper)

That night, my mom finds my dad sitting on the side of the bed looking through my box. She sits at his side and wipes tears from the side of his face. She kisses his cheek and says, "We will be alright. We will get through this as a family."

These words seem to comfort him because he grins and says, "Yeah, we will."

For the next few minutes, my parents enjoy the contents of the box once again, remembering with tears and laughter as they talk about me. Once they finish, they place the items back in the box and lay back onto the bed, arm in arm, holding my box. They turn and look at one another, and then over to the nightstand.

My father asks, "Do you hear that?"

My mom smiles and says, "Let it play."

She lay her head back on my dad's chest and they fall asleep to the sound of my crib mobile playing, with my box close to their hearts. They never turned off the baby monitor.

Piper's Wings

I hate to see my mom and dad hurting. Leaving them isn't something I wanted to do, but my time had come to an end. I know losing me was never a thought, especially one that would have to be processed so soon. I didn't want to cause them any pain. I didn't want to see them cry. I didn't want to see them question their faith. I didn't want to create a wedge between them.

I do want you to know that I felt loved every day. I do want you to know that I am proud to have been your child. I do want you to know I felt safe and secure. I do want you to know there was never a moment where I didn't feel special, important, wanted or desired. My family will no longer be the same after my death. I hurt them so much. My death wasn't their fault, and I don't want either one of them to feel that anything they did or didn't do was the cause. When they are ready, they will feel my presence again.

My mother is part of a prestigious organization, Zeta Phi Beta Sorority, Incorporated, which has a national program called the Zeta Prematurity Awareness Program (ZPAP), that involves healthy mothers and healthy babies. I believe my mom's sorority sisters are going to be a great support to her and my family. My mother is very involved with her organization, and I know she will use this experience as another platform to honor me and other families who have experienced sudden infant death syndrome.

ZPAP occurs annually during the entire month of November in support of March of Dimes and World Prematurity Day on November 17th. Since 2003, Zeta chapters and auxiliaries reach out to over 300 houses of worship annually across the country and distribute information on prematurity awareness, causes of prematurity, and the importance of seeking prenatal care to decrease infant mortality and the number of low-birth-weight babies. Even though I was born healthy and not premature, education and awareness of SIDS will also serve as a role model for proven-risk reduction practices and techniques.

I'm happy that my mom and dad have a strong sense of purpose for life and allowed themselves the opportunity to say goodbye. I finally received my wings and will always be with them as their sweet angel.

National Resources
https://www.nami.org
https://www.samhsa.gov
https://www.counseling.org
https://healgrief.org
https://childbereavement.org

Bible Passages (English Standard Version)
Matthew 19:14
Psalm 34:18
Isaiah 41:10

Buried Alive

By Rhonda M. Lawson

Chapter 1

"Hey, Babe," Neil greeted. It was his usual greeting when he called, but there was no joy in his voice this time. Usually, his sexy West Indian accent was coated with a smile in his voice, sounding like he was aroused just to hear me say hello. It was different this time, and I wasn't a fan.

"What's wrong with you?" I asked, trying to sound nonchalant. We'd been having issues for nearly a year, and frankly, I had grown tired of trying to make it work. Breaking up to make up sounded romantic in music, but in real life, it was exhausting. The song had one thing right, though: it truly was a game for fools. This was why I didn't think twice about moving away from my beloved hometown of New Orleans and taking a job in Seattle. The weather may not have been as sunny, but at least I could put some separation between me and Neil while starting a new life in a totally different environment.

"We need to talk," he said with a sigh.

Here it comes. I rolled my eyes when I heard what I believed to be the four most toxic words in the English language. Nothing good ever followed them. Besides, we'd already broken up months ago, so what more could he really tell me? I already knew he'd started seeing someone else. Some white girl he'd met at his military base. As far as I was concerned, our ship had sailed and I was done.

"What do we need to talk about?" I asked, stretching out my legs on my bed and leaning back on a pillow. Something told me I would need to be comfortable for the shit fest that was about to take place. "You've made it clear, and I agree, that we should just stop trying."

"You know I still love you," he stated.

"And I still love *you*, but sometimes love isn't enough," I replied. I wasn't sure of the point of this conversation, but I had to admit that part of me wanted him to want me back. I imagined him proclaiming that he couldn't live without me and that he was prepared to fly out to Seattle to be with me. It wasn't realistic, nor was it probable—hell, I wasn't even sure it was desirable—but it didn't stop me from wishing. "How is your little friend?"

"Her name is Lauren, Marie. Don't be petty."

"That's about the best you're going to get from me right now."

"Well, we're still together, if that's what you're asking."

He didn't sound all that happy about it, but I let it slide. Instead, I just rolled my eyes at the sound of the woman's name who had basically taken my man. When he'd first told me about Lauren, I was hurt. I blamed her for everything that was wrong between me and Neil. He claimed she wasn't the reason for our problems. Our problems were actually the reason for *her*.

Apparently, they'd started off as just friends, and when we began having problems, he would confide in her. Later, when we broke up, they began dating. I wasn't surprised though. He'd dated white women almost exclusively before he and I got together. I was actually surprised, though that he'd been attracted to me. A thick brown-skinned sista with big, curly natural hair, I was about as far from a white woman as he could possibly get.

Whatever his preference, we had an instant attraction that set the stage for three years of real love. I had never before been in a relationship like that. We were in sync. We cooked for each other, made each other laugh, and confided in one another. We went to church together, attended events together, and met each other's friends and family. When his military duties caused him to work all night, I brought him dinner. When my job stressed me out, he was there to rub my feet and tell me everything would be okay. No one could tell us our story wouldn't end in marriage.

That was until he got sick about two years into the relationship. Instead of allowing me to be there for him, he just stopped calling. If I called him, he wouldn't answer, nor would he return the call. I felt ghosted. And I was pissed. After another two months of not hearing from him, I had written off the relationship.

I found out later that he had cancer and was now in remission, but that just made me angrier. I couldn't believe he'd shut me out like that. It was never the same between us after that. We still loved each other, but the intimacy was no longer there. We began seeing each other less and less, but like Gladys Knight said, neither one of us wanted to be the first to say goodbye. We still called one another, but the conversations were shorter. We still attended events together, but the quality time, the Netflix and chill nights, and family gatherings were gone.

I guess as we grew further apart, he was growing closer to Lauren. I wondered how much he told her about me. I wondered how much of our private lives she was privy to. The more I thought about it, the angrier I got. Yes, I could have understood his mindset about his cancer, but he should have understood how afraid I was when I couldn't be there for him. It was like both of us had been exposed and neither of us knew what to do about it. So eventually, as much as neither of us wanted to, we went our separate ways just short of our three-year mark. I needed a fresh start, so when the opportunity rose for me to lead the Human Resources team at my company's Seattle branch, I jumped at it. But Neil wasn't happy.

"Maybe this is a sign that we should just be friends," he said with a sigh.

Those weren't the words I wanted to hear. He was supposed to fight for the relationship. Maybe there was no more fight left in either one of us. "Yeah, you're probably right."

He sighed again and stayed quiet for a few minutes before saying, "Be safe up there."

Those were the last words we said to each other before I flew out. I tried calling him a few times when I got settled, but I could never reach him. I left him messages, but he didn't return them.

One day, while at work, I checked my personal email. As I scrolled through the spam while sipping coffee, I froze when my eyes landed on Neil's name. He emailed me? I'd been calling him all this time and he *emailed* me? I bit my tongue as I clicked the email.

Hey, babe. I'm sorry, but Lauren and I are getting married. Please be safe out there and know that I will always love you.

Was he serious? A three-year relationship ended with a two-sentence email? That motherf—! At least it was confirmed. We were over. I refused to cry. I couldn't even get mad. It would eventually happen, so why get emotional? We'd been off for months, and I was living in a whole different city.

The crazy thing was that I had been pushing away Thomas, a man whom I'd met at a party out here in Seattle a couple months ago. I didn't feel right letting him get close to me because I still wasn't sure of the status between me and Neil. Now that it was definitely over between Neil and me, I still didn't feel right calling him. What kind of woman would I be to call one man on the day I was dumped by another man? I wasn't looking for a cleanup man. I wanted *my* man.

I read those two lines over and over again, not believing that it had come to this. Did Neil really not love me anymore? Had Lauren won? I refused to believe that was the case. But at the same time, the fight had officially left me. If he didn't want to fight for the relationship, I wouldn't either. I leaned closer to the computer, imagining I was looking him in the eyes. My nose wrinkled and my eyes narrowed as I clicked reply and typed:

Do what you have to do. I hope she makes you happy.

There was no need to curse. No other words were needed. My point was made.

Chapter 2

It's funny, but my shoulders had actually been lighter since Neil and I officially ended our relationship over that heartfelt email last year. After giving myself permission to be depressed, I started enjoying my amazing job and Seattle's rainy weather. My apartment, much like many apartments in Seattle, wasn't equipped with air conditioning, so during the few days out of the year it got hot, I would sit on my balcony with a glass of Sauvignon Blanc and relax in the damp breeze while listening to Smooth Jazz on Sirius XM Radio.

Now, romance remained to be seen. In the few months after the infamous email, I didn't date at all, but once I was ready to get back in the game, finding that special one who could follow the true love I thought I had with Neil became impossible. Many of the men I met were already married or in relationships, or they preferred white women. And I was not in the headspace to lose out to another white woman.

I didn't plan to stay in this rut long. Eventually, I would have to break down this wall and let somebody's son get close to me. In the meantime, I would just have fun and work on being the best me I could possibly be. Sounds corny, but I meant it!

Part of that process included retail therapy. After work, I decided to change into some sweats and go to the gym after stopping at Pacific Place Mall in search of a piece of jewelry that would make me feel better. I enjoyed walking though Pacific Place, wandering in and out of stores, taking in the sights of casual shoppers doing the same thing I was doing.

A young couple walking hand in hand into a clothing store caught my attention. I watched the man smile as watched his girlfriend comb through the racks, probably in search of the perfect outfit for their date that night. My mind instantly teleported to Neil, and my funk was back. That used to be us!

My face hardened as I tried to hide my frown. I walked into a jewelry store mumbling about the variety of bastards that Neil was. Whomever said it was easy getting over a broken heart obviously hadn't met me.

"Marie?"

I looked up and was instantly embarrassed when I saw Thomas strolling toward me while holding an Art of Shaving shopping bag. I must have looked like a nutcase talking to myself while sliding rings on and off my trembling fingers.

"You okay?" he asked, leaning on the counter next to me.

"Hi, Thomas," I muttered, not even bothering to hide my agitation. "I'm good. Just have some things on my mind."

"Must be serious. Care to talk about it?"

"Nah. I'll be alright."

He backed away slightly. At first, I thought my attitude had scared him off, but he moved closer. "Normally, that would be my cue to leave you alone, but I'm scared that if I do, it might be another three weeks before I see you again."

My shoulders jumped as I tried to suppress a laugh.

"Was that a smile?" he asked, pumping his fist in mock victory. Even through his facemask, he was cute. I guessed Art of Shaving made a lot of money off of him, because his skin looked buttery smooth.

It felt good to laugh. "What are you doing here?"

"I'll let you two talk," the jeweler said with a smile. She placed the tray of rings back into the case and walked over to another waiting customer. I didn't blame her. I was taking forever to make a decision, and was having a whole other conversation. I would have left me, too.

"I had to pick up some supplies," Thomas said, holding up his shopping bag. "These damn masks are doing a job on my face."

"You don't have to tell me," I agreed. "I feel like I'm doing a bentonite clay mask almost every night."

"Does that stuff really work?"

"Yep, and it's a lot cheaper than what you have in that bag."

He laughed and lifted his eyebrows. I was sure there was a winning smile under that mask.

"Well, I've seen you without your face cover, so I guess the clay must be doing its job," he said. I shifted under his intentional gaze, trying not to make it obvious. "Maybe I should be coming to *you* for facials."

I shifted again and focused my attention back to the rings. "Maybe one day."

"You good?" he asked, moving closer to me. "You don't seem like the same lady I met at the party."

"Probably because this isn't a party," I mumbled. I knew I was wrong for the attitude that dripped from my voice, but a couple of chuckles with a man with nice skin wasn't enough to get me out of my funk.

"You're right," he agreed, taking half a step back. "You obviously have some things on your mind, and here I am, all in your Kool Aid."

I smirked. "Do people really still say that?"

"I do," I replied with a laugh."

This dude was corny, but maybe corny was what I needed at that moment. "I'm sorry I'm taking my bad mood out on you. I just haven't been in the best mood these days. Just some drama from back home that I'm dealing with."

"You're from New Orleans, right?"

"Nice memory."

"Well, that and the Pelicans hoodie," he pointed out. "Only a person from New Orleans would rep that team."

"At least we *have* a team," I snapped playfully. "Where them Supersonics at?"

He feigned hurt and nodded. "Okay, you got me."

I laughed. "That'll teach you to come for my team. The Pels are good. You'll see them in the NBA championship in a few years. Just watch."

"I'll let you tell it," he said doubtfully.

***

If you ask me how that playful conversation ended with me waking up in his bed, I would have no words for you. Don't get me wrong. The sex was good. Amazing, actually. It was just too soon. I wasn't looking for a one night stand or a friend with benefits. So instead of waiting for him to give me the "I'm not ready" speech, I decided to beat him to the punch and get on out of there.

"Stupid, stupid, stupid!" I shouted as I slapped my steering wheel with the palm of my hand. I was so mad at myself for letting that happen. It was nice feeling wanted during the act, but I couldn't help feeling used once we were done. We didn't know each other. I didn't even know his last name. I wasn't sure I even *wanted* to know anything more about Thomas.

"Call Cassie," I commanded my Bluetooth as I drove onto I-5. Maybe talking with my girl would help me to put this situation into perspective. I pumped my left knee nervously as I listened to the rings.

"Hey girl, what's up?" Cassie's cheerful voice sounded throughout the car, enveloping me in friendly comfort.

"I'm such a slut!" I shouted, jumping right to business. Later for the friendly comfort.

"What? Come again?"

I exhaled and shook my head. "Remember that guy Thomas I told you I met at that party I went to a while back?"

"No."

"You know, the cute one who wanted to talk to me, but I was too busy hung up on Neil's West Indian ass to give him the time of day?"

"Doesn't ring a bell, but I do remember you being wrapped around Neil's finger."

"Shut up," I snapped, sucking my teeth. "Anyway, I met this guy Thomas at a party a few months ago, and we ran into each other at the mall yesterday."

"Okay? And?"

"And we talked for a while, and then he took me to dinner, and—"

"And you finally decided to get over Neil and give this Thomas guy some loving. Congratulations!"

"What do you mean, congratulations?" I asked, as I exited off the highway. I pulled into the McDonald's drive-through. Maybe coffee and a sausage biscuit would give me the understanding that my best friend refused to give me.

"I'm saying you've been swerving these guys for months, and it's about time you gave someone a chance," Cassie said. "Even if it doesn't work out with this guy, at least you got your feet wet."

"Yeah, but you know I'm not one for casual sex," I mumbled. "And besides, I'm over Neil."

"I know, friend, but don't be too hard on yourself," Cassie said. "You've been through a lot this past year. Give yourself some grace."

I nodded. "I think it's time to come home for a few days."

"You know I would love to see you, but you're not just coming home to run away from this man, are you?"

She knew me so well. Maybe by the time I got back to Seattle, Thomas would have moved on to the next best thing. But I wasn't telling Cassie that. "I'm grown. I don't run from anyone, or anything. Maybe I just want to check on my mom and spend some time with my friend."

"When was the last time you talked to your mom?"

"That's not the point! That's why I'm going to check on her. Have you seen her lately?"

"Just in church last Sunday. She looks good."

"As she always does." My mom could easily pass for my older sister, but we didn't always see eye to eye. We loved each other, and there was nothing we wouldn't do for each other, but our time together always ended in an argument. She questioned my career choices, my financial choices, and, of course, my choice to not fight for Neil. Let her tell it, if I didn't think Neil was worth fighting for, I must have wasted the last three years of my life. I vowed not to put up with it during this impromptu visit, but I knew it was bound to happen.

"So, when are you coming?" Cassie asked, saving me from my thoughts.

"Probably in the next couple of weeks," I said as I pulled up to the speaker. After placing my order, I added, "It's really going to depend on flight prices. These airlines are getting out the box."

My call waiting beeped. My dashboard screen told me that Thomas was calling. Curiosity wouldn't let me ignore his call.

"Hey girl, I'll call you back when I work out my flight details. That's Thomas calling."

"Oh, he misses you already!"

"Shut the hell up!" I snapped with a laugh. I switched over and immediately changed my persona to feminine Marie. "Good morning."

"Good morning to you," Thomas replied. "Just checking on you to see if you got home safe."

"I made a pit stop at McDonald's, but I'll be home in a few. Thanks for checking."

"McDonald's? You're too beautiful a woman to be eating junk food."

"That's sweet of you, but I'll be running it off later. Our little adventure yesterday kept me from going to the gym."

"Was it worth it?"

Did he really just ask that? I winced, kind of irritated with the question, but I remembered Cassie's advice about giving people a chance. "Last night was nice."

"Just nice? You're a hard woman. Well, I enjoyed spending time with you."

"Likewise, but I can't be skipping out on my workouts too often. Weight likes to stick to you when you get past forty."

He chuckled. "You're right. I try to get my five days a week in, myself. What are you doing the rest of the day?"

I took my breakfast from the drive-through cashier and carefully pulled back into the traffic. "Well, after I eat, I'm going to be researching flights for my trip back home."

"Back home? I didn't run you off, did I?"

It was my turn to laugh. "Relax, Thomas. I'm just going home in a couple of weeks to visit my family."

"Oh, well, that's nice. How long will you be gone?"

"Haven't decided yet," I replied. "Since I'm still working from home, it's not like I have to rush back."

"What if I *want* you to rush back?"

"Then we'll just have to see."

"You're a hard woman, Ms. Marie, but I'm a strong man. You'll let that wall down sooner or later."

Okay, I kind of liked that. Maybe he *was* trying to be around for a while. But like I told him, we would have to see.

Chapter 3

Two weeks flew by, and before I knew it, I was on a Delta Airlines flight headed to the Big Easy. The flight was smooth, but after two mini bottles of Chardonnay, I was out like a light. Just as I usually do, I waited until the last minute to pack and was up all night getting my house ready to be empty for two weeks.

My flight landed without incident. As we coasted to the gate, I pulled out my phone to let Mom know I'd arrived. The sooner I called her, the less time I would have to wait on the curb while she fought rush hour traffic.

My phone let off an explosion of digital beeps and chimes as every missed call, text, and notification over the last few hours fought to get my attention. One particular message caught my attention. *Call me when you get settled and let me know you made it in okay. Miss you.*

That was nice. I smiled and made a note to call Thomas later that evening, and then called Mom to see how far out she was.

"I'm guessing you're here," Mom greeted after the second ring.

"Yep," I replied. "Just landed."

"Okay, I'm halfway there. You gotta go to baggage claim?"

My eyebrows rose. I would have bet money that she hadn't left home yet. "No. I fit everything into a carryon. You're really already on the way?"

"Don't get too surprised," she remarked. "I was already in Metairie running some errands and there wasn't any sense in going all the way home."

"That makes sense," I said with a nod. "Well, I should be on the curb in the next few minutes."

Since I no longer had the time to kill that I thought I would, I bypassed the Starbucks line and went straight to the curb. I hardly recognized the place. The new Louis Armstrong International Airport had opened a few months before the pandemic, so this was my first time seeing it from the inside. The city had spent over a billion dollars on this new facility, and it appeared to be money well spent. The walkways were wider, the restaurants had been updated, and the place looked brighter. There was even a piano in the middle of the terminal. Nice! It was certainly an upgrade.

I finally reached the curb, and Mom pulled up five minutes later.

"My baby is home!" she exclaimed, jumping out of the car and bear-hugging me. It was

like she hadn't seen me in years. Maybe I should stay away more often.

"How is everything?" I asked once we were settled in the car.

"Ain't too much changed since you've been gone," she replied as she joined the gridiron on Interstate 10. Cars were nearly bumper to bumper heading back into Metairie, the suburb between the city of New Orleans and Kenner, where the airport was located. "You feel like going to the Pelicans game?"

"Yes! I actually lucked up and came home on a game night?"

"It's like you planned it like that, huh?"

I laughed and leaned back in my seat. Sitting in the Club Level of the Smoothie King Center while cheering on Brandon Ingram was a great way to get my mind off of my problems. With any luck, I could avoid my mom's relationship questions, and then it would be a hell of a night.

It was amazing how different the city looked. I'd only been gone a little more than a year, but I already felt like a tourist. Stores I remembered before the pandemic were closed.

A few buildings that lined the highway appeared to have taken their place. Yet, the signs that towered above us still bore the street names and exits I remembered. I was sure I could get to a few places without an address if I needed to.

"You heard from Cassie yet?" Mom asked, breaking the silence.

"Not yet," I replied, as we rode past Lake Lawn Cemetery. It was a beautifully kept resting place that lay directly along the interstate. I'm not sure why it always captured my attention, but I couldn't help looking at its pristine grounds whenever I passed. "I'll text her in a bit to let her know I'm here."

"That's good. I've been seeing her at church, but she's always by herself. She doesn't have a boyfriend?"

"She dates, but no one special yet," I mumbled. If Mom was already asking about Cassie's personal life, it would be only a matter of time before she got to mine. I needed to hurry and change the subject. "Are we going straight to the game?"

"We have a little time," she replied. "The game starts at seven, but you know me. If we go home, I ain't coming back out."

"I don't blame you," I said. I then smiled and shifted toward her. "So, when are you coming to visit me in Seattle?"

She shook her head. "I don't know. Maybe this summer. Definitely before it gets cold. Hell, it's March and I'll bet it's still cold up there."

"It's not that bad. I like it."

"You met anybody yet?"

I knew it wouldn't take long. I shifted back and looked straight ahead. "I date, nothing serious just yet. I'm just enjoying life right now."

"What's the use of making all that money if you're not going to find somebody to be with?" Mom asked, shaking her head again. "You're not still hung up on Neil, are you?"

"No, Mom," I groaned. "I am totally good on him."

"You know, when I saw Cassie at church, she told me she saw him with that white girl he married."

Well, there was some tea. Cassie hadn't told me that. I didn't want to look like I cared, although a piece of me did. "Good for him. I'm sure he's happy."

"I doubt it," she said. "He got married too fast. That boy still loves you. I know it."

"Yeah, well, nothing I can do about that. He made his choice."

"Oh, I know what you're saying. I'm just saying I don't want you being up there in Seattle by yourself when he's living his life."

"I'm fine. Trust me," I said. I didn't dare tell her about Thomas. If it didn't work out with us, I didn't want to have to explain to Mom why I'd let yet another one get away. Time to change the subject again. "Who are the Pels playing tonight?"

"Memphis. They better win tonight. They keep trying to depend on Zion and Brandon to get the job done, but they've got to learn how to close a game. It makes no sense to be twenty points up and then lose by ten."

I smiled and co-signed as she ranted about our beloved basketball team. The Pelicans were about the only thing we could agree on, and one of the few subjects we could discuss without treading into my personal life. We started attending games together a few years ago. Win or lose, the games were fun.

My phone buzzed as I listened to Mom go on. *You here yet?*

Yes, I replied to Cassie. I couldn't help but add, *Mom said you saw Neil with his wife. Why you didn't tell me?*

"I guess we can go to the Smoothie King Center now," Mom said, taking the Superdome exit. The Superdome and Smoothie King Center were right next to each other, and even shared a parking garage. "They don't let us in there super early anymore because of COVID, but we can at least park and stroll up there. Maybe we can get some food before the game starts."

"Yeah, that works," I said just as Cassie texted her reply. *I didn't think you cared.*

I don't, but I figured you would at least say something.

"Who you texting?" Mom asked.

"Just Cassie," I replied. "She texted to see if I was in yet."

You mad? she asked.

No. I'll call you later. Going to the Pels game with Mom.

Cool.

"What's she up to?" Mom asked.

"Not much," I replied, tapping my phone. Why would Cassie ask me that? Why did no one believe I was over Neil? Mom wanting me to fight for him. Cassie trying to protect my feelings. I'm good! Yes, I was hurt when we broke up, but I didn't want him back. And the sooner the people in my life realized that, the easier it would be to get back to normal.

Sadly, I couldn't vent this to anyone. Mom was impossible to talk to about relationships. Cassie obviously didn't feel comfortable discussing him. And this was none of Thomas's business. I guessed I had to do what most strong Black women do: hold it in and pretend everything was awesome.

***

It was a good game. The Pels actually won, although they lost the lead late in the fourth quarter. From there, it was a shootout, but the Pels came out ahead. I damn near lost my voice cheering for them, but it was worth it. It was a damn good game.

Cassie had texted me during the game and asked me to meet her for drinks, so I dropped Mom at home and drove out to our favorite wine lounge. New Orleans was full of tourist spots, but we preferred to frequent the places where everyone either knew you or knew *of* you. The places where the drinks didn't cost almost as much as the main course. The places that weren't crowded with Spring Breakers looking for a little fun in the Big Easy.

I walked in and immediately saw Cassie sitting at the bar. She was nursing a red wine that I was sure was a Merlot. It was her secondary drink when she wasn't sipping on a vodka cranberry.

"What's up, lady?" I asked as I sat on the barstool next to her.

She looked up and smiled. "Aye, girl. I figured you'd be here sooner or later. They showed the game here."

"Yeah, I would have been here sooner, but I had to drop Mom off."

"All good," Cassie replied as the bartender approached.

"What can I get you?" he asked, flashing the whitest teeth I had ever seen.

"I'll take a Sauvignon Blanc," I said. "Do you have any on tap?"

"I sure do, and it's a pretty good one."

"Then that's the one I'll take," I confirmed, smiling back at him. Once he walked away, I turned to my friend. "I'm sorry if I came off like I was fussing at you earlier. Mom just took me by surprise when she said you told her you saw Neil. I just wondered why you would tell her and not me."

"It wasn't even like that," Cassie said, waving her hand at me. "You know how your mom is. When I saw her at church that day, we were actually talking about you. I was telling her that I had heard from you. She said she was proud of you, but she wished you and Neil had worked things out. And that's when I told her I saw him and his wife."

I cocked my head to the side and sipped my wine. "She cute?"

"She a'ight. She looks about ten years older than him."

"Figures. He probably thinks he upgraded."

"I wouldn't say that, but he didn't. Trust me."

"Boys have cooties," I remarked. We both cackled, and the tension was broken. That ended the Neil conversation. We replaced it with updates on the city, the dating scene in Seattle, and our plans for hanging out while I was in town.

It was good being with my girl again. I hadn't found a bestie in Seattle yet. Heck, with this pandemic, I rarely went out, so I really hadn't had the opportunity to make many friends. How do grown women make friends, anyway? We don't do playdates, and I don't belong to a sorority. Maybe someone should create a Tinder for best friends. We'd swipe right on the women we might be able to hang out with, and swipe left on the ones we knew we would never bother with. It would save so much time.

As Cassie and I laughed and caught up, I noticed a familiar face that nearly made me drop my wine. A man with a football player's body and a friendly face sat at a booth across the room with a frumpy-looking white woman. They looked happy. They didn't seem to notice me staring.

"Speak of damn devil," I mumbled, setting down my glass. All of a sudden, I wasn't very thirsty.

"What?" Cassie asked, looking around.

"Neil is here. He's across the room."

Her head snapped up, but she tried not to make it obvious that she was trying to be nosey. That's my girl. "Is he by himself?"

"Nope. I think he's with that so-called wife."

"You're not gonna trip, are you?"

"Not in this lifetime," I said, turning my back to the happy couple. "I told you I'm over the whole thing. I'll admit that part of me will always care about him, but I really don't want him back."

"That's good because he's coming this way," Cassie said, her eyes focused past me.

"The hell?" I shrieked. I refused to look his way. Instead, I grabbed my wine glass and took a gulp.

"Hey, my friend," Neil greeted the bartender as he leaned toward the bar across from us. He looked good. Really good.

"What can I do for you," the bartender asked.

"Can I get two Heinekens with lemon?"

"Sure, give me one sec."

As the bartender walked away, Neil shifted his weight and continued leaning on the bar, taking in his surroundings. It was a habit he picked up from the military. He always wanted to be aware of what went on around him. Once his eyes landed on Cassie and me, his face fell, and he froze.

I didn't know what to say either, so I just lifted my glass to him as if giving him a toast. He stood up and nodded, but before he could say anything, the bartender returned with the beers. Neil took the bottles, pursed his lips, and then nodded at us again before heading back to his wife.

"Well, that was awkward," Cassie said.

"You ain't never lied," I agreed.

We giggled, but before we could jump back into our conversation, I felt a presence behind me. I turned and found Neil standing there. This was turning out to be a hell of a homecoming.

"Marie, can I talk to you?" he asked, sounding like every bit of the teddy bear I remembered.

Eyebrows raised, I asked, "You're not going to get in trouble, are you?"

"There you go, being the petty I remember so well," he said with a chuckle.

"I'm just saying I know you're here with your wife. I really don't want no trouble."

"Hi, Neil," Cassie greeted, peeping around me.

"Hello, Cassie. It's good to see you again."

She pushed her empty glass away and stood. "You can sit here. I'm going to use the bathroom."

I wanted to protest, but I guess Cassie knew this was a conversation that needed to be had. We hadn't seen each other since I left New Orleans, and we hadn't spoken since the infamous email. I wasn't in the mood for a closure conversation, nor did I feel I needed one, but it was obvious that Neil had something he needed to get off his chest. And since his wife was waiting, the conversation wouldn't last very long.

"You look good," he said as he sat in Cassie's seat.

"So do you," I replied.

"Can I get you another drink?"

I sighed. "Neil, something tells me you're on borrowed time. We might want to just get to the point."

He nodded. "She knows you're here, and she's not really handling it well. She always thought I was still in love with you. I think in the back of her mind, she thinks if there was a chance, I would leave her and come back to you."

"Why would she think that?"

"For a long time, she was right," he said, casting his eyes on the bar. "But as time went on, I had to realize that our time had passed, and I needed to concentrate on my marriage. Marie, I'm so sorry for the way I handled all of this. You didn't deserve that."

I nodded as I listened to him. Maybe an apology was all I needed. I no longer felt like I had been cast away. I also realized that I didn't have the urge to take him in my arms. It was actually over.

"Are you happy?" I asked.

"It has its moments," he admitted. "But one thing is for sure. She's a good woman. I'm not going to mess this up like I did with you."

"Glad to hear that," I said as my phone buzzed. I figured it was Cassie asking if the coast was clear, but it was Thomas wondering why I hadn't called him yet. I smirked, and then texted that I was out and would call him before going to sleep. He was two hours behind me, so I knew he wouldn't be asleep when I got home.

"I know it's not my business, but is that a love connection you're texting?" Neil asked.

I chuckled. "Nah, I'm not sure what it is yet."

He tapped the bar slightly and rose from the barstool, towering over me the way he always did when we were together. "I'm going to let you get back to your evening. I'm sure Cassie wants her seat back."

"Yeah, true," I replied. "For what it's worth, I'm glad we talked. It was good seeing you."

"Same here. And just so you know, we may not be together anymore, but I will always be your friend, and I don't mean a friend with benefits. If you need me, I'm there for you."

I appreciated him saying that, but I knew I wouldn't take him up on that offer. I cared about him, but I refused to be the cause of any further tension in his marriage. Maybe one day we could be real friends, but for right now, I think we both knew we would have to keep our distance.

***

I wound up leaving the lounge about a half hour later. I had a great time with Cassie, but my involuntary glances at Neil and Lauren made me feel weird. Especially since I also felt his gaze on me a few times. They left before I did, but Lauren didn't look happy. I guessed she was happier when she knew I was over two thousand miles away. I didn't care. She would just have to get past her insecurities. Hopefully, Neil was doing his part to make that happen.

It was near closing time, so the cars that had crowded the parking lot when I got to the lounge were mostly gone. The walk to the car seemed a little longer, and I regretted not taking Cassie up on her offer to drive me to my car. A year in Seattle had made me forget that the streets of New Orleans could be dangerous, especially for a woman walking by herself. Hell, there were men who were robbed and even killed walking by themselves at night so I had no idea why I thought I would be the exception to the rule.

I reached the car and rummaged through my purse for my keys. Why hadn't I pulled them out at the lounge? I felt like I had lost all my common sense. I knew better than this.

Just as I put my hands on the keys, my cell phone rang. I struggled to balance my purse as I pulled out both my phone and keys in one raggedy motion. The damn phone fell.

"Shit," I grumbled as I unlocked the car door. I placed my purse on the seat and then squatted down to look for the phone, which had stopped ringing. I felt for it with wide hands in the small perimeter near the door. Once I finally put my hand on the phone, I felt a presence standing over me.

"Excuse me, Miss," a youthful male voice said. I looked up to find a young man who looked no older than fifteen standing above me. He wore an oversized Polo shirt and baggy jeans. I stood and faced him, trying not to look afraid. He held up a cigarette. "Sorry to bother you, but I was just wondering if you had a light."

"No, I don't smoke," I said quickly before getting into the car and closing the door. My heart pounded as I started the car and drove off. I couldn't believe how many stupid mistakes I made. Not pulling out my keys earlier, not having someone walk me to the car, fiddling with my phone....

What if that man had been a thief or a killer?

My breathing slowed as I drove away from the area, and I started to relax. There was no way I would tell my mother about this experience. I would never hear the end of it.

I couldn't help checking my phone to see who had called me. It was Cassie who had nearly made me lose my life. When I got to the red light, I sent her a quick text to let her know I was on the way home. I thought about calling Thomas, but decided to wait until I got to the house. The light turned green and I took off.

I never understood how people noticed a car was following them until now. A pair of headlights seemed to be going the same pace as me, turning the same corners I turned. I decided to test the theory and take a different route, but there the headlights were.

My heart rate sped up again. Could it be the same guy from the lounge? My eyes darted back and forth as I wondered what to do. My mind immediately went to Neil. He'd left the lounge not long before I did, so hopefully he wouldn't be too far away. I grabbed my phone and texted that I needed his help.

I was glad Mom had filled the tank before she picked me up earlier. There was no way I would stop at a gas station in this situation.

I checked my rearview mirror. The headlights had dropped back a little, but they were still there. Should I go home? Go someplace public? Drive to a police station? I wished I had a gun. As my mind raced, my phone rang. The dashboard told me it was Neil. *Thank God!*

I pressed TALK on the steering wheel and checked the rearview mirror again. "Neil!"

"I'm going to need you to not text my husband," a female voice said.

"What? Excuse me?" That certainly wasn't Neil's voice. I didn't have time for this. "Lauren, this is an emergency. Can you please put Neil on the phone?"

"I don't think that's such a good idea," she said. "You're going to have to find someone else. My husband is unavailable to you."

"Lauren, this is not the time!" I shouted. "I need help."

She answered by hanging up on me. That bitch! And he said *I* was the petty one. Before I could call back, a crash that sounded like thunder filled the car and I went sailing into a pole. I snatched the steering wheel, avoiding a head-on collision, but the side of my car crashed into the pole. My head hit the window and the world went black.

Chapter 4

I woke up, but there was still nothing but blackness. It was strange because my eyes were open, but I couldn't see anything. I squeezed my eyes shut, and then opened them. Still nothing. I looked around, but my eyes refused to register. I tried to lift my hands to wipe my eyes, but they brushed past something hard. What was going on?

I lifted my hands and felt around me. I began hyperventilating as I realized that I was boxed in. I was in a box. I pushed up. I pushed out. I was trapped. Like I had been buried alive. I wanted to scream, but something told me not to. In fact, I needed to slow my breathing before I ran out of air.

How long had I been in here? Would anyone find me? I'm sure people were looking for me, but who would think to look in a random box? Where was I, anyway? The last thing I remembered was being rammed from the back. All I saw were headlights. And then I crashed.

It was hot. It was nighttime, but it was still hot. And being in a tight, dark box wasn't helping. I slid my hand up my face to wipe away the sweat that was starting to stream into my ears. I wiped more sweat from the side of my face. But this didn't smell salty like sweat. It smelled metallic. Blood. I was bleeding. I was bleeding in a tight, dark box.

I wanted to scream. I wanted to rip myself out of that box. But what if I was underground? How much air did I have left? Damn, this was scary. I needed someone to find me.

The bottom of my leg began to itch, and my back ached. I wriggled the best I could to ease the pain. I longed to get up and stretch. Hot tears streamed from my eyes, down my temples and into my bloody hair. I tried flexing my knees, but I couldn't get them high enough. I wanted to go home, but how could I?

Why did that guy target me? How long had he been watching me? What did I have that he could possibly want? I was driving my mother's Ford Escort, so he couldn't have wanted the car. Plus, he crashed it. He wouldn't have gotten much for a wrecked mid-level vehicle.

I thought back to the lounge. Did he see me pay cash for my drinks? I pulled out a hundred dollar bill to pay a twenty-dollar tab. Maybe he saw that. Maybe he saw my designer purse. It cost a hell of a lot more than a Coach bag. Maybe he knew that? My purse wasn't in the box with me, so he must have taken it.

Did he have help? He must have. How could he have rammed me and put me in a box by himself? What a hell of a way to spend my first night at home. What did I do to deserve this?

I guess I could thank God that he didn't kill me on the spot, but why put me in this damn box? Only a hateful person would want to put someone in a box to make them die a slow death. Okay, I needed to stop talking about death. I wasn't about to die in this box. My God wouldn't let that happen!

My wrist started to itch. I reached over to scratch it and nearly shouted for joy. I was still wearing my Samsung watch! I'd been wearing it since I left Seattle, but had turned it off when I boarded my plane. It had been one activity after the next since I landed, so I had completely forgotten to turn it back on. I actually forgot I was wearing it.

"Thank you, Jesus," I whispered as I pressed the home button, the light from the watch killing what little night vision I had. I didn't care. I just wanted to be saved.

My joy was short-lived. I could barely see the watch face, and my shaky hands refused to dial the numbers. I couldn't even scroll.

"Dammit!" I shouted, hitting the side of the box.

***

My watch told me that an hour had passed since I was able to turn it on. It was getting harder to breathe. The watch face lit up a few times with text messages. Cassie and Mom were looking for me. At least they knew I was missing. The watch even rang a couple of times, but I couldn't muster up enough breath to do much more than grunt. There was no way I could tell them where I was because *I* didn't know where I was.

I was tired, but afraid to go to sleep. What if I didn't wake up? And as scared as I was, even if I did go to sleep, it wouldn't be restful.

I wanted to turn over so badly. My back was sore. I needed water. I desired fresh air. All I could do was pray.

*Father, I need you. Please, in the name of Jesus,
let them find me in time.*

"Marie!"

I thought I was hearing things. Had someone called my name? My eyes widened as I looked around, trying to see if what I had heard was real.

"Marie?"

Another voice. Had they found me?

I wanted to call out to them, but I couldn't. I could barely breathe. I needed to make some noise to lead them to me.

My watch!

I took it off and began tapping the box, praying they would hear me.

"Wait! Do you hear that?"

"Maybe that's her! How did she get in here?"

A few minutes later, I heard banging. It was loud. All I could think of was the thunder of the crash, and I began to hyperventilate again. Inside my head, I screamed as loudly as I could. My eyes cried out. Yet, my voice remained silent, save for a few soft grunts.

Suddenly, cool air rushed over me, and the voices I heard became louder.

"Miss, it's okay," a man said. "You're safe now."

"My God! She's alive?" another man asked.

"Marie, baby, are you okay?"

The sound of my mom's voice was all I needed. Once I heard her, I knew I was really safe. I cried as the emotion overcame me and clung for dear life as the police officer pulled me from the box. I finally received the fresh air I craved, but it was too much. I coughed uncontrollably as I tried to breathe with weak lungs.

"Take your time," a paramedic told me. "Let your breathing catch up with you."

He walked me to an ambulance and tried to get me to lie down on a gurney. The thought of lying down again was too much. I shrieked and backed away, pain shooting down my back and my head wound making me dizzy.

"Please," I huffed. "Don't make me lie on my back again."

"It's okay," another paramedic said. "She can sit."

"Mommy, can you come with me?" I asked, my voice still husky.

"Of course, baby," Mom said as she helped me into the ambulance. "You're safe now."

Chapter 5

A week had passed since I was pulled from my "grave," and although my body was safe, my mind couldn't escape the nightmares. I had finally been released from the hospital, but it would be a long time before I was fully healed. Each time I closed my eyes, my breathing stopped and the tears would flow. I hadn't slept well since that night, and it was both frustrating and scary as hell. This was something I wouldn't even wish on Lauren.

Speaking of Lauren, Neil came to visit me while I was in the hospital. Again, he apologized.

"I should have called you back," he pleaded. "I didn't know she had called you, and when I found out what she did, I was pissed. I didn't hit her, but I cut up. Cussing, shouting...."

He shook his head and balled his hands into fists. I could count on one hand the times I had ever seen him angry.

"You okay?" I asked.

He shook his head again. "It just wasn't her place. Even if she doesn't trust you, she should trust *me*. If she was going to be that insecure about us, she should have never married me. We've gotta work out these issues. I can't take much more of this."

I shook my head and turned away from him. "It's not your fault. But Lauren? She'd better hope I never see her again in life. I could have died that night. I got rammed right after she hung up on me."

He reached over and rubbed my shoulder. "I just thank God you're okay. Did you ever find out what happened?"

I turned back toward him and wiped away a tear. Visions of the headlights speeding toward my rearview mirror flashed in my mind. I shuddered, but pushed forward. "I'm convinced that I was being watched at the wine lounge. And there was more than one of them. When I left, this scruffy-looking kid asked me for a light. I think he might have been the one to distract me so the other guy could mark the car. As soon as I pulled off, they followed me."

"Damn," he said. "But why would they bury you?"

"That's the thing. They didn't. The police told me the guys meant to carjack me, but they wrecked me. So, they just grabbed my purse and sped off. Dumb asses must have forgotten my phone was in my purse and it could be tracked. That's how my mom figured out where they were."

"But how did you get in the box?"

"That's the funny part. Some drunk homeless guy found me knocked out in the car and thought I was dead. I don't blame him for that. I guess I did look dead with my head bleeding and my face kissing the steering wheel. The man figured he would give me a proper burial. I crashed near a construction site, so he used an old metal box as a casket and laid me in it. He was still there sleeping when my mom showed up with the police. He was shocked when he found out I was alive."

"That's crazy!" he exclaimed. "That man almost killed you thinking he was helping."

"Right." I couldn't help but smile at the irony, despite the flashes of darkness that remained in my head. I'd developed a real fear of the dark. It was part of the reason I couldn't sleep. I saw the dark every time I closed my eyes. Another tear rolled down my cheek. "I just thank God those guys didn't take my watch. My mom said the locator on our account was what helped her find me. Technology is a beautiful thing."

"Yes, it is," he agreed.

It was good to talk with Neil as a friend. It taught me that great relationships don't have to end in hate. I probably wouldn't be invited to any barbecues at his home, nor would I want to go, but at least we knew we could talk when we needed to. I think that was what I needed at that moment. It was much easier to enjoy Neil's friendship than it was to bask in being his enemy.

The experience also taught me that life was short. I couldn't continue living my life closed off to the world. My hatred of Neil had taken residence in my mind and refused to let go. It clouded my judgment in more ways than one, and led to a series of events that literally could have made me die a lonely woman. God had given me another chance to get it right. I couldn't mess it up this time.

Funny enough, it was Thomas who reminded me of that lesson. After Neil's visit, I called Thomas and told him what happened to me.

"I don't know if I'm happy you didn't diss me, or sad that this happened to you," he said.

I laughed. "Why do I feel like that's a selfish statement?"

"Because it is," he said. "I'm sorry. I'm glad you're okay. That's scary. I'm guessing you're going to stay home for a while?"

"Yeah, I don't feel comfortable being by myself right now. I still can't sleep, and to be honest, I'm probably going to be creeped out for a long time. Besides, Mom and Cassie are taking good care of me. No need rushing back to Seattle to be by myself."

"I'm glad to hear your family is there for you," he said, "but just know that you won't be by yourself when you get back. I'm here for you."

I smiled. That was nice to hear. "You don't have to feel obligated to take care of me."

"Who said anything about obligation? If you haven't noticed yet, I want to be with you, and I'm looking forward to you coming back so I can show you."

"Really, Thomas?" I asked, smirking. "You don't have to sweet talk me just because of my tragedies."

"One day, you're going to knock down that wall and you're going to find out there are other people who care about you. I could have shown you that months ago if you had let me."

I saw Thomas in a different light after that conversation. He was a good guy, and I vowed to get to know him better once I returned to Seattle. For now, I would continue spending time with my mom. Since the incident, we talked more, we prayed together, and she even sat with me when all I wanted was quiet. She also stopped asking about Neil. If things kept progressing the way they were, I might even tell her about Thomas. But no time soon, though.

As for Cassie, she got over blaming herself for what happened. There was no way of knowing that her phone call caused me to drop my phone. She was just checking on me because I refused to let her drive me to my car. That was my fault. I did know this: I would never let down my guard again, no matter what city I was in. It's the little things that keep us safe, and we should never be so busy that we miss the details.

"Hey, girl, hey," Cassie greeted as she walked into my bedroom with two wine bottles. Mom walked in behind her. I thought they were both crazy.

"Why would you two bring me wine?" I asked. "Y'all know I'm doped up on all these painkillers and antidepressants."

"Girl, relax," Cassie said with a laugh. She held up the bottle in her left hand. "You get sparkling cider. I get champagne. No need in both of us suffering."

I laughed so hard my head hurt. "I hate you."

"You know we don't say hate in this house," Mom said, taking a seat next to my bed.

"Sorry, Mom," I said with a laugh. "So, what are we celebrating?"

My new cell phone rang before she could answer. A vision of me feeling for my old phone under Mom's car in the dark of night flashed before my eyes, but I pushed through and pressed TALK. "Hello?"

I was answered with silence, but I could hear the breathing. Someone sniffed and then stuttered. "M-Marie?"

Mom must have noticed the confused look on my face. "Who is it?"

"I don't know," I told her. I turned my attention back to the woman on the line. "Who is this?"

"Look, Neil wanted me to apologize to you," the woman said.

"Lauren?" I asked, scrunching my brows.

"I'm sorry about what happened to you, but I'm not going to apologize for protecting my marriage," she stated. There wasn't a drop of remorse in her voice. Was she serious? "It's obvious you two still have feelings for each other. It was inappropriate for you to call my husband that time of night."

I looked at Cassie and Mom and pressed my finger to my lips. I tapped the speaker button and continued speaking. "Lauren, why did you call me?"

"I already told you why."

"Well, considering this is the second time we've ever spoken, it's obvious that you don't know me at all. Neil and I are nothing more than friends, but the fact that you would marry a man who you think has feelings for someone else says a lot about your insecurity. You need to get some help."

"You know nothing about my life."

"And bitch, you don't know mine!" I could see Mom and Cassie trying their hardest to hold in their laughs, but I was on a roll. I had waited a year to tell this woman off, and she gave me my opportunity wrapped in a bow. "Now I suggest you get off my phone before I really say something to hurt your fragile ass feelings. I would have thought you'd learned something from this situation, but you're still a silly bitch."

"I don't have to take this disrespect from an ignorant man-thief."

"Girl, nobody wants Neil except you. I'm just wondering now why he wants *you*. You really need a hug. Have a good day."

With that, I hit END, looked at Mom and Cassie, and then burst out laughing. "Can you believe that?"

"I guess I'll drink to that," Cassie announced, pouring herself and Mom a glass of wine. She then opened the cider and passed me a glass. "You did that! I guess you are officially moving forward."

I laughed again and lifted my glass. We clinked glasses and ten pounds of weight lifted from my shoulders. I resolved my feelings for Neil, reignited my relationship with my mother, and I might even get a boyfriend named Thomas out of the deal. It would be a long time before I was fully healed, but I thanked God for the support He placed in my life. Who would have ever thought the most tragic moment of my entire life would bring so much clarity?

Celebrate Our Children

Original Children's Stories

Presents
for Those
Who Pray

By Beautiful Lawson

Many years ago, in a land past the Sinai Mountains, the Red Sea, and the Great Pyramids, there lived a lady named Ursa. Ursa and her husband Re lived in a grass hut along the Nile River near the Valley of the Angels. They were poor, but Ursa always knew her family would someday be great. Each evening, just before Re returned from working, Ursa would sit next to the river and imagine being among the many powerful queens like Hatshepsut and Nefertari.

"Some day," she'd say, "Re and I will rule Egypt."

Unfortunately, she knew it was only a dream. The only way to the throne was through marriage and she loved Re so she would never leave him. She instead hoped for a beautiful daughter who would make her family proud by impressing the prince with her charm and beauty. She hoped that one day the angels would finally bless her with this child after three failed years of trying. She prayed, but she was beginning to become certain that her prayers would not be answered. Little did she know that the angels had heard her thoughts.

The next day, Ursa returned to the river. It was peaceful, soothing her continued troublesome thoughts from the day prior. Just as she sat down in her usual spot, she began to daydream about what life with a daughter would be. She thought about how she would teach her to be a well-mannered and respected young lady.

Suddenly, she saw a lotus flower floating toward her in the river. Picking up the flower, she suddenly felt different. She knew that it could only mean one thing!

"Re!" she exclaimed as she burst into their hut. "The angels have heard my prayers!"

"What do you mean?" Re asked. He was tired and had no patience for his wife's rantings today.

"Look!" she said, showing him the flower. "This wasn't there yesterday. It's a sign from the angels!"

Re refused to believe her. "Ursa, there are probably lots of flowers near the river."

"But not lotus flowers," Ursa assured him. "This flower means rebirth. This could only mean that I am finally going to have a baby!"

Sure enough, months later, Ursa gave birth to a baby girl. She was the most beautiful child anyone had ever seen. All of Re and Ursa's neighbors marveled at the child's beauty and peaceful nature.

"She's beautiful," Re said proudly, ashamed that he hadn't believed his wife.

"What will we name her?" Ursa asked.

Re smiled. "Her name shall be Beautiful."

Everyone in the hut was surprised and amazed by the baby's unusual name. But they knew that with a name like hers, the child would be special.

***

Meanwhile, the king and queen had also had a baby. They named him Tiras, and he was very handsome.

"He is the image of perfection! The crown jewel of Egypt! Let us begin choosing his future queen now. She must be just as perfect as my son," the king boasted. "Whomever our son marries must be bred in the ways of royalty."

"But where will we find such a girl?" the queen asked. "Our neighboring nations?"

"We will start here and keep the royal bloodline Egyptian. Royalty can be trained," the king commanded.

They didn't know it, but Seneb, the king's scribe, overheard the king and queen talking and immediately told Kofi, the king's adviser. Kofi explained to Seneb that if such a girl was found, their dreams of taking over the kingdom were over.

They decided to follow the king's messengers and sabotage any little girl who may stand a chance. Their plan did not prove too difficult, as there were not very many contenders who measured to the king's high standards.

"The future princess cannot just be pretty," the king had told them. "She must also be smart, well-mannered, and have a peace befitting a queen."

The search took years. Each time the messengers thought they'd found the perfect girl, the king found a fault in her. She either was not mannered enough, not well spoken, or she was not graceful enough.

After yet another day of coming up empty, the messengers decided to take a rest near the Nile.

"I'm beginning to believe that there is no girl good enough for the king," one messenger said sadly.

However, just as they had begun to head back to the palace, they heard a woman's voice coming from behind them.

"Beautiful, this is where I stood when the angels told me about you," the woman said.

"Who are they?" Beautiful asked.

The woman laughed patiently as they sat near the river, paying no attention to the three men sitting a few feet away.

"These angels watched over Queens Hatshepsut and Nefertari, and they were women who held great power. They used to rule over all of Egypt and they walked with grace and beauty, just like you."

As the woman spoke with her daughter, the messengers looked at each other and wondered if Beautiful could be the one the king had been looking for. They agreed to take her to the king, cheering amongst themselves and startling Ursa and Beautiful.

"I'm sorry, my lords," the woman said. "Have we upset you?"

"On the contrary," the first messenger said. "You may be just who we're looking for."

Frightened, Ursa held her daughter close and asked, "Why? Who are you?"

"We are the king's messengers, and we have been searching for the past six years to find a princess for the prince," explained the second messenger.

"I'm a princess!" Beautiful said, jumping up and down.

"You certainly seem to be," the second messenger said with a laugh.

"Where is your husband?" the first messenger asked.

"He is working," the woman said. "His name is Re, I am Ursa and this is *Beautiful.*"

"Beautiful?" the third messenger asked. "That's her name? Curious, but befitting."

"Her father named her," Ursa said proudly.

"Ursa, meet us here with your husband at sundown. We will then take Beautiful to see the king," the second messenger said.

"Yes, my lords," Ursa said, bowing her head and quickly taking Beautiful away. "Come, my child, you must look your best if you are to see the king."

Seneb watched the entire scene from behind a bush, knowing there was no doubt that this child was the future princess. He hurried back to the palace to tell Kofi all that he had seen.

***

Ursa instructed Beautiful on how she should present herself to the king. She showed her how to bow and taught her how to sit as a lady should.

"You must always show respect and walk with grace," Ursa said. "Smile genuinely. Keep the peace and beauty that you were born with."

"Like this, Mother?" Beautiful asked, sitting perfectly with her ankles crossed and her hands in her lap.

"Perfect," Ursa said, clapping with joy. "You are ready to meet the king."

With that, Ursa dressed her little girl in her best clothes and perfumed her with rose oil. Once Re came home, they set out for the river. The messengers, joined by Kofi and Seneb, were already waiting there.

"If this girl is truly the one, the spell will work," Seneb whispered to Kofi.

"Good evening, my lord," Re said as Ursa and Beautiful bowed silently. "We have come as you have ordered."

"The king seeks a princess for the young prince," the first messenger said. "We believe your child is the princess he seeks."

"How can you be sure?" Re asked.

"We can't, but the king will know," the second messenger said.

Confused, but knowing better than to doubt again, he turned to his daughter. "Are you ready to see the king, Beautiful?"

"Yes, Daddy," she said.

"Then we shall go," Re said.

The group left the river and headed for the castle by way of the royal carriage. The carriage smelled of rotten fish to Beautiful, but she knew better than to complain. She tried her hardest not to make a face, surprised that the smell didn't seem to bother anyone else in the carriage.

Kofi and Seneb noticed Beautiful's discomfort and smiled to themselves. The first part of their spell was working. Kofi planned to make sure to thank the local priest they conspired with once they had a chance.

As soon as they reached the castle, Beautiful began to cry. The closer they got, the louder her cries became.

"What's wrong, my child?" Ursa asked, taking Beautiful into her arms.

But Beautiful wouldn't answer. She seemed to get smaller, her cries louder. She had become a baby again!

"Beautiful!" Re cried, moving beside his wife and child. "What's happening?"

"She must be cursed!" Kofi shouted. "We can't take her to see the king! Not like this!"

"What's happened to my baby?" Re cried.

The messengers pleaded with Kofi to give them an answer. As the king's trusted adviser, surely he would know what to do. But Kofi decided to take her away from the castle, away from her parents, away from the entire town so she wouldn't pass her curse to others. He then promised her parents that Beautiful's disappearance was only until she made a great recovery.

He placed her in a cave located deep in the woods where no one would possibly find her. This cave bore little light, which was her only indicator for the time of day, as she was never allowed to leave. Strangely, in the dark, damp cave, Beautiful appeared to be her regular self. However, whenever she entered the tiny sliver of light, she was once again a baby.

Each day, Kofi and Seneb would check on her to make sure she had not been found and give her one meal. Beautiful would constantly ask why she was being kept there, desperately wanting to see her family again, but she would never get her answer. Years went by, and Beautiful remained trapped in the cave.

***

The king had still not found a bride, and the prince was now fourteen years old.

"Perhaps we should look to our neighboring countries for the princess," the queen said sadly.

"I'm afraid you are right," the king agreed.

"Sire, perhaps I can help," Kofi said, clearly eavesdropping on their conversation.

"Yes?" the king replied.

"Sire, why not let Sir Tiras rule alone? I have been your trusted advisor for many years, and I can continue to advise your son in the matters of Egypt," Kofi said with a mischievous smile.

The king and queen pondered for a moment, not enthused about the idea of their son ruling without a queen. The perfect girl for the prince had to be out there somewhere. Maybe they just weren't looking hard enough.

"Well, the prince is coming of age," the king said. "He will soon have to learn the laws so that he can rule the country once the time comes. Let me think about it."

"Very well, Sire," Kofi replied with a bow. He then quickly rushed out to find Seneb. "The plan is working. Soon, we will have control of the kingdom."

"But what do we do with the child?" Seneb asked.

"Leave her there," Kofi said.

"But we can't—"

"We must! That child stands between us and the kingdom. She can never be found. No one can know about her."

Neither of them noticed Tiras standing near the door.

"What child?" Tiras wondered. "I must go tell my father."

As he ran to the king's chambers, he ran into one of the messengers.

"Where do you run so fast?" the messenger asked.

"I have to talk to my dad," Tiras said. "I think a girl is in trouble."

"Who?" he asked.

The prince started to tell him, but remembered what Kofi said about her standing between them and the kingdom, so he decided to see for himself.

"I don't know. Can we go for a ride later?"

"Of course, Sire," the messenger said, confused by the boy's words.

***

Later that evening, the prince and the messenger rode their horses in the country. The prince remained quiet for much of the trip, keeping a lookout for anything unusual. The messenger wondered if the prince was okay. After a long silence, the prince finally spoke.

"Remember when I said a girl was in trouble?" Tiras asked.

"Yes." The messenger replied gingerly.

"Well, I heard Kofi and Seneb talking about a little girl. They said they were going to leave her somewhere because she stood between them and the kingdom. What do you think they meant?"

The messenger thought for a while. Why would Kofi and Seneb think a child could keep them from taking over the kingdom? Why would they think they would take over the kingdom in the first place? He then remembered Beautiful and the strange thing that happened to her on the way to see the king many years ago. Kofi had taken her away, but to where?

"Do you think the little girl is the princess my parents seek for me?" the prince asked, seeming to read the messenger's thoughts.

"You knew about that?" the messenger asked, surprised at the young prince's wisdom.

"Everyone knows about that," the prince said sarcastically. "After ten years, it was rumored that she didn't exist."

"Anything is possible. Maybe those rumors will subside," The messenger said with a laugh. He then sighed. "Sire, if Kofi and Seneb are hiding her, it could be dangerous to go looking for her."

"I know," the prince said sadly, "but no one deserves to be lost. What if she misses her family?"

The messenger sighed sadly. He knew the young prince was right, but he feared going against Kofi and Seneb. He'd always felt they were bad people, but he never thought they would hurt a child. Suddenly, he pulled the horse in the direction of the Nile River. It wasn't that late. Maybe she'd still be there.

"Where are we going?" the prince asked. "To look for the girl?"

"You'll see, Sire," the messenger said.

When they reached the river, they left their horses and walked near the bank. Sure enough, they found a woman sitting alone, facing the Valley of the Queens. She was hunched over, as if she had been crying.

"Madam," the messenger said quietly.

When she looked up and saw the messenger and prince standing over her, she scrambled to her feet in fear.

"It's okay, Madam," the messenger said. "I've come to find out if Beautiful has returned to you."

Ursa looked down sadly. "No, she hasn't. We haven't seen her since—"

"Do you remember where Kofi took her?" the prince asked.

"No, Sire."

"What happened to her?" the prince asked them.

"Something terrible," Ursa said, crying again.

"We will take you to get your husband and find your child," the messenger said. Ursa's sadness had given him courage. He knew what had to be done.

Ursa quickly got onto the messenger's horse with him. Once they picked up Re, they set out to find Beautiful.

"I just don't know where else to look," Re said. "She could be anywhere."

"The angels will help us find her," Ursa said. "Every day I prayed that she would come back to us. I had just finished praying when the prince found me today. I know the angels will lead us to her."

"Look!" the messenger said suddenly. He pointed to fresh footprints on the road leading to the woods.

"Where do you think they lead?" the prince asked curiously.

"Let's find out," Re said.

The messenger led the horse to follow the tracks into the woods. They seemed to travel for miles. Suddenly, the tracks stopped at a cave.

"Could this be it?" the messenger asked.

"Yes, I think so," Re and Ursa said together.

They quickly hopped off of the horses and ran to the cave. They tried to remove
the rock that covered the entrance, but it was too heavy.

"Please, help us," Re asked the messenger.

Together, with even the young prince, they tried to push the rock away from the cave. After trying to push the rock three times, it finally moved. Ursa could hardly wait for the stone to be moved completely. As soon as there was enough room, she squeezed into the cave and began calling, "Beautiful!"

But there was no answer.

"Beautiful!" she yelled louder.

The messenger and Re finished moving the stone completely and helped Ursa call for the young girl. The light from the setting sun shone into the cave. "Beautiful!"

But there was still no answer.

"Perhaps this is not the place," the messenger said sadly. "Let us keep looking before night falls."

As they turned to leave the cave, Ursa heard the sound of a baby crying. Everyone searched the cave, thankful for the little sunlight that lit their way.

"There!" Re called, pointing toward a brightly lit corner of the cave.

The group rushed to where he pointed. It was Beautiful! But she was still a baby. Ursa picked up her child and cried. "What could have happened to her?"

"The same thing that will happen to you!" said an evil voice from behind.

The group turned to find Seneb and Kofi staring at them angrily.

"Why are you here?" Kofi asked.

"What have you done to my baby?" Re asked angrily. "She should be ten years old, yet she looks as if she was just born."

Kofi laughed. "She's still ten, but we had to make sure that she would never become princess. We have worked too hard to take over this kingdom, and no peasant child is going to stop us!"

"But she's just a child!" Ursa cried.

"And that she shall stay," Seneb said. He grabbed Tiras as he and Kofi backed out of the cave. "He shall come with us, but you all shall be together!"

With that, he and his men began pushing the stone back into place to seal the messenger and the family in the cave. It was now completely dark in the cave, and Re felt Beautiful grow back into a young teen in his hands.

"Daddy!" she yelled as she hugged him.

***

Meanwhile, Seneb and Kofi began to plan their excuse for having Tiras in their grip.

"Not so fast, Seneb!"

They turned around and found the king and queen and the other two messengers standing near their carriage. Kofi and Seneb dropped to their knees in fear.

"Unhand my son immediately!" the king commanded. Once the prince was free, he looked at Kofi and Seneb angrily. "I trusted you all these years, and this is how you repay me? You lied to me and took my son?"

"But…Sire…how did you know?" Seneb asked.

"I had a feeling something was going on," the queen replied. "I was right. You've been acting strange for years, and when I saw you follow my son today, I had you followed."

"Who is in that cave?" the king asked.

Kofi and Seneb looked at each other, afraid to reply.

"A girl and her family are in there," the prince cried.

"Move the rock!" the king commanded.

Kofi and Seneb scrambled to their feet, their men helping them to push the rock away. They then tried to run away, but the king's men stopped them and held them down.

"Whomever is in there," the king called, "You can come out! It is safe."

"My lord!" the messenger called from deep within the cave. He led Re, Ursa and Beautiful into the fresh air. It was now dark, so Beautiful looked like a regular beautiful ten-year-old. She coughed as she tried to get used to the clean air.

"Thank you, my lord," Re said as he, Ursa, and Beautiful dropped to their knees.

"Don't thank me," the king said. "Thank my wife. She is the one who knew how to find you."

"But how?" Ursa asked.

"It was strange," the queen said. "Queen Nefertari came to me in a dream. She told me that I should watch Kofi and Seneb. When I saw them leaving the castle tonight, I convinced the king to follow them and they led us to you."

"How did our son end up here?" the king asked.

"That is my fault, Sire," the messenger said. "He heard Kofi and Seneb talking and asked me to give him a ride in the country. I found the child's mother and we followed footprints that led us here."

The king turned to Kofi and Seneb, both of them shaking in fear. "What could make you do such an evil thing to a child?"

When they still didn't answer, the prince exclaimed, "They said the girl stood between them and the kingdom. She could be the chosen princess!"

Kofi and Seneb scowled at Tiras for exposing them to the king and queen. The king then shook his head, weary of all the surprises he'd had tonight. He turned to Beautiful, who, even through her dirty clothes and wild hair, was still quite beautiful.

"What is your name, child?" he asked.

"Beautiful," she said quietly, bowing just as her mother had taught her so long ago. "It's nice to meet you."

"It's nice to meet you, too, Beautiful," the king said. "Are you okay?"

"Yes, Sire, thank you for asking. I'm just a little hungry," Beautiful replied, trying to be polite and modest.

"Did they hurt you, Beautiful?" the queen asked.

"No, Madam," Beautiful said, crying. "They just didn't let me see the sun, and whenever I did, I would turn into a baby. I was only fed scraps. I was scared that I would never see my mommy and daddy again."

The king again looked at Kofi and Seneb angrily. "This evil deed will not go unpunished. See if you will enjoy the same fate you tried to set upon this child."

With that, all three of the messengers seized the two men and cast them into the cave, sealing the opening tightly with the rock.

The king took Beautiful and her family back to the castle. The queen's handmaids gave them clothes to wear and helped them get clean. The family was then invited to sit at the king's table for dinner. The royal family smiled as Beautiful and her parents approached the table.

"Young Beautiful, you are even more charming and beautiful now," the king said.

"Thank you, Sire," Beautiful said with another bow.

"Have you noticed that she has not turned into a baby yet?" Ursa asked Re quietly as they ate.

"Maybe the spell is broken," Re said.

They didn't know it, but the spell had, in fact, been broken. After talking with Beautiful and seeing all that Kofi and Seneb had put her through, the king had spoken with another priest to break Beautiful's spell. With a strand of Beautiful's hair stolen from the hairbrush used to get her ready for dinner, Beautiful never had to worry about turning back into a baby again.

The king also decided that she truly was the chosen princess. He told himself that if those two men were willing to go through such efforts to hide her, then she must be something special.

Beautiful and her parents were invited to move into the castle so she could learn how to be the princess she was born to be. She and Tiras played every day, but she always remembered to be a young lady. She also kept her manners, especially in the presence of adults.

Ursa learned that dreams really do come true for those who believe. The angels had helped her family realize the greatness they always wanted. With their help, the royal family made Re and Ursa their trusted advisors.

Years later, the entire kingdom attended a royal ball. They had come to see the beautiful, peaceful young lady the prince had chosen to help rule the kingdom. Young Beautiful had finally become Princess Beautiful!

A Precious Adventure
By Vanessa J. Ross

Once upon a time, there was a little girl name Precious. She was about five years old.

Every morning, Precious would get out of bed and go to the front door. Her mother worried about Precious because she kept going back and forth to the door.

"Precious, my darling, why do you keep going to the front door?" her mother asked.

"I am looking for my angel flying around in the sky," Precious replied.

One morning, she decided to go looking for her angel. The problem was she really didn't know where to look. Her first stop was the garden, where she found beautiful daisies, tulips, roses, and sunflowers, but no angel. So, she continued her journey.

She stopped at a second garden, where she found nothing but vegetables like tomatoes, lettuce, and greens. She continued to look in her treehouse, and then in the wilderness.

"Maybe my angel could be in the forest with all the beautiful animals," she decided.

She continued to explore until it became dark, and she could no longer find her way home. Her mother grew worried because Precious was nowhere to be found. Her family began to search for her, but no one could find her.

"We can't give up," her mother told her family. "My baby is out here somewhere and we must find her before something happens to her."

They continued to search and came across the forest Precious visited last.

Hello there," someone asked. "Are you looking for someone?"

The mother turned to find a deer speaking to her. She asked, "Have you seen a little girl around here?"

The deer replied, "No, but we will be glad to help you look for her."

With the animals' help, the search for Precious continued as the night grew darker. They entered a garden and heard someone crying. It was Precious!

"Are you okay?" her mother asked, hugging Precious.

"I need to find my angel," Precious cried.

A light glistened above them and her mother smiled. "There is your angel above the trees. She has been in the sky keeping you safe until we found you."

Ja'Quay, the Fearless Ant Leader
By Avalon Soulette Brown

It had been a long winter and the food was getting low in Welcome, the Ant Kingdom. Ja'Quay, the fearless leader of Welcome, called a meeting with all the ants to discuss their plans for replenishing their food supply. Everyone came to the meeting because they were anxious to hear his plan.

"Thank you, everyone, for coming," he began the meeting by saying. "It has been a long winter, and we have survived. I know the food supply is getting low, the winter is gone, and the weather is warm now. We know during this time, people put more trash and garbage in the garbage cans. People are cooking out more, which means more scraps for us. I will go out and scout the land and come back and give you a report on our next move. After that, we will gather the men together and go out on a hunt for food."

The next day, Ja'Quay carefully crawled out of the hole to scout the land, realizing he was in the backyard of a house. It was such a lovely day. The yard had bushes that were nice and green, and the flowers were starting to bloom. Ja'Quay could smell the aroma of food in the air.

He crawled all around the yard in search of ways into the home, and he noticed a hole in the house. He decided to crawl in and see where it led. He continued to crawl until he noticed a light at the end of the hole. Ja'Quay peeped out of the hole and noticed bread on the counter, and then saw another table with different foods. He quickly turned around and crawled back out the way he came. He could not wait to get back to the others to tell them what he had found.

Ja'Quay crawled faster and faster, through the hole, down the side of the house, and back to the hole that led underground, excited to let everyone know he had found a place to go to replenish their food. Ja'Quay called all the men together. When he reached the kingdom, he called all the men together.

"We must prepare to go out tomorrow and bring back food to our storage house," he announced. I found a place just above ground that has enough food to last us through next winter. The women will stay here and prepare the storage house."

Everyone cheered. They were so happy, they started dancing and playing music. When the music stopped, Ja'Quay said to all the men, "You should get some rest because we will start out early in the morning.

When the morning came, the men assembled at the beginning of the hole with Ja'Quay at the head of the line. They all marched out of the hole one by one, each with a basket on his back. What they did not expect was the lady in the backyard pulling weeds from her garden. As she pulled up the weeds, she looked around and noticed the army of ants crawling toward the house. She grabbed a push broom and began sweeping toward them.

"Scatter everyone!" Ja'Quay yelled.

All the ants ran in different directions, making it back to the hole that led underground.

"Is everyone okay?" Ja'Quay asked.

"Some ran in the bushes to hide," his commander replied. "They will come back later."

"We'd better stay in for the day and try again tomorrow," Ja'Quay said. "The lady will not be in the yard. So, let us all meet here again tomorrow."

Ja'Quay was extremely disappointed. He knew where the food supply was and was sure he would be able to lead them back to it. Now that he knew the lady came out into the yard, he needed to produce a plan to go out when she was not in the yard. He rose up early the next morning to scout the yard before everyone assembled. By the time everyone came together, he was back underground and let everyone know it was safe to go out.

He led the line of ants in a single line. There was no sign of the lady anywhere, but as the ants headed to the house, Ja'Quay spotted white powder along the wall.

"Stop!" he yelled. "I'm not sure what this white powder is, and I don't want to walk across it."

"So how do we get to the house?" asked one of the other ants.

"Just stay around the outside of it," Jaquay instructed. "It has to end somewhere. Some of you go to the left and the rest go to the right. When we find the end, we can climb up the wall."

The ants crawled around the edge of the white powder, careful not to step in it, realizing the lady had put down ant powder to kill them so she could stop them from getting into the hole.

Once the ants climbed up the wall from both sides, they met at the hole that led into the house. Ja'Quay led them down through the hole. When they reached the kitchen, he saw the bread sitting on the counter, just as it had been before. All the ants scrambled around the bread, chopping off pieces with their tools and putting them into their baskets. Once everyone's basket was full, they all crawled back through the hole, down the wall and around the white powder.

Just as the last ant was coming down the wall, the lady came out into the yard. She just stood there in amazement as she watched them crawl down the wall and bypass the powder. These ants were smart. None of them crawled across the powder. The lady stood there with her hands on her hips, realizing the powder would not get rid of the ants. They would keep coming. After seeing them maneuver around the powder, all she could do was shake her head and go back into the house.

Ja'Quay and the others made it safely to their underground home and unloaded their baskets in the storage area. He knew this would not be enough food to last the winter. They would have to go out again and gather more food. The only thing that could stop them would be the lady in the yard. Ja'Quay knew the lady was trying to kill them, so they had to be careful.

He decided they would not go back out for a couple of days so he could get an ideal of when the lady would come into the yard. Ja'Quay decided to set up surveillance just to see how often the lady came out.

Each morning he noticed the lady normally came out in the garden at a different time in the morning. He monitored her for about a week, going out at various times to watch for her, wanting to get a sense of the exact time, so he could tell the team.

During the surveillance, Ja'Quay noticed she did not come out at noon when the sun seemed to be hottest. He did the surveillance for another week, making sure she would not come out at noon. He went back to the group, called the new meeting, and let them know that noon would be the best opportunity for them to return. He then told all the men to assemble the equipment and meet in the morning so they could make it to the house before the lady came out.

The next morning, Ja'Quay led the men with their supplies and baskets across the yard. The whole army had made it across the yard without seeing the lady. They made it to the house and started crawling up the side of the house just as the mail carrier set a package inside of a wooden box near the house. Ja'Quay was not worried about the mail carrier, and the mail carrier did not notice the ant army, so they continued crawling up the wall to the hole that led inside the house.

"We have to hurry and fill our baskets and get back to the hole before someone sees us," Ja'Quay instructed once they reached the kitchen. All the ants began filling their baskets and began leaving the house back through the hole. Ja'Quay thought he heard a noise and told everyone to stop for a minute. They did not hear anything, so they continued their journey back home. Once they reached the hole that led underground, Ja'Quay suddenly noticed the lady coming out of the house.

"Hurry everyone! Hurry!" he commanded. "We must run and get back to the hole. The lady has come out into the yard."

The lady picked up her package out of the box. She looked over her right shoulder and noticed the army of ants marching in a line as usual down the side of the house. She ran to the side of the house, returned with a hose, and started spraying them with water. The ants started scattered, but twenty of the ants were washed away. It was too much water for them to get away. Ja'Quay could hear them yelling for help as they drowned. The rest of them made it back to the hole that led underground or ran into the bushes.

"I will get you ants," the lady vowed. "You think you're smart, but I'm going to get you all.

When the ant army made it back underground, they realized they had lost half the men. The ants were sad they had lost their friends.

"Thank goodness the lady did not get us all," Ja'Quay said with a sigh. "If it weren't for the package, the lady would have never come into the yard. I thought we would be safe this time. We will try again another day, and hopefully the lady will not come out. Get some rest."

Ja'Quay was glad they were able to bring some of the food back with them, but he would have to produce another plan to lead his men back to that house without the lady catching them in the garden.

***

Meanwhile, the lady told her husband about the ants and how she needed to figure out what to do to get rid of them. Little did she know both she and Ja'Quay were determined to conduct their plans.

"We have to go to the store and find something to help us get rid of those pesty ants," she said. "They are trying to get into the house, and we cannot let that happen."

Down in the ant hole, Ja'Quay was formulating a plan of his own. The food storage cabinet was only half full. The ants had to fill up the storage cabinet before winter. Ja'Quay knew he would need someone to look out for the lady when she came into the yard. He came up with a plan and shared it with the rest of the group.

"What if we disguise ourselves as a caterpillar and creep across the yard so the lady in the garden can't see us?" he asked. "Let me see a show of hands of those who think that this might be a clever idea and can work."

Everyone raised their hands.

The lady from the garden had her own ideas.

"Let's go to the store and see what other things can get rid of those pesty ants before they make it into the house," she told her husband. "Once they get into the house, they are going to be all over the kitchen, and then we will have another problem."

Her husband replied, "Okay, we can do that this morning. "There must be something that might help us get rid of the ants. We must see how they are getting into the house and then plug up all the holes."

"Follow me," she said, leading him to the backyard. She showed him where the ants had been coming from.

Once her husband saw the antihole, he said, "We can also pour dirt or cement down the hole so they can't get out."

The spouses only saw the one hole, but Ja'Quay the Fearless was smart. He made sure there was more one than one hole in case of emergencies. He watched them walk behind a bush in the yard and heard what they planned to do. He then scurried back down the hole.

"They are trying to close all possible ways that we can enter the house," Ja'Quay reported. "We must get our disguises together now so we can get our food and store it away or we will be hungry when the wintertime comes."

The ants agreed with Ja'Quay. They would have to hurry and put their plan in motion before the lady and her husband could put theirs in motion.

"We have to keep the lady in the garden from seeing us," one of the ants said. "She will try to kill us. The caterpillar disguise will work; let us try it."

Now, Ja'Quay had to figure out how he would get enough caterpillar disguises for all his men. He decided to ask the women to immediately sew their disguises big enough for ten ants to fit in. It would take them three days if they all worked together.

The next day, the women began sewing the disguises. While the women sewed, Ja'Quay snuck up to the garden to watch the lady and her husband. He knew they both took an early morning walk together. The rest of the day, only the lady came into the garden. Her husband did not come out unless she called him.

As the women promised, they completed the disguises in three days. Ja'Quay had the men try them on, and then they practiced walking like a caterpillar. After three days of practicing, Ja'Quay wanted to do a test run using only ten men. He would be the lookout and let them know when to start coming out of the hole.

Ja'Quay left the hole first. He looked around the garden to make sure the lady had not come out yet. When he saw the coast was clear, he waved his hand for the ants to start coming out. They slowly came out as a caterpillar and made it across the yard to the house. They then began to slowly crawl up the wall to the hole that led to the kitchen. As Ja'Quay watched the ants crawl up the wall, he continued to look out for the lady and her husband.

"Hurry, crawl as fast as you can," he said. "I will continue to watch out as the rest of you get to the house."

Ja'Quay continued peeping out the top of the hole, searching for the man and his wife. He knew they were trying to produce something to keep them from getting into the house, but he did not know how much time he had to try out his plan or how soon the husband and wife would be back to the garden.

The ants continued crawling up the side of the house into the entrance. When they got into the kitchen, the counter was clean. Nothing was out on the table, so they hurried out of the kitchen and ran back to the hole. Ja'Quay realized the plan worked.

"We will continue to watch the people's schedule before we can go out again," Ja'Quay told the assembly. "Tomorrow, we will try to go out again in the disguises."

***

The next day, Ja'Quay went to the top of the hole to see if the coast was clear. He saw the man and lady drive into the driveway and ducked back into the hole, telling the men they would have to wait until it was clear for them to go out.

He returned to the top of the hole to watch the lady and man. He saw them take big bags out of the trunk. He was not sure what was in the bags, but he remembered hearing them talk about closing the holes. The man put the bags on the ground in the back of the house, and then went back into the house with the lady.

Once they were inside, Ja'Quay decided to sneak over to the bags to see what it was. He saw the writing on the bags: CEMENT. They were serious about closing the hole. Ja'Quay raced back and told the other ants to get into the house again and look for food. He made plans to wait until the afternoon or closer to dinner time, when the family would leave food crumbs or something for them to bring back to the storage house.

When the evening came, Ja'Quay told the men to get into the caterpillar disguise and crawl across the ground. He went to the top of the hole first. Once he saw it was clear, he called for the others to come out. The ants came out in the disguises and began to crawl across the yard. They made it to the house and crawled up the side until they reached the entrance of the hole that led to the kitchen.

When the ants reached the kitchen, they saw the family sitting at the table eating. They noticed a loaf of bread, a bowl of fruit, and a bag of candy out on the counter. The family was at the table laughing and talking and did not see the ants crawl over to the counter and began filling their baskets. Once their baskets were filled, they hurried back to the hole, down the side of the house, and back to their hole, where they met the rest of the happy and excited ants. The food was taken straight to the storage room, and then the ants met in the meeting area.

Using the caterpillar disguises turned out to be a success. Ja'Quay decided to send out more than one group of ants. Since the disguises held ten ants, he felt they could send out four groups so they could bring back four times the amount of food.

The next day, Ja'Quay decided he would send out the group of four. He went up to check out the surroundings in the yard. He saw that the coast was clear and signaled to the ants to start coming out. The ants inched across the yard as if they were caterpillars until they reached the house, and then made their way up to the hole that led to the kitchen. As they crawled in, they noticed no one was in the kitchen, but there were rolls and nuts on the counter. They filled their baskets and hurried back into the hole, down the side of the house, and back into the ant hole.

Just as they made it back to the ant hole, the lady came outside. Ja'Quay could tell she was looking around to see if she could spot any ants. He continued peeping out of the ant hole to see what she would do. The lady walked all around the garden looking at the wall on the side of the house. She did not see the ants, so she turned and went back into the house, as the ants brought the food to the store house and put it away.

"Men, excellent job," Ja'Quay announced once the men were assembled. "We were able to get plenty of food today. We must wait until we get another opportunity and then we can go out again and get some more food."

Each day, Jaquay went up to the top of the ant hill to see if the lady was in the yard. He knew they were up to something because he saw them bring in those bags of cement.

A couple days later, he went to the top of the ant hole and noticed the husband carrying bags of cement out of the garage. He poured the cement in a big bucket, added water, and began to stir.

"Today, we will fix those pesty ants," the husband said to the lady. "I am going to fill up all those holes so they cannot get out."

When Ja'Quay heard this, he hurried back down the ant hole to tell the others.

"Come, come, everyone! I have to tell you something," he announced. "I just heard the lady and her husband saying they will be pouring cement down the hole today. We must work together and put up dirt bags so the cement does not reach our houses."

The ants began to fear for their lives, but they did as they were told. They started filling bags with dirt and piling them near the hole to make a wall to block the cement. Fortunately, Ja'Quay had thought of making another hole at the other end of the colony that came up through the grass where the lady and her husband could not see.

Ja'Quay went back up the hole. When he saw the husband with a bucket, he ran back down the hole, as the husband kicked down the dirt to flatten the hill. Ja'Quay could see the dirt falling into the hole. He then saw the cement coming into the hole. He just stood there and looked at what the husband had done. Thank goodness they had the dirt bags piled up.

Ja'Quay ran to the other hole that came up through the grass and peeped out the hole to see what the lady and her husband were doing. The husband had smoothed out the cement and left it to dry. He also found the opening to the house and sealed that up, too. Ja'Quay could see them laughing,

"That should fix them ants," he said. "Let's see them get out now."

Ja'Quay also laughed, knowing they did not see the ants' new hole. However, although they had another hole, they now had to figure out another way to get into the house. This meant Ja'Quay would have to scout again.

He went back down the hole and informed the ants that the lady and the husband had sealed up the opening to the house.

"Rest," he told them. "Tomorrow, I will be responsible for going out and scouting around for another opening. Most houses always have more than one little entrance."

All the ants turned in for the night, knowing their leader would find a way.

***

The next day, Ja'Quay went up to the top of the hole to peep out. The lady and her husband started their morning walk. He watched as they left the house and started down the driveway, and then crawled out of the hole. He then crawled down the driveway to make sure he saw them going down the street. Once he saw them turn the corner, he ran back up the driveway and began crawling up and down the side of the house, looking for an opening. Finally, after crawling all over the side of the house, he found another opening. This opening did not lead directly to the kitchen. It led to the bathroom next to the kitchen. This meant the ants would have to crawl a little further once they got into the house.

Ja'Quay went back down the ant hole to report what he found.

"We will have to sit and think about how to get to the new entrance," he told the men. "We will have to go a different route to get to the kitchen. Tomorrow, we will wait until the lady and her husband come back from their walk. The lady usually does not come into the garden for a long time after that."

The next day, the ants assembled their caterpillar costumes and followed Ja'Quay up the hole. He peeped out first to make sure the lady was not in the garden. The coast was clear. He turned to the other ants and said, "Follow me, but be careful."

The ants crawled across the yard like caterpillars. Ja'Quay showed them the way up the side of the house to the new entrance he had found. Once they were in the house, they had to crawl through the bathroom to get to the kitchen.

Ja'Quay told them to split up into groups and meet back at the bathroom. When they reached the kitchen, one group of ants crawled up the cabinet to the kitchen counter, where they found the bread. The other group crawled up the leg of the kitchen table and found that someone had left a piece of toast on a plate. The last group crawled into the cabinet and found an open box of crackers. The ants filled their baskets and crawled back to the bathroom as Ja'Quay had instructed.

"Now hurry," Ja'Quay said. "We have to get out of here before someone comes."

They all ran to the entrance where they came in, crawled down the side of the house, and back into the hole where they lived. When they made it back home, everyone cheered because they did not lose anyone.

It had been a successful trip, and Ja'Quay was happy. Everyone took their food to the storage house and put it away. When Ja'Quay came to see the amount of food they had collected, the storage house was almost full.

"We just need one more run and the storehouse will be full," he announced. "We will wait a couple of days and try again."

Three days had passed, and Ja'Quay was ready to go out one more time for food. He watched out for the lady and her husband. When the lady came into the yard, she did not seem concerned about the ants. She knew her husband had poured the cement in the hole and closed it off. She also knew her husband closed the spot where the ants were entering the kitchen. Her mind was no longer on the ants. She just focused on watering her plants.

Ja'Quay waited for her to go back into the house, and then went back to the other ants to let them know it was time to try again. "This will be our last run. After today, we can relax."

As the ants started putting on their caterpillar disguises. Ja'Quay went up to the top of the hole to make sure the lady was not in the garden. He signaled the ants that it was clear for them to come out. Once again, they crawled across the yard to the house, up the wall and to the opening in the bathroom.

They went into the house and split up in search of food on the counter, the table, and in the cabinets. They filled their baskets and started for home. They went back through the opening and down the wall. Just as they were crawling across the yard, the lady suddenly came out into the yard. They began running, but an ant in the last group tripped and fell on top of the ant in front of him.

The lady looked down and saw the caterpillars. They seem to crawl faster than caterpillars usually crawl. She turned her head and noticed the last group of ants. When the two at the end fell, the back of the disguise came off. It was the ants again!

She ran to the side of the house to get a broom and started hitting at the ants. They weaved side to side, ducking the broom, but the lady managed to hit the last two ants and send them flying in the air.

The rest of the ants made it to the grass and got to the hole in time. They informed Ja'Quay what had happened, but they did not know what happened to the other two ants. Ja'Quay was sad to hear he lost the ants, but was thankful that he did not lose everyone. He told them to put the food into the storage house and rest. They now had enough food to feed everyone when the winter came.

"If you have to go out into the yard, just be careful," Jaquay told the ants. "The lady is always out there waiting to kill us. But this time, we won. We have our food and do not have to worry about the winter."

All the ants cheered and thanked Ja'Quay for being a fearless ant leader.

***

The lady ran back into the house to tell her husband the ants were back.

"I thought they were caterpillars crawling, just to find out they were really ants," she said.

The husband began to chuckle. "Those ants are smarter than I thought. This will be a never-ending fight. During the summer, there will always be ants; we just do not want them to end up in the house."

He went out into the yard and looked around for the ant hole, but could not find it. He checked the one he sealed before to see if the cement was still hard. It was, but this time Ja'Quay had their hole hidden in the grass. The husband shook his head and went back into the house.

"I could not find the hole," he told his wife. "I do not know where they are coming from this time. I will go out and spray the whole yard. Maybe it will kill some of them. The only other thing to do is to hire an exterminator."

"Will that cost a lot of money?" the lady asked.

"I do not know," he replied, picking up his phone. "We have to find out. If we want to get rid of those ants, this is our last resort."

The next day, Ja'Quay was out crawling in the yard when he suddenly saw a van pull up into the driveway. He saw pictures of a bug on the side of the truck and read the exterminator sign. He knew what that meant.

Ja'Quay ran back to the hole and warned the other ants. Everyone grew scared, knowing exterminators had chemicals that could kill them. If they sprayed the yard, they would not be able to go out.

Ja'Quay went to the top of the hole and peeped out. He could see the man getting a big canister out of the back of the truck with a long hose on the end. The man started spraying around the yard and house. Ja'Quay went back into the hole and warned the others.

"You may smell a strong odor, but please stay in your houses," he said.

The smell of the spray lasted for weeks, but the ants remained in their holes. They remained underground for the rest of the summer and through the winter, but their storage house was full, and their families were safe.

The lady was happy again because she could come into her garden and no longer had trouble with the pesty ants. Little did she know, they would be back. The battle was not over.

About the Authors

Debra Thompson

Debra A. K. Thompson is an author, songwriter, singer and instructor who has published two inspirational books. Her first book, *Enlightenment: Looking Back to Move Forward*, is a book of short stories that engages readers to examine their own past experiences to learn how God uses those experiences to shape their futures and their lives as they move toward their destiny.

Debra's second book is *Enlightenment II, Building Self Esteem through Poems and Positive Affirmations*. This is a book of awe-inspiring poems and affirmations designed to reinforce and encourage appreciation for the uniqueness that God gives to each of us along with the characteristics that make us unlike any other person He has ever created.

Both books are available on Amazon, Books a Million and anywhere digital books are sold. Print copies are also available through Debra's website at

www.debrathewriter.com

Additionally, follow her on Facebook, Twitter, Instagram, Pinterest, and Linked-in to receive your daily dose of affirmations and encouragement so you can learn to enjoy that richer, fuller life even more.

Debra also plans to release her first children's book series in 2022, which will explore the joy of saving money and building wealth. To book Debra for speaking engagements or workshops, contact her at (813) 442-6702 or email her at dethomgirl@gmail.com.

B. Danielle Watkins

New York is not only known for its famous hot wings, its historical museums, and its beautiful One World Observatory where you can see the skyline and the stars from high above, it is also the "City of Dreams", and the place where rising star B. Danielle Watkins began her journey. B. Danielle Watkins, international award-winning filmmaker, and author is a native of Buffalo, New York. Watkins is on top of her game, rapidly paving her way to success with her many accomplishments.

B. Danielle began laying the groundwork for her career at the age of nine, not aware that her gift of writing would take her to higher heights in her future endeavors. By the age of 15, Watkins had her first poem published in the "Poetry Gems Collection", presented by the Famous Poets Society.

It did not stop there, this tenacious young lady put her talents to work by publishing a three-novel trilogy entitled "The No other Man Three Part Tragedy" released in 2011/2012. In 2013, Watkins began working her way up the ladder to join the ranks of some of the greats when she was officially named the head of the Creative Writing Department for M Power Productions, LLC based out of Atlanta, Georgia, the same place that the great Tyler Perry studios is located.

Working with M Power productions allowed this fierce lady to advance her way onto stage and screenwriting. In 2014, Watkins produced her first sold out show respectively titled "BlacButterflii: The Saigon Ruse Story" which premiered in Atlanta, Georgia. During this time, she was also creating a name for herself in the industry. B. Danielle decided to try her hand in writing the Gender Diverse Digital Series, "Girls Just Don't Do That", giving way to a fresh new perspective of the

LGBTQ community and the real-life circumstances that are addressed and often marginalized. This series portrayed an open honest common-sense view to relationships, hardships and intimacy.

In January 2016, Watkins made major power moves by launching her own production company, Dream N1 Productions, based in Las Vegas, Nevada. Later the same year, her newly formed production company produced its first major production, *Parallel the Documentary,* based on her true-life experiences as the first African-American filmmaker at the first all lesbian film festival in Paducah, Kentucky. This documentary has since been screened internationally in two countries, winning awards such as Best Director and Audience Choice, causing her name to circulate through the film festival circuit.

Taking her career to the next level Ms. Watkins became the first and only African American filmmaker to write, produce and star in a REVRY original series, "3030". 2019 proved to be one of her most defining years in her film career. After winning four Telly Awards for the documentary entitled "GRRRL: The Beauty of the Beast" and launching the second season in her original series "3030". She has earned a plethora of accolades and acknowledgements in the film industry, making her an alchemist in the game.

Starting at the end of 2020, Watkins added another amazing title under her belt, becoming the chief programmer as well as long form content coordinator for the new, Black LGBTQ+ led and centered television network iElevate +TV. In 2021 Watkins filmed, wrote, and contributed to over 20 projects for the network including the number one watched series written and directed by Watkins *Love & Stuff.*

Watkins added journalist to her resume when she became staff writer for MIM Magazine. A graduate of the HBCU Winston Salem State University, and a member of the Zeta Phi Beta Sorority Inc., B. Danielle Watkins gives new meaning to the saying "Black Girls Rock." Author, filmmaker, screenwriter, actress, and producer, B. Danielle is breaking barriers, shattering glass ceilings, and propelling her way to the top. Watkins is a woman on the move, a rising star, and as Hip-Hop Artist Tobe Nwigwe would say, it's time to "EAT"!

To learn more about B. Danielle Watkins and her exciting endeavors, please visit
https://www.bdanielleswatkins.com/

(Henry, SC 2020)
Author

C. Damon

C. Damon is a native New Orleanian, and has been teaching for over twenty-five years. He holds degrees in psychology and education. C. Damon is a man of God who values spiritual growth above all things. His hobbies include reading, shopping, and mentoring youth.

Avalon Soulette Brown

Avalon Soulette Brown is the author of six books, and has co-authored six anthologies. She is currently drafting a book of spiritual poems, which will be released soon.

Avalon grew up in Newark, New Jersey, and now has two children, seven grandchildren, and two great grandchildren. As a children's book author, her goal is to write a book with each one of her grandchildren as the main character. This will be her legacy to them. She is also working on a project with my grandchildren. Each grandchild will write a story about Nanna. The stories will be compiled into an anthology.

Avalon has been a registered nurse for thirty-nine years, working in post-op GU/GI surgical floor for 18 years. She decided to change her specialty and started working in an outpatient clinic for dialysis., where she was promoted to a charge nurse. I stayed in that position for seven years. She became a manager by the age of fifty.

Avalon obtained her bachelor's degree in the science of nursing at the age of sixty. She is a member of the American Nurses Association, the New Jersey Nurses Association, and the Association for Professionals in Infection Control.

In her words: "I am thankful for all the blessings he has given me. When I add God along with my nursing career, I know he wants my light to shine. I can now be a greater comfort to those who need just a kind word and a smile. As I walked through the halls in the hospital during this pandemic, there were so many staff that needed their spirits lifted. I am thankful that I had that word they needed that let them know they were making a difference. I find joy in being that comfort to those that needed it. Avalon just wants to make sure she is always putting out a spirit of love."

LaRita Dalton

LaRita Dalton is a native of Memphis, TN. She is a single parent of a son, who is the light of her life. She joined the military shortly after high school with the hopes of providing a better life for herself and her son. She served on active duty for 18 years before retiring in Savannah, GA.

Her passion is advocacy, research, social service and justice. In all that she does, especially regarding the health and well-being of others. She uses her personal experiences, education, knowledge, and skills to be the voice for those who have lost their voice or feel that their voice will not be heard. She has a genuine compassion for humankind and will always work to the best of her ability in all that she finds in her heart and hands to do.

Her drive is discipline and education. She believes that you must have discipline and education to succeed in life. She herself is a life-longer learner and never passes up an opportunity to learn something new. She believes these opportunities are designed to help her help others to reach up and not out. LaRita loves giving back. She does not know the impacts she makes in the lives of many but is assured that they are long lasting and makes a difference in the communities and organizations she serves.

Her favorite phrase is "All is well and will continue to be so."

Her favorite quote notably is her own: "The world is a stage, and we all have a part to play."

Tracey Jackson

Tracey Jackson is a South Florida-based speaker and author. She has four self-published works: *Impressions* (Poetry), *From The Valley To The Mountaintop – Lessons from the Journey* (Inspirational), *The Summer of Chances* (full-length African American fiction novel), and *From Yaad* (Caribbean Short themed novel). She's written for various newspapers and online magazines. She is also a member of Zeta Phi Beta Sorority, Incorporated.

Keesha Dancy

Keesha Dancy, a native of East Saint Louis, IL, currently resides in Memphis, TN. Keesha is a U.S. Army retired soldier, author, and current substitute teacher. Keesha's first book (inspired by and co-written with her eight-year-old grandson), was published in February 2022. *Boys Breathe: An ABC Introduction to Self-Confidence* is designed to build esteem, empower youth to learn about self-love and confidence at an early age, and expand vocabulary. It also develops mindfulness through positive words and takes children through the process of meditation.

Keesha is currently working on children's books number two and three (one of which is co-written with her ten-year-old grandson). It is Keesha's desire to continue authoring books that educate, engage, entertain, and inspire. Keesha's books are available on Amazon and through her website at www.pearledbutterflypublishing.com. Keesha is also the Founder of All Things Are Possible, Inc., a nonprofit organization committed to empower and inspire youth through Travel, Education, Mentorship, and Service and the owner of Pearled Butterfly Publishing, LLC, a book publishing agency dedicated to developing books with diversity.

Keesha earned her Bachelor of Science Degree in Resources Management from Troy University and her MBA (Human Resource Management) from Columbia Southern University.

Keesha's hobbies include reading, writing/journaling, crafting, and giving back to her community. Keesha is an avid traveler, she has traveled the world to over 50 countries and counting. Keesha is on a personal mission to complete her

"Living to Do" list, which includes visiting all the continents (she has one more to go) and the Wonders of the World.

Keesha is a Diamond Life Member of Zeta Phi Beta Sorority, Incorporated, a member of Blue Nile Toastmasters Club (Memphis), Junior League Memphis, and other charitable and social organizations. Keesha lives by the saying, "Be Blessed and Be a Blessing to Others." She believes that ALL Things Are Possible, and it is a daily reminder that even though you may have obstacles, failures, or disadvantages, you can overcome them. To book Keesha for speaking engagements and/or author reads, contact her at 901-518-2018 or via email at keeshaldancy@gmail.com. Find out more about Keesha by following her on IG @keeshadancyauthor.

Beautiful Lawson

Twenty-two-year-old Beautiful Lawson was born November 19, 1999. The Clark Atlanta University graduate strives to be a well-known actress and later a director for Broadway, movies, and TV shows. She has appeared in such television shows as NCIS New Orleans, Claws, and Queen Sugar, as well as the movie Happy Death Day 2.

She began acting in Belgium at the age of 12 in order to make friends in the community before starting class at her new school. Now this young actress is a role model for young girls who are afraid to come out of their shells. While in college, she served as the vice president of the CAU chapter of Revolt, a member of the National Society of Leadership and Success, an organization on campus that emphasizes being the person you were created to be, AUC Vybz, which celebrates cultural awareness of the Caribbean, and the AUC African Students Association.

Dr. AudreyAnn C. Moses

 Dr. AudreyAnn C. Moses is the owner, coach, and consultant of NeverSayCain't Christian Life Coach and Consultant. She is a certified Christian life coach, mental wellness counselor, speaker and workshop facilitator, and author.

Dr. Moses is a retired Chief Navy Counselor, U.S. Navy and a Human Development Psychologist and professor. Her specialty is personal, spiritual, and family growth. She is involved in several community-based programs focusing on personal and professional behavior, and is an experienced program facilitator, keynote, and topic-specific speaker/trainer for seminars and workshops.

She has published several professional articles and four novels. She has been a contributing author for three anthologies, including *A New Renaissance*. She lives in Cokesbury, SC, and is married with four adult children, ten grandchildren, and one great-grandson.

Learn more about me on https://linktr.ee/neversaycaint

Vanessa J. Ross

Vanessa J. Ross is an author/co-author, songwriter and inspirational/motivational speaker. She is the second oldest of nine children, born to Jean T. Jack and the late Paul M. Jones Sr.

Vanessa is a devoted mother and grandmother, but most of all, a God-fearing woman who loves the Lord with all her heart. She is the owner of #Be Encouraged Christian apparel and I Am Free Active Wear. She is a member of Believer's Temple of Faith under the leadership of Pastor Kenneth Davis & First Lady Fay Davis, and sings in the Chorale Choir under the leadership of Bro. Sam Lovely. Additionally, she sings with Jeffrey Pelrean and Created to Worship.

Vanessa is a member of Le Bon Ton Baby Dolls, which serves the community. She is also on the Board of Directors of 108 Organization LLC a Nonprofit organization for men in Baltimore MD

Her favorite scriptures: Psalms 27:1-3 and Jeremiah 29:11

Motto: I take nothing for granted but, I owe it all to my Lord and Savior Jesus Christ. All I can say is that God has truly been good to me and without him I would be nothing.

Favorite Song: If I Can Help Somebody, Then My Living Shall Not Be in Vain

Favorite Saying: Be encouraged

Angie Wyatt-Braden

Angie Wyatt-Braden is a celebrated writer, speaker, educator, and counselor. She has a BA from University of North Texas in Communications, as well as a MED in Counseling and MA in Communications from Texas Southern University. As an African American woman who is blind, Angie is compelled to pen stories that acknowledge and celebrate the broad yet unique stories of women and girls of color, people with disabilities, and individuals from underrepresented cultural groups.

You are welcome to follow Angie via Facebook at www.facebook.com/bradenspeaks.

About the Editor

Dr. Rhonda M. Lawson is the founder of Meet the World Image Solutions, LLC, a boutique public relations firm based in New Orleans, LA, and the award-winning author of *Cheatin' in the Next Room*, *A Dead Rose*, *Putting It Back Together*, *Some Wounds Never Heal*, *Twylite*, and *Trust*, and contributed to eleven different anthologies, including *Second Chances*, *Crimes of Passion*, *Gumbo for the Soul*, *The Heart of Our Community*, *Surfacing*, *Heart of a Military Woman*, *The Color of Strength: Embracing the Strength and Passion of Our Culture* and *Keeping it Finer: What it Means to be a Finer Woman in the 21st Century*. She is also the co-host of Black Authors Matter TV and host of Horizons with Meet the World Image Solutions, both of which highlight and promote authors, entertainers, and entrepreneurs.

Rhonda is a twenty-three-year Army veteran, having served during Operation Enduring Freedom, Operation Iraqi Freedom and Operation New Dawn. Rhonda's career as a Soldier-journalist has also taken her to various parts of the world, including Japan, Hawaii, Korea, Afghanistan, and Egypt. Her work has appeared stateside in various Army and civilian publications, including Soldiers Magazine, the Seattle Times, and the Army Times. Throughout her career, she edited various military publications, earning many awards, including the 1997 Training and Doctrine Command Journalist of the Year. She also taught journalism for two years at the Defense Information School, and served as an adjunct professor for the University of Maryland University College-Europe.

She is currently the National Director of Publications for Zeta Phi Beta Sorority, Inc., and the Literary Correspondent for the National Black Book Festival, which takes place in Houston each October. She holds a Bachelor of Arts in Communication Studies from the University of Maryland University College, a Master of Human Relations from the University of Oklahoma, and a Doctorate in Business Administration with an emphasis in Organizational Leadership from Northcentral University. Dr. Rhonda values education and literacy, leading her to found the Black History Month Literary Weekend in February 2017 to celebrate Black History while promoting literacy.

Additionally, she launched the Meet the World Image Solutions Eighth and Ninth Grade Essay Contest in February 2018, and the Meet the World Image Solutions Graduating Senior Scholarship Fund in April 2020. Rhonda also added playwright to her repertoire in 2018, when she adapted *Cheatin' in the Next Room*, and later *Twylite*, into stage plays. She plans to bring more of her stories to stage, while still promoting the many authors who have trusted her with their publicity and literary needs.